Camera Obscura

A Novel

Dennis Hicks

MARCO PRESS

Marco Press
11600 Washington Place, Suite 201
Los Angeles, CA 90066
drhicks2@yahoo.com

Printed in the United States of America

First Edition, 2007

Library of Congress Control Number 2006908992

ISBN: 978-0-9709092-1-3

TO STEFFI
For Love, Patience and Support
Thank You

WRITING IS A SOLITARY undertaking sustained by many. In particular, I thank Randi Johnson, Steve Wolf, Sean O'Neil, Robert Templeton, Stephanie Waxman and Phoebe Larmore for their careful reading and thoughtful critiques of this novel at different stages.

A special appreciation goes to the Rough Writers Group: Tony Abetamarco, John Binder, Maryedith Burrell, Dale Eunson, Randi Johnson, Phoebe Larmore, Leon Martel, Beth Ruscio, Rob Sullivan and Stephanie Waxman for their insights and comraderie. For their steady encouragement, thanks to Garry Francell, Stephan Cohen, Howard Wallman, Mark and Paula Waxman and especially, my wonderful daughters, Tessa Hicks and Jessica Williams. Also, thanks to Susan Dworski (susan@ theblueone.com) for bringing the cover to life and Cory Juvitz for line editing (info@thethreecs.com).

I am grateful to Monsignor Larry Purcell, Phillip Walters, Dittnay Lang, Detective Ray Terrones, LAPD, Lt. Gary Gallinot, SMPD, Tony Abetamarco, Michael Vest, Hala Khouri, Sarah Sorice and others who shared personal experiences and/or information vital to this work of fiction.

Many non-fiction books have contributed to this effort including *Rich Church, Poor Church* by Malachi Martin, *Papal Sin* by Garry Willis, *The Calvi Afffair* by Larry Gurwin, *A License to Steal* by Ben Stein, *Liars Poker* and *The Money Culture* by Michael Lewis, *Plants of the Gods: Their Sacred Healing and Hallucinogenic Powers* by Richard Evan Shultes, Albert Hoffman and Christian Ratsch, *Jefferson's Pillow* by Roger Wilkins, *Secret Knowledge: Rediscovering the lost techniques of the Old Masters* by David Hockney and *The Future of Nostalgia* by Svetlana Boym.

Lastly, a bittersweet thank you to two dear friends whose determination and creative spirit inspire me even after passing on: Dale Eunson and my soul brother, Josh Hanig.

1

September 11, 2004

IN A BEDROOM OFF the dim hallway, Peter's dad was yelling about his fishing pole. Like a thunderstorm, the outburst rumbled away to an apprehensive silence. Dementia. Who wouldn't be pissed off if he couldn't remember a damn thing? How many functions can a man lose before his life is no longer worth living?

Peter fanned through the bills on his father's oak desk. He wrote the checks now, supporting an existence that Martin Winston had long ago made clear he wanted no part of. And Peter had agreed to never let this misery drag on. A door slammed. Peter began to go to him, then stopped himself. Juanita could handle it. She was used to these tantrums. He had to write the checks. God knew the old man couldn't.

Peter's sadness dredged up the memory of the first time his dad had mentioned his own death. It had been forty years earlier, summer 1964, deep in the High Sierras. He saw himself, a puny twelve-year-old with skinny arms watching the signature of a cold breeze zigzagging across Muir Lake. The boy shook off the chill and cast his bait far into the lake. Squinting at the late afternoon sun as it neared the jagged teeth of the 14,000-foot peaks, he asked, "Dad, why does the sun move faster as it sets?"

His father had just knocked off forty push-ups and was stretched out on a flat granite slab. "It doesn't do anything different. It's us earthlings on our spinning orb who turn away from the sun."

"But it doesn't look that way," he argued.

"You can't always believe your eyes."

"But if you can't see it, how do you know for sure? That doesn't seem very scientific." He slowly began to reel in the line.

"The physical world doesn't yield its secrets to just anyone, my boy. It's why I hound you about doing your math homework. It's the language of the invisible."

"But when Mom says she knows there's a God even if she can't see him, you say she's nuts."

"Mom uses God as an answer to mysteries we haven't been able to explain yet. That is nuts. But I will admit that if faith means believing things you don't experience personally, then even scientists have to take certain things on faith." He sat up, cackled a scary, madman laugh and added, "That's what makes being a scientist so much fun." He jumped to his feet. "Can you imagine what it was like for the first person who proved that the earth rotated around the sun and that what everyone thought was wrong?" He looked across the vast basin. "It wasn't easy being Copernicus." Shivering, he slipped on an old woolen sweater. "Let's call it a day, Peter. The fish have voted, and it's Dinty Moore canned stew for dinner again."

Peter's groan of protest and fisherman's frustration was cut short as a large trout made a big mistake. Overcoming nerves and cold hands, he managed to keep tension on the line as something surprisingly strong played tug-of-war with him. Gradually, under his father's approving eye and encouragement, he reeled the prize in close to shore.

As his dad stepped to the water's edge to grab the fish, Peter shouted, "I want to get him!" and pushed past him. Keeping the tip of the pole up and the line taut, Peter leaned down into the shoals, where the twenty-inch, two-and-a-half-pound giant had finally run aground. He grabbed the flopping beauty and hefted it exultantly.

In a flash, the slimy German brown trout squirted out of Peter's hand and spat the shiny lure into the air. Too late, Peter yanked his fishing rod back sharply as their dinner plopped onto the watery mud next to him. "Sh…shinola!" he yelled, observing the no-swearing rule even if his dad had broken it several times on this trip. He dropped the pole and leapt into the reeds. He managed to latch onto the muscular, writhing fish behind the gills. He lurched to his feet with a wide grin. Eyes glistening with joy, he once again held up the slippery devil for his father to see.

"Pete," his father said through tight lips, "put that in the creel and find me the needle-nose pliers. You hooked a 140-pounder, but I think you'll have to throw me back."

Peter shrieked when he saw the blood oozing from his dad's hand, where his barbed hook had taken up new residence. His father's flinty gray eyes silenced him. Bursting with guilt, Peter dropped the fish into the wicker basket and rummaged madly through the tackle box.

"You gave that pole a hell of a jerk, boy. It's in there past the barb," he explained as if it weren't his own appendage. He took the pliers and snipped the lure off above the hook. He grabbed the spine of the hook with the pliers and tried to yank it out. "God dammit!" he swore.

After catching his breath, he scrutinized the blood pooling in his palm. "We've got to wise up, Peter, or I'm going to have a hand so ripped up we'll have to hike out." Peter looked at his dad wide-eyed and nodded. "I can't get a purchase on it from this angle, so you'll have to take the pliers and push the hook farther into my palm. If you do it right, it should curve around and come out about a half-inch away."

"I can't, Dad!"

"Not true, Son. You don't want to, but you can." He squinted in pain at Peter. "It may be a little premature, but it's all part of an inevitable process: sons taking over for their dads." He mimicked the movement with his good hand before giving him the pliers. "Practice giving it a quick, strong twist of your wrist. The tip of that son of a bitch should pop right out."

Peter took the pliers and tried to copy his father. "That's it, Peter, like scooping ice cream. Now get a good grip on the end of the hook and do the same thing while you press down slightly."

"I can hardly see it!" the boy complained. His dad touched the edge of his handkerchief next to the hook, and the cloth rapidly absorbed his blood.

"Now," his dad said, "forget it's my hand. It's just a piece of meat. Do it firmly and you won't have to do it again." Peter flicked his wrist twice more, took hold of the hook, and did it for real. Like the claw of a monster, the barb emerged from the middle of his dad's hand. "Shit!" the older man exhaled sharply. "Excellent! Now pinch the tip and pull it out with that same curving motion, but slowly this time."

"Son of a bitch," his dad uttered, slowly enunciating each word as the hook curved out from a crimson pool. As it pulled free, they both swore loudly with relief, and Peter's "Fuckin' bitchin'!" came echoing back from the granite wall that rimmed the other side of the lake.

With the sun behind the mountains, the speckled alpine granite glowed with a soft peach color. Peter cleaned and fried the big fish all by himself. His father sat gazing at the shimmering lake, sipping whiskey and dabbing it occasionally onto his wound. "This is heaven, buddy, as good as it gets for us Homo sapiens." Peter silently nodded, his concentration on the sizzling fish. "I want you to promise me," his dad continued, "to scatter my ashes up here when I die."

"Da…ad," Peter squawked, almost overturning the frying pan, "don't talk about that."

"You might as well get used to it, pal. Death is what makes everything else so wonderful, knowing that it all has to end sometime." He tapped his scratched-up, metal Sierra cup against a rock to get Peter's attention and delivered the first of many similar edicts: "As a matter of fact, when I get too old, I want you to bring me up here and leave me." When Peter didn't say anything, he added, "I'm serious, Son; it may be up to you."

PETER WINSTON SNAPPED OUT of his reverie as his father charged into the living room, muttering and swearing. "What's wrong?" Peter asked.

Martin Winston, a small, wiry man who looked younger than his 78 years, scrutinized his son before he recognized him. "Goddamn maid or housekeeper or whatever: She's an idiot. Can't find my fishing pole."

"You want to go fishing, Dad?"

"Well," he paused, confusion deflating his upset, "hell, I might. That's not against the law, is it?"

"No, Dad, of course not."

Standing in the middle of his living room, Martin's posture shifted. Sagging replaced vigor, and he looked about him as though he had entered for the first time. Peter asked him a question to send him back to the comfort of the past. "Dad, do you remember the times you took me backpacking in the Sierras?"

Martin perked up. "Sure!" he said enthusiastically, then stopped, open-mouthed.

"I was just remembering when I snagged your hand with my fishhook."

Martin sat on the edge of the couch and rubbed the two faint scars in the middle of his palm. "I bawled you out pretty good for that?"

"No, you didn't. You were great."

"That was after your mother died?" It was another question longing to be a statement.

"No, it was two years before Mom died," Peter said gently.

"It was? What happened?"

If there were a blessing to his father losing his mind, it was this: forgetting what he had hated to remember. "She was killed by a truck."

"Geraldine?" Confusion pinched Martin's eyes, but before Peter could construct a face-saving segue, his father's countenance slipped into blankness and he sat staring at the scars.

A woman emerged from the hallway carrying a bundle of sheets and towels. As she passed through, she said, "Mr. Peter, may I speak with you?"

Peter stood and followed Juanita into the comfortably worn kitchen.

"I can't take it any longer. Your father swears at me and calls me names, and I know he doesn't really mean it, but sometimes I get afraid of him."

"I realize he's difficult, Juanita, but please don't leave. You've been a godsend. Believe me, compared with the others, he likes you. How about finding someone to relieve you? You hardly get any time off except when I can get free."

"My cousin Carmen just finished working for another family."

"Great! I'll continue paying what you are getting now plus whatever Carmen gets for, let's say, two days. If you pay her directly I won't have to pay taxes for her. Okay?"

Juanita smiled wearily. "That would help a lot. I just hope Mr. Winston can…" She stopped as Martin appeared at the doorway, a bright and curious look on his face.

"What are we doing now?" he asked as a glance and a nod between Peter and Juanita finalized their agreement.

It had taken Peter quite a while to realize how far gone his father was. The deterioration seemed minimal for a long time because Martin keyed off of whatever human activity there was around him. In this instance, he had followed their voices and found where the action was in the house. It was his way of masking his inability to keep track of what was happening, a way of hiding the fact that without a sense of time every moment was mysterious. In Peter's own four-year-old child, this condition was often exhilarating, a delicious process of discovery. In Martin it was tragic. Even though Peter had known that Martin would eventually decline, it was shocking how quickly his lapses had gone from rare to commonplace.

"Are you hungry, Mr. Winston?" Juanita asked. An agreeable look from Martin suggested that he thought he probably was, but didn't know how to be sure. "Why don't you and your son go sit on the patio and I'll bring you your favorite sandwich: liverwurst and Swiss cheese on rye with a glass of buttermilk."

"And mustard!" Martin blurted out, a few brain cells suddenly clicking. "Don't forget the mustard," he repeated as he strode out of the kitchen.

Gloomily, Peter followed him. For years, they had talked at great length about how the end of life should look. The working model of what Martin was trying to avoid was a slow, painful death by cancer and its assorted treatments. Alzheimer's was different, and worse. It robbed Martin of a meaningful existence, but it didn't kill him.

Martin took a chair at the table outside. He motioned to the newspaper Peter had brought. A photo of an airplane hitting the Trade Center tower commemorated the third anniversary of 9/11/01. "Plane crash?" Martin asked, trying to make conversation.

"Yeah, it's terrible." Peter came up behind his dad and

massaged his neck while the old man moaned with pleasure, blissfully unaware of what he had forgotten. It was becoming impossible to deny that they were in the kind of situation that his dad had adamantly wanted to avoid, and it was only going to get worse. The poorly imagined future had become the present. Peter had promised to pull the plug, but where was the plug?

2

SATURDAY, JANUARY 29, 2005

T HE WORLD'S FIRST SOLAR-POWERED Ferris wheel slowly rotated in the bright sunlight, discharging and picking up voyagers. Near the top, the winking, shimmering ocean and thirty miles of Southern California coast spread out far, far beneath four-year-old Samantha, who clamped onto Peter's arm with both hands. She squealed in wonder as she peered down from their gently rocking perch. "Everybody's so little," she whispered excitedly as she took in the miniaturized people on the Santa Monica Pier one hundred feet below them. "Daddy!" she cried out. "Look at all those sea-girls!" She pointed to the beach where a pulsating cloud of gray and white birds lifted up and over the crashing surf only to settle again in the choppy green sea behind the waves.

"Gulls, Honey," he muttered, not wanting to dent her enthusiasm.

"What?"

"Nothing. Yeah, they're beautiful." *And so are you, my little lifeline to sanity,* he thought. He kissed the top of her head, with its tangle of curly black hair, and looked inland five miles to the reflecting towers that marked the Westwood area of Los Angeles. He'd grown up just a few blocks to the right of those office buildings. His father lived there still and Peter imagined him, standing in front of that prototypical Southwestern tile-and-stucco house, eyes blank, just staring. Memories beckoned, but reminiscing was dangerous, holding as it did many painful pockets. The Ferris wheel took off in earnest, sweeping them backward in space and, in spite of himself, sending him backward in time.

He'd taken Shirley Blackstone to a nearby beach when he was thirteen. It was Pacific Ocean Park back then—POP—and he recalled the Ferris wheel as even higher and more bedazzling. He was as innocent and Catholic as they came. His mother had made sure that an endless parade of nuns and priests brainwashed him into believing that sex was sinful and unhealthy. But a kiss at the top of the ride had encouraged Shirley, a girl from what his mother insisted was a good family, to take her hand and put it down his pants. This was Peter's introduction to sexual liberation, and he was too shocked to halt her manipulations as they rotated through that evening sky. With a stain on his pants and his conscience, he accepted that he'd have to be highly vigilant in order to eventually gain admission to heaven. For a year he avoided being alone with girls, until one March day in 1966 his daydreaming, saint of a mother stepped into the path of a pickup truck and was killed instantly. He was repeatedly told it was God's will, but that only killed his faith, too. His dad was morose for a year, so Peter veered down a stoic path that confused maturity with emotional control. He grew up quickly. He remained idealistic, but the context changed. In the aftermath of his mother's demise, no vision of heaven could compete with the throbbing beat of the cultural revolution of the late sixties and seventies. The ferment of the times made it seem obvious that if you took away hypocritical rules and restrictions, people would be free, honest and responsible. He embraced radical politics and free sex as passionately as he had the rules of the Catholic Church and the Boy Scouts' pledge. He might have become an Eagle Scout if they'd given merit badges for fucking and cunnilingus.

"Daddy! What's that?" Samantha pointed to the beach as a giant bird with a long tail climbed into the sky.

"That's a kite," he said as she gripped his arm harder. "We're okay, Honey. It won't come near us."

He couldn't imagine how he would handle Samantha when she hit puberty. If she ever brought home a boy even remotely like he had been when he was young, he'd annihilate the punk. Coming back to the top of the arc, Peter acknowledged he'd do anything for Sam, even leap off the Ferris wheel if it was called for. He frowned at the irony. It was crazy. He, as a father, was ready to die for his daughter while he, as a son, was concocting ways to put his father out of his misery—at least, that's what he was supposed to be doing. He kissed the top of Samantha's head again to drive away the thought. He'd planned this day so he could forget that mess.

As they came off the ride, Samantha announced she had to go to the bathroom. Peter waited for her, leaning against the graffiti-covered wall of the women's restroom, jiggling keys in his pants pocket. He gnawed on his salt-and-pepper moustache. His lovely wife reassured him that the gray in his hair looked distinguished rather than old. He wasn't convinced. An unnatural blonde in shorts and a red halter-top emerged from the parade of people walking by. She glanced at him, sizing up this short, thick-bodied man in an Italian knit shirt, unwrinkled khakis and loafers before she disappeared into the bathroom. He liked to think he was still attractive, but he was glad he was no longer single, no longer a player. He'd retired that attitude when he got married, which was only a few years after he retired from the supercharged world of junk bonds, leveraged buyouts and cocaine.

His cell phone rang, and he read his wife's number on his caller ID. "Hi there, Vice President," he responded.

"Hi. I just got away for a second, but I was missing you and Sam. Did she have her maiden voyage on the Ferris wheel yet?"

"Yep. She was thrilled, and I still have her fingernail marks on my arm to prove it." He chuckled. "She's in the bathroom now. I don't know if it's connected to the ride."

"I can't stand missing these 'firsts' in her life."

"Don't worry, Honey. If you want, I'm sure she'll come back with you tomorrow and be excited and happy all over."

"Damn, here comes someone who needs me. I hate working on weekends."

"We'll see you tonight, Judith. I'll have dinner waiting." The phone went dead after he heard, "Bye. I love you."

After ten years, marriage had become predictable, just as he'd feared it would. But, instead of hating it, he found it comforting. He had resisted becoming domesticated for a long time, but he was glad he had finally given in.

Two dazzling young teenagers with enough eye makeup for a Broadway musical passed by, giggling. Peter smiled. They took it as flirtatious and shrugged him off like lunch at their high school cafeteria. Peter saw through their face paint and attitude and glimpsed two girls who might have been his students. A career change into teaching high school history had been part of the domestication process, but not as important as having a child of his own.

The pier shuddered as waves crashed beneath him, remnants of a storm the day before. He crossed his arms across his soft belly and mourned the wrestler's body that once was. He wasn't too much over the 150 pounds he had carried in college, but what had been hard muscle had melted and spread out. He wasn't sure he was even five foot eight and a half anymore. Creeping up on fifty-three, he was confronted with a body that was shrinking and expanding simultaneously.

The blonde reappeared. "Is that your little girl in there?" she asked.

"Is she all right?" Peter responded, ready to run in.

"She's doing fine, Daddy. She's so cute. She got all upset 'cause there wasn't any toilet paper, so I gave her some tissues." She smiled, hips and head cocked at the same angle. "Girls gotta be prepared, you know." Peter wondered if her smile said that she was turned on by his parenting and was willing to overlook any marital complications. Or maybe he was imagining things, turning plain friendliness into an invitation. It irritated him that he couldn't read her. He had always known what was what when he was a player. Now, her body language was like hieroglyphics.

He was midway through "Thank you," and, "Yes, she's a doll," when Samantha came running out of the bathroom, tugging at her black tights.

"Daddy, I had to poop and there wasn't enough paper," she explained. Then she saw the woman and grabbed his leg. "She gave me some," and looked up at him to see if that was all right. Peter reassured Samantha and straightened out her blue jumper as the friendly lady waved and slipped away into the crowd.

They headed down the pier hand in hand, caught up in the sideshow of mimes, face painters and the eccentric urban dwellers that swirled around them. In the crowd were representatives of every racial and ethnic look imaginable: tattooed physiques, people barely clothed and people arrayed in tribal costumes. Los Angeles had become a body representative of the whole planet, and they were at its pierced navel. A pelican landed on a tall piling only fifteen feet away and Samantha joyfully greeted the old bird. Its big eyes stared down from under its baldhead. "He looks like Grandpa," she giggled. Peter disguised his discomfort by joining her in talking to it with squawks and chirps. The bird took off, and he put his child on his shoulders and ran so she, too, could fly.

Breathing hard, he stood with Sam at the end of the pier and watched the community of fishermen and their families: the poor, the recently arrived, the hopeful and the desperate. It satisfied the radical who persevered in Peter that, despite constant attempts to be gentrified, the heart and soul of Santa Monica Pier was still free fishing and carnival games. The place entertained both grubby bikers and relaxing executives—and dope dealers who sold to both. Even so, it was a family place, a middle ground between chaos and conformity. Whether Russian, Nigerian or Filipino, they could look past the breakwater and out to sea, pondering what they had left and what might be in store for them.

An Asian family—they might have been Korean—finished looking through the heavy commercial telescope mounted on the deck of the pier. Peter dropped in a quarter, swung it around toward the coast and followed the busy street that ran along the top of the cliff. His eyes finally rested on a slanted yellow building with green trim that blended comfortably into the many bushes and tall trees surrounding it. The Senior Recreation Center was modern in the fifties style with shifting angles and heights in its roofline. It was the only building situated in the thin, green park that ran along the cliff on the ocean side of Ocean Avenue. The unique placement of the center testified to the great political clout that the elderly had carried in Santa Monica years before.

He picked Samantha up and held her close to the view piece. She squinted, popped her head up to look in the same direction and then back to the telescope. "I can't see anything, Daddy."

Peter pointed across the waves and beach. "See that building in the trees? We're going to a special room in there. It's called the Camera Obscura, which means "dark chamber.""

"Is it scary?"

"Oh, no. It's really neat, Sam. It was invented at least 700 years ago. Artists using it became famous because their paintings were more realistic than anything done before. It was an important part of the Renaissance and one of the birthplaces of the scientific tradition and the Age of Enlightenment.

Sam wrinkled her nose. "You promised me an ice cream, Daddy."

Each carrying a mint-chocolate-chip ice-cream cone, they walked from the pier across a sloping concrete bridge to the edge of downtown Santa Monica. They sauntered up the narrow park, joggers bounding past them, while elsewhere people gathered on the benches and lawn. They passed tired-looking flowers in a planter, then an extensive mosaic of large rocks that covered the front of the slightly worn Senior Recreation Center. Once through the plate-glass doors, they encountered old folks in varying degrees of declining vitality. Some were playing card games while others dozed in their chairs. A sense of depletion hung in the air. Peter had forgotten that they would have to go through this gauntlet of the elderly in order to get into the Camera Obscura. Automatically, he scanned the room. Before the dementia had become too noticeable, his father had spent many hours in these chairs. That seemed long, long ago, although it was no more than two years. He had been embarrassed for his father then, but compared with Martin's current state of deterioration, Peter thought of that period as the good old days. He felt himself teetering on the abyss of his dilemma, and he resisted. It was a tar baby: Once he started thinking about it, he only became more stuck.

"Daddy, come on." He felt a tug on his shirt and gratefully looked down at Samantha. At the office window of the Senior Center, Peter exchanged his driver's license for a key to the Camera Obscura. They went through a side door and up a stairwell that led to the only room on the second floor. Peter let them into a small, windowless compartment with a white, round, four-foot-wide table in the middle. It was encircled by a metal railing and, at one spot, there was a steering wheel. Samantha ran to it and began to turn it, pretending she was driving a car. A grating squeak filled the room.

"Where's the camera, Daddy?" Sam asked as she cranked the wheel.

"I have to turn off the lights, then what is outside will show up right in front of you." He threw the light switch, and the round table glowed in the center of the dark room, hovering like a suspended altar or a miniature spacecraft. Peter and Samantha stood at the perimeter, vaguely illuminated by the cold, reflected light. With Samantha rapidly turning the wheel, the luminous surface reflected grainy scenes that whisked by too quickly to register anything but a sense of trees and buildings. What seemed to be a broad street with cars quickly gave way to sky and ocean.

"The picture is fuzzy, Daddy."

"Stop turning the wheel," he said, and she did. "Now, do you see the ocean?"

"It looks all shiny."

"That's right. Those big waves we saw when we were on the pier seem tiny from up here. Look," he pointed with his finger on the table, "there's the Ferris wheel we were riding."

"I see it!" she shouted happily. "And there's the dragon ride." Then Sam looked around in the dark for a moment. "How can we see outside when we aren't looking outside?"

"Because there's a mirror on the top of this building that turns with that squeaky wheel, and what is outside shows down here on this table."

"So?" she questioned, not understanding.

"It's like we were in a submarine and we sent a periscope above the water to see what was happening," Peter explained.

"What's a perryscope?"

Peter pushed away a surge of impatience and updated his example. "Forget about the periscope. Imagine that there is a tiny video camera on top of this building and that you can aim it any direction you want with the wheel. What is outside gets shown on this table here." He put his hand on the table, and the images covered his skin like a faint tattoo. "What's neat is that no one outside knows we can see them."

"I wanna see more things," Sam said.

"Okay. Turn the wheel slowly. That turns the mirror at the top so we can look in other directions. Now stop. See, there's where you dropped your ice-cream cone on the sidewalk."

"And you let me have the rest of yours. That was nice, Daddy." Samantha looked back at the table. "Look, there are those two men juggling."

"Good, Sam. How many people are sitting on that bus bench?"

"One…two…three…four. And there's an old man like Grandpa waiting to cross the street."

"You're right, Sam, and there's a tall man walking up behind him and looking all around."

"He walks like Big Bird, Daddy. This is like television, 'cept it's harder to see."

"Right."

"Here comes a bus…"

"Jesus Christ!" Peter shouted.

"Daddy," Samantha screamed, "that old man fell and got run over by the bus!"

"He was pushed!" Peter shouted and watched bug-eyed as the tall man in a checkered cap stepped back from the curb. The bus had abruptly halted twenty feet beyond him with its rear end sticking into the street.

Peter yelled, "That guy in the cap shoved him!"

Samantha grabbed onto his leg in the dark. "But what happened to the old man?"

"Look, Sam! That one you called Big Bird…with the checkered cap." Peter leaned forward and put his finger on the table, following the image as the man looked about and distanced himself from the scene.

"I'm scared, Daddy!"

"It's okay, Sam. He can't see us. He doesn't even know we're watching him." Peter stepped closer to the wheel, dragging Samantha, who was attached to his leg, and followed the guy's movement. "Look, he's crossing the street. That son of a bitch is running away!"

Samantha began to whimper.

Peter reached down and picked her up. "Jesus! Okay, Honey, I'm sorry."

Struggling to control her tears, Samantha gasped, "What about the old man, Daddy? Turn it back."

Peter rotated the wheel back to the accident. Passers-by had been drawn in, and a tableau of about ten people stood on the sidewalk, leaning and pointing toward a dark form under the bus. Peter and Samantha observed the silent movie before them. Two people approached the rear wheels and peered underneath. Others inched closer, while from the periphery many more came flocking to see what had happened. Peter hugged Samantha tightly and said, "Let's go see how that old man's doing." Just before they left, Peter turned the wheel and checked out the other side of the street for several blocks. The man in the cap was nowhere to be seen.

3

Continuing: Saturday, January 29, 2005

PETER RUSHED OUT OF the Senior Center carrying Samantha. The bus had stopped with its rear stuck diagonally across the southbound lane, backing up traffic. Horns blared as Peter searched for the murderer among the rubberneckers collecting across the street. When he didn't see him, he veered toward the bus, toward the old man somewhere underneath it.

Samantha began to suck her thumb as they wove their way through the growing, uneasy crowd. Peter didn't want Samantha to see whatever there was to see, but he couldn't think how to avoid it. From inside the bus, the faces of two dozen riders—curious, horrified, impatient—pressed against the windows, staring down at everyone. Peter jostled past the final ring of onlookers and almost fell over a kneeling woman. She was reaching past the rear wheel well, gently touching the old man. There was no blood. There was no movement either. The woman released the old man's wrist and looked up. In a matter-of-fact voice, she said, "This man is dead." The crowd started to buzz as the information made its way outward.

On the other side of the woman, the bus driver sagged heavily against the bus. Immediately, Peter questioned him, "Did you see him get pushed? He was pushed!"

The driver responded defensively. "I only saw the cars in front of me. That old man popped off the sidewalk out of the corner of my eye. I didn't have a chance."

"But didn't you see the guy behind him shove him?"

"I told you, I was looking left, the way I was turning. I didn't see anything...nothing except a blur and then the sound." He seemed to deflate and slowly sat down on the pavement, holding his head in his hands. The woman who had pronounced the old man dead turned to the driver and said, "I'm a doctor. Are you okay?"

Peter glared at the bus driver, then turned to the crowd. "Who else here saw the old guy get pushed?" The crowd shook its many heads, and several people turned away, declaring they hadn't seen anything. "Come on!" Peter said louder and more urgently. "I saw a man push this poor old guy behind his knee so he'd fall under the bus. Who else saw that bastard?" Once again, no one responded. Peter shouted, "He had on a dirty tan windbreaker and a checkered cap!" He lost all calm as he stepped back onto the curb and pointed across the street. "He ran over there," he yelled over the horns and voices. "The cap was orange and brown." Again, no one had anything to say to him.

Searching the other side, Peter thought he caught a glimpse of the guy nearly a block away. In an instant he would replay many times, he demanded, "Hold my little girl!" and pushed Samantha into the incredulous doctor's arms. To Samantha, he vowed, "I'll be right back." She started to cry in unison with the sound of approaching sirens as Peter whirled around, wove through the stalled traffic and began to race up the block. The bum was nowhere in sight. Just past where he figured he had been standing, Peter came to a building under construction. He rushed headlong into the dim, cool interior and almost crashed into two workmen smoking.

"Did you see a guy run in here?" he demanded.

"There's people going in and out all the time, pal."

"What'd this guy do, steal your American Express card?" the other one cracked.

"I think he killed someone!"

"Yeah, right, and you're Batman."

"He looked like a bum, with a cap on."

The other guy shrugged and pointed toward the back of the building. Peter took off running to the rear and looked out onto a small lot, empty except for some construction equipment. Then he charged up the stairs onto the second floor. He darted from empty room to empty room. When he encountered other workers, he hurriedly described the man he was looking for, but no one had seen him. Up he went. Finally, on the fifth floor, after he had heard another variation of, "Buddy, I haven't seen anyone who doesn't belong here," he slumped to the floor.

Peter lay on the cold concrete, gasping. A man with a face like a pre-Columbian sculpture and plaster dust in his black hair appeared. He knelt next to him and looked into Peter's eyes with concern. Suddenly self-conscious, Peter smiled to cover his embarrassment and stood up shakily. He tottered toward the stairwell, clumsily moving faster as thoughts of Samantha replaced those of the bum.

Emerging from the building, Peter took in the flashing lights at the scene of the accident down the street. His lungs ached and his shirt was soaked. With foreboding, he hurried toward the corner to cross the street. How could he have done this to Sam? And yet, he had only been doing the right thing. Worried and defensive, he started to cross, but a policeman blasted a whistle at him and waved him back. Chafing, he returned to the crowd of spectators and watched the police and paramedics hard at work. Uniforms were on the street and inside the bus talking to people, gathering statements. It was as if time had slowed and the experts were trying hard to get it running normally. The air was cooling and a chill added to his dazed condition. Eventually, a cop stepped into the single line of traffic that was worming its way around the accident and stopped it cold. Slowly, silently, an ambulance trailed away with the dead man. There was no need for a siren.

Finally, the group he was part of was allowed to cross. He hurried to the other side and jostled his way into the large crowd surrounding the bus. A tight cluster of some of the regulars from the Senior Center who had been drawn outside by the accident slowed him.

"It was Adrian. I'm sure it was," said an old man with a cane. "He goes home this way every afternoon."

"Dear God!" an elderly woman with white hair cried out. "Adrian Montero. I was just playing gin rummy with him," she said to no one in particular.

"At least it was quick," a man standing next to her said. "That's more than most of us can look forward to," he added with a wheezy laugh.

"Somebody should call his daughter," said another.

"We could walk over to his house," the woman with the white hair said. "It's only a few blocks." She hesitated, not getting any support for her plan.

Pushing his way through, Peter recognized the doctor as she stepped out from behind the bus. Samantha was still in her arms, intently sucking her thumb and looking curiously at a policeman who was interviewing the doctor. Peter continued, dreading the impending moment.

"Daddy, Daddy," Samantha cried when she saw him. She wriggled out of the doctor's grasp and raced to Peter. "You ran away!" she said after she jumped into his arms.

"I know, Honey. I'm very sorry. Are you all right?" Peter asked in a hushed voice.

Samantha's brow wrinkled. "No! You ran away."

"I'm really, really sorry, Sam, but I had to."

Sam glared at him. "I don't like you, Daddy."

"Right." He hugged her tightly. "You're mad, and now I'm back."

"Right," Sam agreed. With one arm, she held on to his neck and said over her thumb that had found its way back into her mouth, "There are lots of police people here."

"I know; I need to talk to them."

"But the man who got dead isn't," she added.

Peter told his story to the police, but it was rushed, cut short by his whining, increasingly impatient daughter. The supervising cop at the scene assured him they would pursue the case rigorously, gave him his card and said to call if he remembered anything else. Samantha cried all the way home, because she didn't want to sit in the car seat in the back. It was too far from him. When they got to their exclusive "north of Montana" home, she wouldn't even let him make a phone call to tell Judith what they had seen. She didn't want to play with dolls, color or sit in front of their big-screen television. She wanted his complete attention.

She whined steadily as Peter carried her throughout the house from room to remodeled room. They ended up in the inner courtyard with the Moorish fountain. Not even the goldfish helped. With his head throbbing, he started to read her *The Runaway Bunny* on the suede couch in the living room. Even though it was a twist on the original story, Peter was able to reassure her that he would always come back and find her. By the time they had read it twice, she had conked out.

Peter stroked Sam's hair as her breathing slowed and considered his lovely daughter. She was growing out of her toddler pudginess and elongating into a young colt. She was becoming more and more like her mother. A nauseous tension gripped his stomach: guilt for leaving her. He knew what had happened, but he didn't understand it. And, if he couldn't understand why he'd acted like he had, he was sure that Judith was going to have an even harder time of it. He'd fallen in love with her, in part, because she was independent, a liberated woman. But now that she had a kid, a high-powered job and a husband who shared in everything, she was also worried—too worried for his taste—that Samantha was suffering from lack of parental contact. Since he had more time with Sam, Judith's concern often centered on his parenting choices. It was a tender spot even when things were going smoothly.

He sat staring at the sweat dripping down his bottle of beer onto the egrets engraved in the glass coffee table and replayed the events of the afternoon over and over. By the time he heard the sound of the front door opening, he was convinced that by handing Samantha to the doctor he had done the only logical thing. Quietly, he unwrapped himself from Samantha and hurried into the foyer. Pointing to Samantha, he signaled his wife to be quiet before she even had a chance to kick off her heels. "Judith," he whispered, "you won't believe what happened. We saw someone get murdered right on Ocean Avenue."

Judith's green eyes widened. Fear quickly replaced surprise, and she dropped her briefcase and purse and rushed to look at Samantha. "Sam's fine," he whispered. "She conked out from all the excitement." Judith looked at him skeptically, and they both headed for their bedroom where he started to lay out what had happened. She said very little until he got to the part about chasing after the man. "What?" she burst out, "You handed Samantha to a stranger and ran off after this…this… murderer?"

"For Chrissake, I gave her to a doctor," Peter said, "and a woman at that," he added quickly.

"But you left Samantha with a stranger at the scene of a murder!" she exclaimed.

"Look, I knew she was safe. I realize it seems extreme, but it was my only chance to catch that son of a bitch. You know me: Either you stand up to the crap in this world or you don't have a right to complain. And this guy was evil. Besides..."

Judith marched back into the living room in the middle of his rationale and knelt next to her daughter.

Peter followed her in. "She's exhausted," he whispered. "We just got home a while ago." Then he added into the silence, "You're going to have to trust me that she really is okay."

"I'm trying, Peter," she whispered earnestly and walked back to the bedroom. "Okay," she said, taking a big breath and trying to relax, "tell me more about how she reacted."

"Like I said, we were up in the Camera Obscura watching the street when it happened. All of a sudden this old man caved in under the bus. Sam was freaked out. She knew he had been hurt, but she didn't really understand that the man behind him had pushed him." Peter sat on the edge of their bed. "It was done subtly. That's a strange word for something that was so violent, but it fits."

Judith's eyes narrowed. "What about when you left her with the doctor?"

He sighed and looked at her. "I won't lie to you. She got upset and scared." Peter started to carry on with a more vivid description, but stopped himself.

"What about when you got back?"

"She was mad at me. I apologized, and after a few moments she let it go. I think for her the whole thing was kind of like a dream. For me it was a nightmare." He smoothed out the silky, lime-green coverlet he was sitting on. "It was hard to believe what we were seeing."

The edge came off of Judith's voice. "Do you think there's anything we should do?"

"I feel like I should, but the police said they would keep looking for this guy. I mean, I talked to them until Sam got too, too...restless."

"I wonder whether we should take Sam to a therapist."

"Come on, Judith. This isn't going to be some big trauma that she'll have to deal with for the rest of her life. I left her for ten or fifteen minutes. She was upset and pissed off, and, believe me, she let me know it when I got back. When we got home, I had the brilliant idea to read her *The Runaway Bunny*. She accepted that I had been both the runaway bunny and his mother who always finds him. End of problem as far as I can tell, at least for her."

"Let's hope so." Judith looked down at him and touched his cheek, then removed her gray suit jacket and unpinned her name card:

Welcome to the **JOB FAIR**
Judith Goldman, Ph.D., R.N.
Vice President, Human Resources
The Wellness Corporation

"So the police didn't find this guy in the cap?"

"Hell, no," Peter said with disgust.

"I don't understand how he got away. Weren't there others who saw him push the old man?"

"Montero. He has—had—a name, Adrian Montero," Peter reacted, then explained his conundrum. "One or two people remembered seeing the bum. But so far, nobody else has come forward to say that they saw what I saw."

"Do you think they're scared to testify?" Judith asked from her walk-in closet, where she was hanging up her stuff.

"Worse than that." Peter continued, "It could be that, except for me and Sam hidden away in our secret tower, nobody else was watching that bastard and Montero as the bus came. Long after it happened, I remembered that as he approached Montero he'd been looking around, as if to make sure no one was watching him. He stared right at the Senior Center, but, of course, he couldn't see us. Even so, he was real sneaky. He stepped in behind Montero and bent at the knees so that his right knee nudged behind Montero's left knee. Then he gave Montero a little push: just a little dip into the knee and a subtle shove. All this happened just as the bus was closing in, and Adrian Montero melted under the bus like—" he paused— "like fucking angel hair pasta dropped into boiling water. Then, the bastard slowly backed away as if nothing had happened."

"But he couldn't have gotten too far away," she called from the dressing room.

"That's why I ran off to find him," Peter's voice rose, "and the cops went to look after I told them what happened, but it was too little, too late." Peter lay back on the bed, exhaustion setting in. "I've got to assume that the police believe that I could have seen what happened from the Camera Obscura."

She returned to the bedroom in jeans and a blouse. "And you're sure you saw this old man get pushed?" What had started out as a statement ended up sounding like a question, and she reached out to touch him to soften the effect.

He pulled his head away. "Of course I am. Why else would I have freaked out like I did?"

She dropped her hand. "I don't know, Peter. The whole thing is hard to imagine."

"What's hard to imagine is that old man being killed like that: I mean for no fucking reason!" He paused. "I went a little crazy. I made up for all the aerobics I've put off for the last five years." Silence. "I hate feeling helpless. I mean, I'm used to taking charge. I'm not …"

"Peter?" Judith said with a questioning tone in her voice, verbal shorthand that had developed over their ten years together that meant he was going off on a tangent. This time it worked.

"Anyway, some of the people just stared at me like I was crazy for saying it was a murder. It was shoot-the-fucking-messenger time."

She sat next to him and put her hand on his shoulder. "What

happens now?"

This time he accepted her touch. "I don't know. I've got to assume the cops will track this guy down, even though they may be as skeptical as you are. The only thing I'm sure of is that somebody got killed today and I'm the only one who noticed."

"The whole thing is bizarre, Peter. Mysterious. You don't do well with mysterious."

"Meaning?"

"You like to nail things down. You're a moralist. I know you." She patted his leg.

He smiled tiredly. "I wish you'd been there."

"I do, too, but what if I missed what you saw, just like everybody else did?"

"Well, there's a supportive thought." He stood up.

"I'm trying, but it's a lot to take in all at once."

"Tell me about it," he said with a mixture of frustration and sarcasm. He looked at his watch. "I think we'd better get Sam up, or she'll never get back to sleep tonight." As he headed out of the bedroom, the doorbell rang. "We ordered some Thai food. I was going to poach salmon, but there was no way she was going to let me cook."

Between bites of mostly white rice and carefully avoiding green peppers, Samantha told her mother the story of the man who got dead and all the policemen and the nice doctor and her bad, bad daddy. Cuddled in the attention of her parents, the terror of death and abandonment was absorbed into the fabric of a story with a beginning and an ending. Soon after dinner, she announced she was too tired for a bath and that it was Mommy's turn to tuck her into bed.

There were no disagreements. Together, there was a fluid ease to their childcare. It had always been that way, and it had become the glue of their marriage.

Peter tried to correct some student papers, but he couldn't

concentrate. Finally, he went into the den. Using Samantha's crayons, he drew little sketches of the palisades with the Senior Center and the bus on the street, then crumpled them up and threw them toward the trash can.

In bed after the lights were out, Peter was too wired to sleep. He caressed Judith's hip, looking for a release. She lay still, unresponsive. Mercy sex, as they called it, theoretically wasn't out of the question. But worry and what-ifs had spread a shadow over their bed and added to a collection of resentments, some petty and some deserved, that lay between them. As random images from the day bombarded his mind like a dartboard, Peter tried to unwind. When Judith finally touched his arm, it didn't register as encouragement. When he became aware that her breathing had deepened into sleep, he turned away to a long, fitful night.

4

Sunday, January 30, 2005

P ETER AWOKE WITH A mission. He leaned over the
slumbering body of Samantha, who had crawled into bed
with them in the middle of the night, and excitedly whispered
to Judith, "Wake up! I want to go back to the Camera Obscura
so you can see for yourself."

"Peter," Judith groaned, "it's Sunday; let me sleep."

Undeterred, he rocked her gently and continued, "I'll go to
the street and act out what I saw, and you'll see and understand
what happened."

Judith opened her eyes enough to peek at the clock. "It's six
o'clock. They won't be open for hours."

"Right." He retreated for a moment. "I'll call and see when
they open, but I want to do it today, as soon as possible."

"I don't want Samantha to go back there," she whispered.

"You're probably right. Shit, here's a reason we shouldn't have
let her nanny go.

"What do you mean, "we," you cheapskate?" She squeezed
his hand affectionately and rolled away, toward sleep.

"I don't regret letting that nanny go. It's ridiculous how most middle-class families live like royalty did a hundred years ago, except that takeout food had replaced cooks. But this is a crisis. I'll call your mom. She'll be thrilled to have Sam for a while."

"Not if you call her at six, " she mumbled.

Peter jumped out of bed. He put on slacks and a sports coat and went to an early Mass to help kill time, but left right after communion. He buzzed around impatiently for the next few hours until he finally had Judith situated in front of the glowing table at the Camera Obscura with the view of the crosswalk and bus stop plainly visible. "Stand here and don't move. Watch right there," he pointed, "and I'll run down and show you what happened."

"Peter, I feel silly. This isn't going to prove anything. I mean, I told you that I take your word for what happened."

"Taking my word isn't enough. I want your outrage over what happened. I can tell you're skeptical, so it's important to show you that, at the very least, I could have seen it, and maybe, if there's someone down there whom I can stand behind, you'll get a sense of how it happened."

Judith cocked an eyebrow at him. "Don't kill anybody."

"Very funny," he said seriously. "If anyone comes in, don't let them turn the wheel."

Approaching the street, Peter pivoted and waved awkwardly toward the mirror in the odd metal hat attached to the top of the little tower that constituted the second floor. He felt strange being watched, but even stranger occupying the same space where Adrian Montero had been pushed. He dipped at the knee a few times, but backed away as a couple of middle-aged tourists approached the curb and stood waiting for the light. Then he walked up behind them and did a little dipping motion until the woman glanced over her shoulder and gave him a look. He stepped away and, with a self-conscious grin on his face, motioned to Judith to come down.

Waiting for her, he looked thirty feet away to the bus stop and then to the people who were coming and going around him. There were more people stirring about than the day before. He felt a faint surge of hope that the bum was lingering nearby. But, for all the meandering people, there was no one who looked the least bit like that tall, gawky bastard with his big Adam's apple. Big Bird was way too benevolent an image for this bastard. He was a mad man: He was Mad Max.

Peter suddenly felt very self-conscious, flooded with the sense that trying to solve this was ludicrous, impossible, a fool's errand. His litany of doubts was interrupted as he looked across the street. The big Blue No. 7 bus idled ominously opposite him, where Broadway ended at Ocean Avenue, perched just like it had been before it ran over Adrian. The light changed, and the bus lunged forward into a wide-arcing left turn. Mesmerized, Peter watched as it approached, accelerating rapidly. As it loomed, wind poured off the front of the bus, pushing him slightly away from it until its bumper swept over the curb a mere foot from where he was standing. At that point, the wind curved around and began to pull him under the bus as it passed by. Peter's entire being recoiled in terror as he resisted the vacuum that suddenly pulled at him. His body experienced what his eyes had seen the day before. While he could easily withstand the suction, if he were to fall at that moment, or were shoved, he too could be sucked under.

The bus whooshed to a stop thirty feet beyond him to pick up a passenger. Then, expelling its exhaust on Peter, it was gone as quickly as it had swept in. With the vibrations still in his chest and his knees shaky, he teetered to the bus bench and sat. Fear simultaneously constricted and spread out from his chest. Mad Max was smooth. And he was deadly.

"You're right, Peter," Judith laughed and slid in next to him, "I could see things quite clearly, including that woman who was about to punch you out for trying to spoon her husband." She was having fun now. Her high-energy, idealistic, preoccupied husband wanted to spend the morning with her. It had been a while since that had happened. Maybe she could get him to go to a gallery in Bergamot Station and turn it into a real date.

Peter's ashen face silenced her levity. He led her back to the crosswalk and pointed out the chalk marks on the street where Adrian Montero had lain the day before. "I didn't want it to be true, Judith. Bringing you down here, I was thinking maybe I was wrong, that maybe I'd overlooked something. But I'm right, God dammit. That poor bastard was murdered."

"You've done everything you can to help the police catch him," Judith insisted. Peter's countenance flushed, ready to argue, but he had no retort. Sullenly, he returned home, forgetting to return the key to the Camera Obscura as he had planned.

That afternoon, he took his dad to a big-band concert at Disney Hall. Peter always thought of jazz as a gift from his dad, a language they shared. It sometimes seemed like the only thing that had saved them after his mom died was Gerry Mulligan or Dizzy Gillespie pouring out of the speakers when they were at home. Duke Ellington had filled a lot of empty spaces, and Dave Brubeck soothed the hungry ghosts that roamed that house. But on Sunday, even the A Train had lost its magic. The part of Martin's awareness that controlled audience behavior was lost. He was anxious, and he kept trying to dance or leave. Finally, Peter gave up trying to keep him in his seat, and they walked through downtown Los Angeles until Martin was worn out.

On Monday at school, Peter got a message from Sergeant Jones, the supervising officer who had interviewed him, asking to talk to him again. Peter eagerly called back, but Jones just wanted to know if Peter had remembered anything new. After Peter went over his story for him, Jones assured him they were doing everything they could and hung up. For the next few days, scenes from the murder flashed in Peter's head, but he told himself to be patient. His tenuous equilibrium was shattered on Wednesday, when a local paper called Montero's death an "apparent accident." At lunchtime, he marched the few blocks from the high school to the new police station and was ushered into an interview room. In a few minutes, Sergeant Dan Jones, a muscular man of about forty whose body was going to fat, entered. He'd been lifting pizzas and donuts instead of barbells. It soon became obvious that he didn't like being pushed. "Why in the hell are the cops downplaying the possibility of a murder?" Peter blurted out.

"Slow down, Mr. Winston. We interviewed everyone who was on the bus or standing nearby," Jones said. "Two bus riders recalled somebody who looked like your murderer, but neither one saw him push Mr. Montero. On the contrary, they both stated quite emphatically that they didn't see the guy do anything suspicious. The bus driver particularly denied seeing anything. He also mentioned that he had told you the same thing."

Peter shot back, "He also told me he was looking the other way. Anyway, that's only three people: Go back and interview the rest of the people on the bus again or those construction workers I mentioned. And how about putting a notice in the paper asking for witnesses? There's probably some tourist out there who saw it all, but took off before you guys got there, like the murderer did. I mean, it's not like you showed up right away."

"Besides interviewing over twenty people, including those construction workers, we also went to all the businesses near the corner of the incident to see if their security videos caught anything suspicious."

"They have cameras on all the time?"

"Some do, twenty-four seven. But the only one that shows that corner is in a restaurant across the street, and its view was blocked by a plant. So we came up empty."

Peter insisted, "Listen, Sergeant, I know what I saw."

Jones countered, "With an eyewitness account like yours, we have even more reason to push for corroboration. But, because you indicated there was no murder weapon, no shell casings or other physical evidence to be found, we didn't call in Homicide. We call it a 'traffic,' but that doesn't mean we've ruled out murder."

Peter hesitated a moment, then asked, "Do you guys actually believe what I've told you?"

"We don't just take people's word. I checked you out a little. Your principal vouched for you. She said you're reliable, and a top-notch teacher."

"You checked me out?" Peter looked insulted. "Well, since I'm 'reliable,' I guess all we have to do is catch him."

"Yes, but there's another potential problem. My partner and I staged a re-enactment of what you described happening, and we were less than impressed by how clear the image is from the Camera Obscura."

"So now I'm lying?"

"Not at all. I'm just saying that things aren't very clear from up there, and that's going to create problems if we ever find this guy and go to trial."

"What?" Peter began to argue.

"Reasonable doubt, Mr. Winston. If this has us wondering if you could see clearly enough, imagine the fun a defense attorney would have taking a jury up there to see for themselves."

"But people don't normally get pulled under buses. That's got to be unique."

"Not necessarily. Most years there are two or three deaths from slipstream accidents in the L.A. area."

"'Slipstream?'" Peter repeated. "You mean there's even a fucking name for it?"

Peter crumbled at that point. As he trudged back to school, what he was up against began to sink in. After repeatedly going over what had happened in those few seconds, he began to accept that he and Samantha, from their hidden aerie on the second floor, were the only ones to see Montero being pushed.

Everyone else was focused elsewhere, lost in his or her own little world. That meant that even if the cops picked up Mad Max, he'd deny it, and with no other witnesses, he might get away with it. Frustration pulsed through Peter's body. The old wrestler wanted to get his hands on that son of a bitch. There were dozens of ways to force a confession out of him. Otherwise, proving there had been a murder seemed like a lost cause.

Back at his desk, Peter's anger disintegrated into nausea. He felt like a victim of circumstance, and that was unacceptable. People were never stuck in their situations. They only ran out of imagination or courage. He'd lived by this belief since he had decided that the failure of the 60's cultural and political revolution wasn't going to stop him from succeeding in life. He'd made millions of dollars before "retiring" to teach history. If he could do that, he could solve this.

Peter reviewed the situation. He knew there was a murder and who had done it. He knew who, what, when and where, but he didn't know why. What was missing was the motive: Why would someone want to kill Adrian Montero?

After school, Peter found Montero's obituary in the *Los Angeles Times*. "Bullshit," he swore under his breath as he read that Montero had died in an accident. He had lived in Santa Monica all his 83 years, a Mexican-American native son. He had been an Army photographer in World War ll, then went to work in the film industry, where he patented some gizmo that he sold to Motorola. Eventually, he opened his own photography studio, where he had worked until he had retired. He left a daughter and a stepson and had outlived his wife by twenty years.

Peter found Adrian Montero in the phone book, but he couldn't believe the address: 817 Ocean Avenue was more than exclusive; it was unique. It was about seven blocks north of the Camera Obscura, on the other side of the street. But, as far as Peter could remember, there weren't any private homes left on that street. There were office towers, expensive multi-story condos and fancy hotels. Montero's address meant he had not only made good money, but had also been very astute. He'd had the good sense to buy himself a little piece of paradise in the fifties or sixties, before the price of paradise rose so high that only corporations could afford it.

Peter called Sam's nursery school and explained that he'd be late picking her up. He felt a twinge of guilt, but he told himself that he had to get to the bottom of this, that Sam was flexible and other kids stayed a lot later. He also called Juanita, who told him that his father was in his garden in the backyard.

He pulled to a stop in front of 817. He wavered between excitement and apprehension as he took in the rambling, two-story wooden house set back among overgrown bushes and trees. The retired investment banker deep inside Peter was suddenly wide-awake. There was a shitload of money at stake in the affairs of Adrian Montero, even though the place itself had exhausted its charm. The carved wooden beams on the wraparound porch were splintered and weathered. The Greene and Greene handcrafted elegance had been badly betrayed. Peter turned away from the house and looked across Ocean Avenue to the narrow greenbelt of the park that hugged the top of the cliff. From there, his eyes shifted to the limitless horizon of the Pacific Ocean. What couldn't deteriorate was the view of the Santa Monica Bay. That went for over four or five hundred dollars a night at the hotels nearby. This joint was a funky, multimillion-dollar diamond, just waiting to be picked up.

He knocked on a heavy oak door several times before a tall, thin, haggard woman with dyed, eggplant-colored hair down to her shoulders tugged it open over the protest of squeaking hinges. A palpable cloud of despair and confusion surrounded her as she stared at him in silence, a rag in one hand and a spray bottle of lime cleanser in the other. Except for the hair, her resemblance to the ashen corpse he had seen just a few days before was staggering. He wanted to ask Montero's daughter if her father had had any enemies, but it seemed like too cruel a question, especially coming from a stranger.

"Sorry to bother you. My name is Peter Winston. I was there when your father died, and I wanted..."

"You were there?" she interrupted, and then lamented, "I should have been there." The timbre of her voice was irritating, a whine that even grief couldn't soften.

"To be honest, there was nothing anyone could have done for him," he responded, but his words only provoked tears. "At least, it was quick," he added. She wiped at her eyes and looked at him as if he were happy about that fact. "I mean, he didn't suffer," he explained.

The woman began to speak as if she were in the middle of a story. "He had lunch at the Senior Center nearly every day: It was free. On his way home, he'd take Broadway to the Third Street Promenade, then up the Promenade through all the crazy street entertainers to California Avenue, back to the palisades and home for his nap. That was his route." Recounting her father's routine seemed to comfort her. She added, "He was a walker, like me, though I prefer the beach. At least we had that in common." The tears returned in full force.

Uncomfortable with her naked grief, Peter said, "My father used to go to the Senior Center."

"Is he dead?" she asked through her gloom.

Peter winced and shook his head.

"You're lucky," she said. "You can still help him be content." She put down the cleanser. "I shouldn't have left my father." Mechanically, she pulled some tissue from the sleeve of her black high-neck sweater and blew her chafed nose. As she finished, she suddenly fixed on him with a quizzical look, as if he had just appeared. "What do you want, Mr. Winston?"

"I'm sorry to tell you this," he began, "but I saw someone push your father." She stared at him, and he couldn't figure out if she was shocked or was waiting for him to make his point.

"The newspaper and the police are wrong. Your father was killed, and I'm trying to figure out who would want..."

"Who did it?" Her voice dropped an octave.

"A bum, about six feet tall with a long red neck and a big Adam's apple and a checkered cap. Probably an alcoholic, maybe homeless."

"That doesn't make sense. Why would some homeless man want to kill my father?"

"That's what I'm trying to figure out. He might be crazy, you know, pathological: getting commands from the CIA through the fillings in his teeth or something like that, but that's not what it felt like. It seemed like he was just doing a job."

"Whoever killed my father must pay for it," she stated with authority.

"I completely agree. But it's going to be even harder to figure out who paid some guy to do it." Peter shrugged and gestured with both hands. "It could be anyone."

She cocked her head and looked at him suspiciously. "You're not another detective?"

"No, I teach history at Santa Monica High School."

"Because I already told them it wasn't me, even if there were times I wanted to."

"Okay," Peter said slowly, unsure of how to read her defensive tone. "I wasn't suggesting…"

"I moved out six months ago. I told the detectives that when they interviewed me." Her voice had climbed back to the higher, grating lament. "The neighbors and some people I work with know I was angry—enraged, to be honest. I didn't tell the police that. Maybe I should have. Maybe people suspect me."

"But it wasn't you I saw," Peter said.

"I could have hired someone. Isn't that what people do?" Her eyes seemed glued to his. "I certainly had murderous thoughts, before and after I moved out." A humorless cackle erupted, then faded to a whisper. "I dyed my hair instead and tried to live a little." Tears leaked down her cheeks. "I guess the joke's on me."

Peter was too embarrassed to know what to say.

"Don't feel sorry for me," she said, wiping her eyes while looking at him intently. "I'm sure I've inherited lots of money." She awkwardly gestured around her. "I thought this would always remain my home with the garden that my mother started. My father destroyed that dream, and instead, I'm going to be rich. That's supposed to be wonderful, isn't it? I've never been rich before. Are you rich?"

"Uh, well, sort of."

"Does it make you happy?"

"Uh, not exactly," Peter stammered.

"That's too bad, though it doesn't surprise me." Her look changed from piercing to aloof scrutiny. Peter felt like he was being evaluated by an alien being. "Is there anything else? I have to get on with the cleaning."

Confused and at a momentary loss for words, Peter finally asked, "Does that mean this house is for sale?"

Her face lost all of its color once again. "This was very cruel, Mr. Winston, to pretend to care about my father so you could worm your way into buying this house. You are heartless, a vulture!" She slammed the door behind her.

Peter slunk back to his car. His first attempt at playing investigator couldn't have gone worse. The woman was grief-stricken, but that didn't mean she didn't have something to hide. She seemed unhinged, but was she crazy or greedy enough to concoct a plot to kill her father? He didn't know and he didn't want to care, but he did. He looked at the old house nestled amid an unruly growth of banana trees tangled up with other overgrown foliage. He needed to explain to someone close to the family, someone saner, what he had seen and get them to solve the mystery. He nodded to himself; it was the ethical thing to do.

He grabbed the obituary from the passenger seat. The funeral would be the next afternoon. He'd have to take off the last period from teaching, but then he could forget this mess.

5

Thursday, February 3, 2005

The funeral mass had already started when Peter slipped into the back of St. Monica's Church on Thursday afternoon. He had stopped off to put a lock on the side gate of his father's house. The day before, Martin had wandered out of the backyard shortly after Peter had spoken to Juanita. It was only a matter of luck that she had found him before he got lost or injured.

St. Monica's was Peter's neighborhood church as well as Adrian Montero's, but it wasn't where Peter went to Mass. Logically, it should have been, but when he had reclaimed his Catholic faith fifteen years earlier, logic hadn't been the decisive factor. Losing his shirt in the junk-bond crisis of 1989 had left him in crisis and, out of desperation, he had gone to Mass at the church of his youth, St. Paul the Apostle in Westwood. To his relief, he found that comfort was still available to him in the pews he'd sat in as a boy.

Initially surprised by his return to the Church, Peter came to appreciate that he had been raised not only to believe, but also to know things in a way that transcended logic. Sitting with his mother every week in Mass as a young child had established that there were answers to life's mysteries. A seemingly innate sense of knowing what life was all about was something that had never left him, even when he stopped going to church following her death. For many years, he had rejected God. He had absorbed his father's scientific explanations of the natural world and still found them true. But his return to the fold was proof of the Jesuits' insight that if the Church had reign over a child's mind for the first seven years, it would determine what kind of man he'd become.

Peter was aware that his faith wasn't the same as when he was young. Nothing in him would ever again be that pure, or that simple. The second time around, he had to decide to believe and doubts and questions littered his path. He agreed with others who said that faith without doubt was either nostalgia or addiction and since no one could solve the mysteries of life rationally, believing seemed like a better choice. To Peter, God was everywhere. He was all the phenomena that had created life, starting with the big bang. Peter was no Creationist. For him, the Bible was divinely inspired because humans were creations of the divine. God was evolution. God became manifest as chemistry begot life, life begot consciousness and consciousness was struggling to give birth to something else. No one knew what that was, and that's where faith and responsibility came in. But that there was a God and a universal design, he had no doubt.

Peter watched as the priest genuflected and carried on with the 2,000-year-old ritual. He liked being in church. It was where humans confronted their faults and their higher selves as represented by Jesus. Peter had lived without Him for almost twenty-five years, and it was frightening how lost he had become. In Jesus, he rediscovered forgiveness for his own failings and a reason to be optimistic. Though he hadn't walked down the church aisles proclaiming it, he indeed felt born again. In church, with Jesus, he was safe, even though he didn't trust most of the sexually naïve priests who wanted to speak for Him. No wonder that so many of these men who had stopped their sexual development in adolescence had, later in their lives, turned to adolescents for sexual outlets. Peter could feel himself getting ready for a good rant, but dropped it as the priest, a tall, handsome man with silver leavening his thick, black hair, began delivering his homily from Romans 14: 7-13.

"For none of us lives to himself, and no one dies to himself. And if we live, we live to the Lord; and if we die, we die to the Lord. Therefore, whether we live or die, we are the Lord's."

Peter agreed. He had decided that Jesus was the best model for living a meaningful life that he could find. People needed guidance in this crazy, fucked-up world.

"For to this end, Christ died and rose and lived again, that He might be Lord of both the dead and the living."

Peter had trouble with this as a literal event, but he had returned to his religion because he believed in Jesus' saying that the kingdom of heaven was within, right here, right now. The only death that resurrection required was ego death. He had only rarely achieved that ecstatic state, but he knew it existed.

The priest finished his reading with, "So then each of us shall give account of himself to God. Therefore, let us not judge one another anymore, but rather resolve this, not to put a stumbling block or a cause to fall into our brother's way."

That was the core lesson, Peter thought. The choice of how to be in this world is between each person and God. But someone had put a big stumbling block in Adrian Montero's way, and Peter was simply trying to bring justice to that situation. If each person didn't do his part to control evil, then the whole experiment of life was in peril.

The priest continued his comments, but he never mentioned Adrian Montero directly. Peter wondered if it was purposeful. If you viewed death as impersonal, as the priest seemed to, there was no cause to focus on who died, even at his own funeral. Whatever the reason, there was a cool, businesslike quality to this guy.

The priest turned back to the altar as he prepared to consecrate the host, to perform the event that constituted the core of the Catholic experience. To many Catholics, turning bread and wine into the body and blood of Jesus was a miracle performed solely by priests. But Peter knew that that wasn't something the Apostles had done, and it wasn't part of Church teaching for several hundred years after Christ's death. The problem was that it created a hierarchy of holiness. To Peter, the body and blood of Jesus were all the people emulating Jesus. What made Jesus present was the congregation gathering in Jesus' name, replicating Jesus' radical example of love and forgiveness in their own way. Belief didn't require some macabre miracle or hocus-pocus. Catholics committed a multitude of good works in Jesus' name, like supporting orphanages, battered-women's shelters and AIDS services. This is what helped Peter to believe in transubstantiation. To him, it signified that change was possible when people trusted and worked together. Peter watched the priest as he slowly raised the host overhead. *We should all be up there*, he thought.

Peter quickly left the church as the Mass ended in order to get to the cemetery before everyone else. He wanted to observe those who showed up from a discreet distance. That seemed like what a private eye would do in order to pick up clues about Montero's murder. The cemetery was on a hill on Fourteenth Street, close enough to the ocean that brisk sea air mixed with the smell of the pine trees on the cemetery grounds. The sky was a deep blue and the light almost painfully clear. The sun shimmered off the ocean like melting diamonds, so vivid that Peter couldn't look at it. It was the sort of midwinter Los Angeles day that enticed bored and freezing souls to migrate to Southern California after seeing it on TV while watching the Rose Bowl. Even though it was real, it was also illusory, because it gave the impression that things could be perfect if only you were in the right place. The day, he thought ruefully, was like the murder, real but illusory.

He sagged against a tree as he watched the hearse and seven cars wind their way through the cemetery toward him. He was used to controlling situations, but this one was getting away from him. He could tell that Judith wished he would let it go, and Sam had lost interest in it completely. She had stopped sucking her thumb, the habit she had started again during the "dead yelling time," as she had poetically named it, and had moved on to more serious matters, like trying to pee into the toilet while standing. As far as he could tell, that was the only evidence of penis envy. Otherwise, she seemed quite content with herself.

The entourage pulled up at the gravesite. From the limousine emerged the tall priest and Montero's daughter. Two other priests and about fifteen other mourners made up the rest of the burial party. He recognized several of the old card players from the Senior Center. There was even a good chance that the poor guy had been a friend of his father's. For a brief moment, he thought of asking his dad about Montero, but Martin hardly remembered his own son.

Peter stood at the back of the group until the graveside service came to an end. His palms became sweaty. He hadn't uncovered a single clue, and he was having a hard time getting up the courage to talk with the family. He didn't want to upset them further, but he felt an obligation. When the mourners began to exchange condolences and disperse, Peter approached the priest who had said the Mass.

"Excuse me, Father. Could you point out Mr. Montero's son to me? I need to speak with him."

The man turned and removed his dark glasses, revealing tearless, dark brown eyes. "Adrian Montero was my stepfather. He had no biological sons."

"I'm sorry for your loss, Father," Peter replied automatically. The priest gave only a slight nod. Peter tried to contain his judgment of this aloof man. "So, you are Father Montero?"

"No, I am Father Frank Greening."

"Well, my name is Peter Winston, and I was present—sort of present—when Mr. Montero was…"

"Yes, the police mentioned your name."

"They did? What did they say?"

"They said that you thought that Adrian had been pushed, murdered. They wanted to know if we could think of anyone who might have wanted to kill him. We tried to think of someone, but I'm afraid that the idea seems implausible."

"How can you be sure?"

"How is one sure of anything, Mr. Winston? What we do know is that as Adrian grew older, he became more and more a creature of habit. He not only had no enemies, but, except for his card games and lunches at the Senior Center, he barely had any friends."

"It may be that he had no known enemies," Peter declared, "but I want you to know that what I have isn't a theory. I saw a man stand behind your stepfather near the bus stop and intentionally push him so he'd fall under the oncoming bus."

The priest eyed him carefully. "You saw this yourself?"

"Yes! Absolutely!" Peter insisted. "The problem is, I saw it from the Camera Obscura. I wasn't on the street." Peter resisted looking away, afraid of being disbelieved. "I know it seems like a long shot, but I swear to you that I really could see what happened." Peter's voice became louder, and some of the others looked their way.

"For what it's worth, I know that what you are suggesting is technically possible." Father Greening's manner warmed. "I was born a year before the Camera Obscura was installed on the palisades in 1955. Ironically, perhaps, it was Adrian who took me there for the first time when I was four or five." The priest cleared his throat, seemingly affected with more emotion than he'd shown during the Mass he'd said. "As I grew up, I spent many an hour observing the world from it. It offered a rather intoxicating anonymity. More to the point, I know what can be seen from up there."

Peter felt himself relax for the first time in nearly a week. "It's one of my favorite places, too."

"However," the priest continued more sternly, "I am sure that you could be mistaken about what you saw. Adrian had become a little unsteady, and he could have fallen. Or, it might have been an accidental bump, one that many people these days, especially a man who didn't want to have to explain himself to the police, might run from. That doesn't make it acceptable, of course, but it isn't murder. Therefore, unless the police come up with a suspect or, at least, a plausible motive…"

"Frank?"

Peter turned to see Montero's daughter approaching and lifting up the black lace veil that shaded her face. As she recognized Peter, her eyes flared.

Father Greening responded, "Marta, this is the man the police told us had witnessed the accident."

"Well, he is also another bloodsucking real estate leech."

"I apologize. I'm really not… "

"Save your sales talk, Mr. Winston. You're too late. We're all too late, at least ten years too late." She expelled a piercing yelp, a convulsive "Haw!" wrapped in helplessness. "He sold our house without telling anyone." Again she barked at her own obscure joke.

Peter looked at her brother to see if he found his sister as strange as he did, but Father Greening was looking away.

"Can you imagine?" Marta continued, "He found fools who bought him out, gave him the money and then agreed to wait until he died before they took possession of it. He was clever, my father was, more clever than anyone knew." She glared at Peter, then turned back to her brother. "Paco, let's go."

Peter became alarmed as they turned to leave. He was being left to solve this mystery all by himself. "Father, who bought your father's place?" he called out.

"You're too late, Mr. Winston," Marta snapped as she walked away.

Father Greening stopped. "Marta…" He gave up and turned to Peter. "I'm sorry. Marta was very close to her father, and this has been very upsetting."

"Yeah, I can see that."

"It's a development company, TMF and Associates."

"What do you know about them?"

"Nothing, actually. Sergeant Jones spoke with them or investigated them, whatever it's called." He shrugged. "Evidently, they are above suspicion."

"Didn't you know about them before?"

Father Greening's handsome face hardened, and his mouth turned down. "That's personal, Mr. Winston, family business that doesn't concern anyone else." He began to leave, but turned back and softened his response: "That arrangement was handled by Adrian himself."

"I'd like to stay in touch with you, Father. I could use some help trying to solve this."

"You see what's happened as a mystery, while I see it as something to accept. I appreciate your conundrum, but…" A keening sound erupted from the gravesite. They turned to see Marta grabbing handfuls of dirt and throwing them into the slot in the earth. Over his shoulder he said, "I'd rather you didn't contact me again," then hurried across the green grass toward his wailing sister.

"Even if I come up with a suspect?" Peter's question chased after the priest.

"That's what the police are for," Father Greening pronounced without turning around.

6

Friday, February 4, 2005

ADRIAN WAS BELLOWING AT him, but Frank couldn't understand because Adrian was also pounding on the dining room table, which resounded like a kettledrum: explosive, thunderous…

Thunder launched Frank upright, shocked awake into a dingy, gray light. Recognition of his childhood bedroom oriented him for a moment until he became worried that the old house wouldn't hold up to the sudden winter storm. That would be symbolic of how Adrian operated: He used up people and things until they wore out and were dispensed with. Frank pulled his sleeping bag around him and fell into the sticky arms of another foreboding. He was on the cusp of jeopardizing his entire career, but he couldn't stop. No, that wasn't truthful: He didn't want to stop. But his weakness, his corrupt humanity, created a dilemma for him at a particularly bad time. *Trust in God*, he told himself. *Give it over to Jesus*.

The bare pine planks creaked as he roused himself. He stuck his head out the bedroom door. Marta was thumping about in the kitchen, no doubt trying to find some instant coffee in Adrian's cupboards. She had pleaded with Frank to stay in the old place with her one last time. The transfer of ownership could happen as soon as the police decided there had been no foul play. He tried to talk her out of her painful nostalgia, but she insisted it wasn't for sentimental reasons, but to better communicate with Adrian's spirit, which had been wrenched so violently from this world. She was convinced that Adrian's soul was lost, and she thought he could find them more easily if they stayed there. As their evening wore on, she admitted that besides releasing Adrian for his journey, she hoped he would tell them who had killed him. Frank shuddered at the depth of his sister's primitive yearning for revenge. He had argued that she was resisting the simple truth that her father was dead, but she insisted it was her duty to free Adrian's soul to journey to the other side.

He had tired of her pantheistic mumbo-jumbo years before and was still shocked at how casually she shifted between that and her heartfelt Catholicism. He found her spirituality naïve and opportunistic. He wouldn't have made a good missionary. Nonetheless, he stayed, out of guilt. He dreaded the moment she would discover that Adrian had cut her out of his estate. Adrian had bragged to Frank about it, but sworn him to secrecy. Adrian had made him feel complicit, even though Frank had neither done nor said anything to encourage his stepfather. Marta still didn't know how far that mean-spirited old man had gone to pay her back for moving out on him. Her years of service to Adrian and the forfeiting of her own dreams had meant little to her father.

When she moved out, Adrian had demanded that she take everything she wanted from the house. Then, he had begun to throw things away before she was out the door. It appeared he had taken a grim satisfaction in selling or dumping most of his past. It was harsh, but it wasn't surprising. It underscored what Frank already knew: Adrian abhorred nostalgia. He militantly refused to dwell in the past. It was an odd insistence for a man who had made his living as a photographer. Adrian had been the instrument of remembrance, capturing endless weddings, birthdays and graduations for thousands of families. Maybe that's what soured him on the past, but Adrian had always been sour. What turned memory into an enemy was the untimely death of Cerfina, Adrian's wife and the mother of both Frank and Marta. It wasn't so much that Adrian changed. He had always been unsentimental, hard-edged and quick to judge. But Cerfina softened him, or at least she provided a place for him where he didn't have to be hard. When she passed on, hard was all that was left.

Frank dressed hurriedly in the unheated room. He hated to admit to being influenced by Adrian, but he had a similar lack of sentimentality, while Marta was the very opposite of her father. She wouldn't let Adrian throw out anything pertaining to their mother. It was just one of the many points of tension between them over the twenty years they had lived together in this mournful, old place. Frank hadn't seen her much the last several years, but she was even more irrational and fragile than he remembered. Grief could do that, he knew, but she seemed mired in something even deeper than grief. She was holding onto a past in a way that suggested that she found the present intolerable. At any rate, she had been inconsolable most of the previous night, even to the point of insisting that she was somehow responsible for Adrian's death because she had left him.

Frank had been relieved when Marta agreed to put off going through the boxes of Adrian's personal papers. He didn't want to deal with Adrian's will while Marta was feeling so raw. She had appreciated Frank's offer to move the boxes to his own house for safekeeping, safe from the razing of the property that the new owners planned.

By 7:30 A.M., they were on their way to a little church a few miles away in Venice, where he was to say Mass. They silently watched as the impossibly tall and skinny Washingtonian palm trees on Ocean Avenue were flailed about by a freezing, whip-lashing front that had slid down the Pacific Coast from the Arctic. Frank felt a chill, but it wasn't only Mother Nature that caused it. He was concerned that his all-too-human nature was threatening his carefully structured life.

A ghostly Marta commented on how lucky they had been to have the funeral the day before, before the storm moved in. They talked intermittently, exploring the details of the funeral over and over: who had shown up and who hadn't, the remembrances of Adrian that people had shared. They agreed it had gone as well as could be expected. Everyone was shocked by Adrian's sudden demise, the pain slightly mitigated by the fact that he hadn't suffered.

Marta went on and on about what a gift it was that Frank could honor Adrian by saying another Mass for him. Frank nodded. He knew Marta was about to tell him once again how blessed he was to be a priest. If he questioned his good fortune in any way or even if the conversation went on long enough, he would then hear how unbearable it was that women weren't allowed to be priests and that there was no sound scriptural reason against it. What she wouldn't bring up was that she hadn't become a nun because she hadn't wanted to leave home. She didn't see it as her choice, but then again, in his experience she usually blamed others for her plight. That made most conversations with her tedious and predictable.

At the stoplight on Lincoln Boulevard and Ocean Park, he looked over at his dour sister, facial skin sagging in folds of pain like a basset hound wrapped in black. He felt a rare moment of compassion for her and wanted to offer her comfort. For all his disdain, he admired her faith, much simpler than his own. Not that he was losing his faith, but he was being tested.

For the second time, Marta thanked him for making special

arrangements so he could say a Mass today. She knew that because he didn't have his own parish he had planned ahead with another priest. All priests were expected to say Mass regularly—daily if possible—but what she didn't know was that he had been lax in the last few years. Even though he had rationalized that the Archdiocese was facing a crisis and he was one of the few who were in a position to deal with the financial challenge, he suddenly sensed how dangerous it was to his soul not to be saying Mass regularly. For him, and for most of his colleagues, saying Mass was an act of intimacy. The consecration of the host was like sex. The priests joked about it among themselves, but that made it no less true. He missed, and needed, that grounding intimacy.

Absorbed in their thoughts, they fell silent and watched the rain or, as Marta called it, God's tears.

Frank stepped out from the sacristy and saw the faithful few arise, the ones in every parish who always showed up for Mass on a weekday, rain or shine. He began the Penitential rite and had moved into the Gathering rite before he became aware that he wasn't concentrating on Adrian or the Mass. He was on automatic pilot. Rather than fight it, he reluctantly faced his quandary.

A month ago and only six weeks before he was to be sworn in as a Monsignor, he had fallen in love. He quickly countered that it could hardly be called love, since he had known the person such a short time, but it was certainly the strongest feeling of lust that he could remember having to contend with in many years. It had come at a most inopportune time, but that was part of the magic of desire. He reminded himself that he had experienced other "crushes" before and that he could enjoy these short-lived pleasures as he had for the last thirty-three years as a priest without ruining his life. It was a test from God. "Christ have mercy on us," he said with a deep sonorous sincerity, and the tiny congregation echoed it back.

He was sure that losing eighty pounds had had something to

do with it. Frank had promised himself and God, if He cared, that he would rid himself of that excess baggage before he rose further in the Church's hierarchy. Being a fat person had never felt right to him, but he had been powerless over it until recently.

He should have been scared away from overeating by the experience he had had as a young altar boy, when corpulent Father Dougherty tipped slowly off his chair at the side of the altar at an early morning Mass, as dead as the statues that haunted that little parish church. But the dangers of obesity hadn't registered with him. Instead, he had started putting on weight when he turned sixteen in the seminary and had spent his life as if in another man's body. Nonetheless, Frank believed that Father Dougherty's death had provided a powerful warning about gluttony that belatedly took hold when Frank heard from the Cardinal that he was going to be promoted. It was in that very conversation that he had been struck with a sensory memory of the sour smell of old Father Dougherty and realized with embarrassment that it was his own body odor that triggered that awareness. In that moment, he accepted it as a warning from God and vowed that he would reject alcohol and excessive and inappropriate food with the same cool dispatch he usually applied to his sexual desires. To his own surprise and relief, he did.

His renunciation slowly led to transformation, and eventually his cassocks began to billow like the curtains in his parents' house on a warm summer afternoon. He wouldn't miss his former body, just like he wouldn't miss his rundown childhood home. He was glad that Adrian had already sold the place. It would make it much easier to settle his estate and put his inheritance to work for the Church. This resolution made up for how it offended him that his stepfather hadn't let him help with his financial affairs.

Frank came back into the moment when it was time for his sermon. He had prepared a little talk on forgiveness in honor of the mutual acceptance he and Adrian had arrived at in the last two years. Forgiving Adrian for being so judgmental and mean had brought them closer. It made his death far easier to accept. He didn't mention this personal history as he spoke, being far more comfortable dealing with these issues in the abstract. However, as he ended, he said, "In addition to any others you are remembering, I would like to ask you to pray for my recently departed stepfather, Adrian Montero. May his soul rise to heaven." The faithful responded, "May it be God's will." Frank turned back to the altar to prepare for communion, but his mind went back to his problem.

When he had arrived at his goal of 185 pounds last month, he realized that it was time to have his finery taken in. Safety pins wouldn't do any longer. He decided not to avail himself of the ladies in the altar guild and instead went to a small tailor shop that the Cardinal had used. An old man there, Gino was his name, had mended some of his Excellency's most valuable garments, and Frank thought that his own new look deserved that same special attention.

When Frank entered, he found himself face to face with a younger Italian man who explained that Gino had passed away, but he, his nephew, whom Gino had trained himself, was there to serve him. Frank was immediately attracted to him, but that hardly seemed like a good enough reason to not use his services. Salvatore showed him into the dressing room and waited as Frank emerged in his first gown. Frank stepped up on a little raised platform, and Salvatore sat at the foot of Frank's newly svelte body while he took in his gowns, praising Frank for the change he had wrought in his body so that he would need such major alterations. They spoke in Italian until Frank felt too intimate using the language he had become fluent in while being stationed at the Vatican. He forced the conversation down to earth with an insistence on speaking English. Salvatore wasn't as comfortable in his adopted tongue, and even his movements— the pinning, the shaking out of the fabric—became less fluid.

But it wasn't just the language that created the intimacy. Frank realized that for the first time in many, many years, he was being looked at with desire.

Frank had been so unnerved that he was trembling as he drove home from the tailor. He had put an end to the shaking in his forearms by gripping the steering wheel of his car as if it were the cross itself. "But deliver me from evil," rang over and over in his head. He had challenged himself: *Have I served God and His church all these years just to have the same refrain bleating in my brain as it did when I was a young man? Is this the best I can do, running from myself, from my lust, from my member swollen with sin and erupting like the devil's own fountain? After what I've accomplished, is this all I can claim, to be back where I began?*

Marta and three parishioners approached the altar, interrupting his silent excoriation. He handed them communion wafers and exchanged blessings, but as he turned back to the altar, his memory reclaimed his mind.

That fateful day, he'd found himself parked safely in the alley at the back of his house, where the previous Sunday's calla lilies stuck out of the trashcans, browning trumpets of a splendor passed. When he finally released his iron hold on the sweat-blackened leather steering grip, he emitted a sob, then stopped. That wouldn't do, crying in the alley like the homeless. But he hadn't been able to move. He idealized himself in his mind's eye: fat and jolly, impervious to the temptations of the flesh, yet enjoying the pleasures of the flesh all the same. It had been a wonderful resolution to an impossible situation, and he had never appreciated its simplicity and brilliance before that moment, after he had destroyed it. He had become ravenously hungry, and the dragon in his belly propelled him into his house. He endured a protracted minute slamming cupboards in search of his hoard of sweets before he grasped that a year of low-fat living had left him no choice but an apple that sat on his counter, taunting him. He had restrained himself from throwing it only because devouring it made his drive to the donut shop easier.

Before he knew it, Frank was in the Sacristy again, changing back into his collar. He would take Marta out to a nice breakfast before he dropped her off, and then he had a day of meetings. Later that afternoon, a bit heavier and one month later, he would return to Salvatore, pick up his garments, and that would be that.

FRANK'S RESOLUTION REMAINED FIRM as the string of bells that hung from the tailor shop's door announced his entry. Salvatore emerged through maroon curtains that shielded the back of the shop.

"Bon giorno, Monsignore."

"I'm not a Monsignore quite yet, Salvatore."

Salvatore shrugged and reached around Frank's shoulders and helped him off with his sport coat. Frank watched, transfixed, as Salvatore shook the coat gently and slid in a wooden coat hanger. All the while his fingers brushed, stroked and spoke to the fabric as if soaking up information from the wool about its origins and how it had been treated since it had left the lamb.

"Tutto bene, Padre?"

"Si, bene, grazie," Frank said automatically, then took a breath. "Well, not really. My stepfather died since I last saw you. I just said a Mass for him."

Salvatore's eyes immediately filled with tears. He didn't attempt to wipe them away or seem embarrassed in the least. "Mi dispiace per la scomparsa di tuo patrigno, Padre." The condolence seemed to emerge from the pools of his dark eyes. It was the same expression of regret and sorrow that Frank had heard for days, but, somehow, from Salvatore, it was different. Frank didn't feel like he had to attend to Salvatore's feelings or explain his own conflicted feelings about Adrian.

"Grazie," Frank said.

After sharing a sweet, tranquil silence, Salvatore pulled aside the curtain and delicately gestured for Frank to enter. Frank stepped into the fitting area to the small raised platform in the center, aware again of the spell that was threatening to unleash his heart. "Salvatore, I'm afraid I don't have much time," he said, careful to use English. He slipped out of his loafers and took off his slacks with what he hoped was nonchalance. Salvatore took Frank's pants and shook out the material. The gentle undulations suggested that a man should not miss out on his own life. Frank held his breath as Salvatore helped him slip the first of his gowns over his head. Frank stepped up onto the platform.

"Un po' stretto?" Salvatore asked as he pulled at the waist that was now a bit snug. Frank saw concern in his eyes and a slight pinching of his upper lip. *Professional pride*, he thought. *How lovely*.

"It may be a little tight, but it isn't your fault, Salvatore. I'm afraid I've been out of control this month. I'm not the man I presented to you originally." Frank swayed in the garment and felt, despite the weight he had put on, how perfectly his shoulders were encased and how gracefully the cloth fell around him.

"Out of control?" Salvatore asked as he walked slowly around Frank, his fingers pulling and shaking the blood-red fabric while gently caressing Frank's body with every adjustment. A bead of sweat formed on Frank's upper lip.

"I went off my diet. I've been eating like a pig, too much of everything. Golosità, Salvatore," Frank nearly shouted, and then laughed too loudly. "Gluttony!"

"It has been a difficult time," Salvatore stated matter-of-factly. "É normale mangiare troppo durante i tempi tristi." He stopped his circling and looked directly up at Frank from under dark swooping lashes. He was four inches shorter, about five foot ten, slender with long muscular arms and tapered fingers. There were lines radiating from the corners of his eyes, but it was impossible to tell if they were a result of sun and laughter or if he was closer to Frank's age than he had originally thought. Frank stared at him, then registered what he'd just said.

"I didn't overeat because of my stepfather," Frank explained. "We weren't that close." Salvatore listened with a deep stillness, and Frank continued, "I was very nervous, anxious, after leaving here last time."

"Hai un problema, Padre?" Salvatore asked and stepped back, indicating that he should step down. Frank imagined that a slight mocking challenge flitted across Salvatore's face. He felt himself withdrawing as he started to step down. Thoughts of everything he had to lose crowded his mind as his toe got caught in the hem of his gown and he started to topple. Salvatore's hand shot out and grabbed Frank's wrist with an iron grasp. Frank pressed into it and freed his foot so that he didn't fall, but he bumped hard into Salvatore as he came off the platform.

Frank began to apologize, but instead said haltingly, "Yes, I have a problem." Salvatore did not step back. Neither did Frank. They stood very close, staring into each other's eyes in silence. There was no challenge in Salvatore's expression now. Frank slowly leaned forward and kissed him.

"This is dangerous," Frank said, snapping his head back, ready to release Salvatore's hand. "Troppo pericoloso."

"Secondo chi? Dio?" Salvatore asked, holding tight while searching Frank's eyes for an answer.

"Yes, because of what God will think and of what the Cardinal would think, for certain, and most parishioners, too. But while I trust that God will forgive my weakness, I doubt the others would be able to, since those pedophiles ruined everything." A look of confusion flashed in Salvatore's eyes. Frank rushed on, "I'm sorry. That doesn't have anything to do with us, except that everyone is watching each other closely now, and there is no forgiveness for our weaknesses." Salvatore's confusion was replaced with a look of sweet compassion and longing. In spite of his fears, Frank relaxed.

"E tu?" Salvatore asked. "Is dangerous because of what you think?"

"I'm not thinking, Salvatore, can't you tell? You seem to be able to tell so much just by looking." Frank smiled, and they kissed again. This time, their hands began to roam over each other and their breathing sped up. Once again, Frank pulled back. "We must stop," he said. Salvatore looked at him with dark, sad eyes. "There's too much to lose. It's too dangerous."

"Is dangerous not only for you, Father," Salvatore said.

"Please, don't call me that, now," Frank interrupted. "Chiamami Franco."

"Is dangerous for me, Franco," Salvatore said. Frank looked at him doubtfully, but Salvatore continued. "People don't come to my shop if they think I make the fall of a man of God."

"It would be easier if we only had to worry about God."

Salvatore dropped his head. "I fear God's judgment."

"I think God only judges us harshly if we don't work to increase his domain here on earth. What we are doing would only disappoint him."

"Disappoint," Salvatore repeated, nodding and smiling thoughtfully. "I would like to know better this God of yours, Franco." Frank watched as he went back through the curtains, locked the front door and flipped the sign so to those outside it said "Closed." But to them, it said "Open."

7

Earlier: Friday, February 4, 2005

NATURAL FORCES HAD EVERYONE'S attention that Friday morning. The same thunderous crash that jolted Frank out of bed found Peter and Judith eyeing each other worriedly over coffee. Despite The Weather Channel's flash-flood warnings for the desert area, Judith drove off for a daylong meeting in Palm Springs, trusting that highway engineers were a match for Mother Nature's capricious ways. As Peter dropped Samantha at nursery school, his cell phone rang. "Mr. Winston, this is Carmen, Juanita's friend. I just started taking care of your father yesterday, but this morning he didn't remember who I was. He's locked himself in the bathroom, and he's afraid to come out. I don't know what to do."

Peter raced over. His father accepted Juanita, but he'd scared away three others before her. Once Martin had breakfast, he calmed down. Upon learning that Carmen was from Nicaragua, he enthused over the botanical richness of the jungle. The old scientist, carrying on about bromeliads, had moments when he almost seemed normal. Peter was only slightly late to his first class.

At the end of teaching, Peter went to pick Sam up. She came running over, followed by several other children, who stood watching them hug and kiss. He told her that he wanted to talk to Sandy, the director of the school. Satisfied that the ritual greeting had been satisfactorily enacted, the tribe of short people ran back to their train of tricycles and wagons and continued snaking their way through the playground. Peter crossed the yard and entered the office.

Sandy Jensen greeted him with a cup of coffee in her hand. "Hello, Peter. Want some coffee?"

"No, thanks," he replied and sat on a well-worn couch facing her. "I wanted to check with you to be sure that Samantha is handling this, this incident we saw. I don't think that leaving her with the doctor traumatized her in any serious way," he stated quickly, "but Judith is concerned," he admitted. He liked Sandy, though he always imagined she looked at the children and saw faults in the parents.

Sandy let his defensive tone dissipate. "Trauma is sort of a buzzword these days. If Samantha was either anxious or ignoring what happened, I would be concerned about trauma. But it's neither of those. If anything, she's a little preoccupied."

"With what?"

"Death."

"Death?" he repeated. Then, slowly shaking his head, he asked, "Well, that makes sense, but what about death?"

"Come into the classroom. I want to show you something."

They went through a door and into a large room, partitioned into sections for different activities. Whenever he entered this room, Peter felt something like deja vu, only he didn't recall ever having such a room or school when he was little. The feeling, he decided, was more like a longing. There was a corner with blocks, a dress-up area with a big trunk filled to overflowing with clothes and hats, painting easels with plastic cups filled with rich primary colors, a reading area with a couch and a rug that Peter and Judith had donated. Sandy led him toward a small table with a tray of sand on it. They sat on the little seats, their knees bumping the edge of the table. Peter looked at a scene in a sand tray. It appeared to be a jumble of small, wooden people, buildings and vehicles of all sorts.

"Samantha has been re-enacting the accident she saw several times since it happened."

"Is that bad?" Peter worried.

"No, not at all. In fact, it has generated a great deal of openness in all the children in talking about death. It's been wonderful."

"Wonderful?"

"Contrary to our adult expectations that sex rules our consciousness, my observation is that death is primary." Sandy paused. "That's why Samantha's retelling of the story has been so important for her and for the group. She breaks the taboo."

Peter was fascinated. "But why do you think she has been telling the story over and over?"

"I think that's how humans of any age gain control over events. It's a primitive, unconscious need. I work with children, and I live in the middle of the filmmaking capital of the world. Both provide powerful evidence that humans are storytelling animals."

"A historian could hardly disagree," Peter concurred.

"Right!" Sandy gestured enthusiastically. "And it's especially true around things that are hard to accept and understand, like death, which is always scary and, in this instance, dramatically so, since it involved lots of people, the police and a daddy who ran off for a while."

Peter started to defend himself, but Sandy smiled compassionately and continued. "Samantha's trying to figure it out. She's trying to understand death and to see if there's anything she or you or anyone could or should have done differently."

"So it's been a good thing that I've kept talking about it to her,"

Peter said. "I mean, it hasn't been a morbid preoccupation."

Sandy picked up some of the figures from the sand tray. "Not in the least, and it's much preferable to repressing it."

Peter began picking up sand and letting it fall slowly back onto the tray. "I don't think I'd be able to do that even if I wanted to." Without thinking, he moved a truck through the sand on the tray until he knocked down a little wooden man. He felt a jolt, electrifying and satisfying. Slightly embarrassed, he dropped the truck and stared at the tray.

Sandy sat, musing. "I suppose storytelling accounts for the impulse in adults to return to the scene of an accident or crime. I've read that it happens often, because people need to try to resolve their feelings of guilt or whatever." Peter was now looking at her intently. "They usually show up on some anniversary of the event, but I suppose it could happen anytime."

"That would be convenient," he said.

"Convenient?"

"That old man who died was pushed," Peter's voice was suddenly ragged. "But no one but Samantha and I saw it."

Sandy's brow furrowed, "Samantha hasn't mentioned that."

"Sam didn't realize what she'd seen," Peter insisted. "It was done very subtly, but it wasn't an accident." He continued in a more hushed tone, "I guess that's better for her, even if it leaves me all alone to deal with a murder."

"That's terrible, Peter, I had no idea."

Peter nodded at her sympathy. "Thanks." He paused. "Convenient was a stupid way of saying it would be great if that son of a bitch returned and I could prove what I saw. That would be a much better story."

Sandy silently acknowledged his conundrum as the children trickled into the room, then said, "There is one more thing. You've been late three times recently picking Samantha up." Peter started to interrupt, but she continued. "When you let us know, it makes it easier for the teachers. But if it's going to happen regularly, we should change the time officially so Sam isn't disappointed. Kids like a routine."

Peter wanted the extra time, but made himself ask the question he knew Judith would ask. "Do you think Sam can handle a longer day?"

"She may get cranky sometimes, but I think she'd be okay. And," she added, "we'll have to charge a little more."

"Okay, let's add an hour," he said. "I could use the time. I'll tell Sam on the way home."

"You look funny in that little chair, Daddy," Sam giggled as she approached.

"I better be careful or I might break it," Peter said and stood up.

"Like Goldilocks!" Sam piped up.

"Just like poor Goldy," Peter said as he picked her up and headed for home.

THAT NIGHT, JUDITH STEPPED into Peter's office after getting Sam to sleep. She came up behind him as he sat staring intently at his computer screen that extolled the virtues of the various projects of TMF and Associates.

"What are you doing?" she asked.

"Research."

"For?"

He hesitated, then said, "This is the development company that's getting the Montero house. I thought I might find something."

"Why play at being a cop? Why not hire an investigator?"

"Because I wouldn't know what to tell him to look for."

"How do you know what to look for?"

"Male intuition. Just leave me alone."

Judith moved into the shadows beyond the circle of light from his lamp. "Sam and I just had a little chat. When were you planning to tell me about her new hours at school?"

He forced himself to look up. He couldn't see her face clearly, but he knew what she looked like from her tone. "It wasn't a secret," he said evenly and went offline.

"Why didn't you mention it when I called to tell you the roads were clear?" Sadness mingled with frustration in her voice. "Do you think it's okay to make a big change in Sam's schedule without even talking to me about it?"

"I was worried about other things. This morning my dad got all paranoid and I had to go talk him out of the bathroom."

"I'm sorry," Judith commiserated, "I really am, but that doesn't change doing what's best for Samantha, and I feel…"

"And you feel guilty," Peter interrupted.

"You jerk!" Judith blurted out and walked over to a wall switch. Suddenly, Peter's office was flooded with light.

"Turn it off, Judith. I don't like it when I'm working." He tapped a stack of students' tests with his finger.

Judith left the light on. "Dammit, Peter, it's not fair to use my career against me. You know I feel bad about not staying at home. And when I think that Sam isn't getting what she needs, I count on being able to talk to you about it."

"Judith," Peter said coolly, "I need more time. If I had told you, you would have jumped on me because I supposedly wasn't thinking about Sam. But I *was* thinking about her, and I concluded, along with Sandy, that Sam could handle it."

"Why didn't you talk with me, too?" Judith exclaimed. "How am I supposed to know what you are thinking unless you tell me?"

Peter sat back. He could feel the pressure building in his head. She had no idea how close he was to exploding. "I've been a bit preoccupied for the last week."

"You were preoccupied before Mr. Montero died, Peter, that's your nature. But I need you to communicate, especially on things that concern Sam. You get more hours with her than I do." Judith stood rigidly in the middle of the room. "I don't want Samantha to have to grow up too fast. She still needs to be babied, and I can't always do it. You're a good daddy, but your mommy died when you were young, and…"

"Don't fucking analyze me and my mother just because you feel guilty!" Peter yelled.

They stared at each other, both trapped in righteous anger. A quaint marching tune erupted from Peter's cell phone sitting on his desk. As he answered it, their home phone rang, and Judith hurried away to answer that. Peter had been finished with his call for several minutes when Judith returned, her face pinched with worry. "That was Juanita. She had just relieved Carmen when Martin fell. The paramedics just took him to St. John's Hospital with a broken hip." Peter groaned and collapsed into his chair. "Poor Martin," she began to cry, "it's just not fair." Peter didn't move. "Don't you think you should get over there?" she finally asked.

He sat immobilized as Judith dissected the situation. "I'm sure they'll operate in the morning, but it's so sad. The poor guy is healthy, except for Alzheimer's. He should handle the operation pretty well, but this sort of shock can really accelerate the dementia. I'm sure we'll have to put him in a nursing home once he gets past this. There are a number of good homes if we can get him in and…"

"No!" Peter cried out. He waved his hand in the air vigorously as though trying to erase her words. "I won't! I promised Dad he'd never have to go away," he anguished.

"Peter, I warned you not to, but you promised him the moon. It's a fantasy to think we can have an easy, controlled death. Besides, you know Martin is, or at least was, a hardheaded realist." This time it was her turn to be gentle. "I'm sure he'd understand you couldn't deliver."

Peter knew it was meant to calm him, but all it did was twist the dagger of guilt that was stuck in his gut. "No!" he blurted out and walked to the door, as his tears began to fall. "That's not how it was, ever. There wasn't a wink and a nod between us. You don't understand my father or me if you think that."

"Peter, I'll help, but you…"

"I can't!" Peter screamed into the ether, and the room fell silent. "Whatever's involved"—his voice fell to a hoarse whisper—"you've got to do it. Please. You go to the hospital. I'll stay with Sam. You decide where, when, how, everything." He flicked the overhead light switch on and off with each decision.

"Stop it," she said, shading her eyes.

He kept the light off. "Please," he entreated. Once he heard her agree, he left the room mumbling, "I'm sorry, I'm sorry."

8

Saturday, February 5, 2005

MARTA GRUNTED AS SHE tugged the eighteen-inch marble Virgin from the alcove it had graced for over forty years. Bent around the heavy statue like the old woman she was rapidly becoming, she trudged through the house to the kitchen sink and lowered it gently into warm, soapy water. Other than her garden, it was the only thing she cared about that she hadn't taken when she had moved. She had left it because she hoped that the Madonna in her shrine just outside the front door would bless this house. But she had been a fool. The soul of this house had disappeared twenty-two years before, when her mother had died. She scrubbed at the grime, silently condemning her sentimentality. Neither she nor her mother nor the Virgin had been able to reach her father's heart. After a few minutes, though the white marble remained pitted with gray, she pulled the plug in the sink and rinsed the welcoming Madonna over and over, stroking her cape and caressing her cheek. Her tears disappeared into the water as it swirled down the drain. She didn't even know she was crying. It had become that commonplace.

Her stomach pressed heavily against the counter. Her hair escaped the bun and sagged lifelessly to her shoulders. The sound of dripping water continued even after the faucet was turned off and the sink was empty. The pipe under the sink had shifted again. In the past, she would have gotten down on her knees to push the trap back on tight, but no longer. The irony didn't escape her. Her leaving home had begun with the plumbing when she told her father she was so tired of the terrible water pressure and constant leaks that she would use her own meager savings and have the house replumbed. It wasn't until she had called a plumber that her father had revealed his big secret: He'd sold the house.

She lifted the statue onto the counter and began to carefully dry it. With brutal casualness, he had told her that the house would no longer be theirs once he died. He knew that she expected it to pass to her, but he didn't care about her life beyond his. As her dream of restoring the old place and living out her years there disintegrated, so had the last remnants of her sense of obligation to her father. If he could decide such things without her, then he could live without her, too. It had taken her forty-six years, but when she finally made up her mind, she was gone in two weeks.

Marta tapped her finger on a cracked blue tile of the counter to the beat of the dripping water. Adrian had sucked every bit of use out of this place, just like he had drained her. A familiar heat of resentment burned its way up her face, only to be smothered by her sweaty fatigue as she placed the statue in a heavy canvas bag. Her anger had helped her to leave, but being on her own didn't really improve anything.

Lugging the statue, Marta thumped across the thin, crackled linoleum in the kitchen onto the scarred oak planks in the darkened dining room. She put the bag down next to the tired, old couch in the living room. She brushed at the print on the cushions: the blue and purple morning glories on their faded yellow background. Her mother had bought this couch less than a year before the cancer took her. Other than Adrian's photographs, the couch was one of the few ways her mother had lived on in this house after her death. By contrast, she had remained vibrantly present in the land surrounding the house. Cerfina's secret garden, Peruvian plantas medicinales y purgas, had flowered and regenerated year after year. The garden was more than her mother's legacy. It had kept Marta living here and came to represent Marta's most lasting relationship. It was at the heart of why she had never left home, until Adrian's callous betrayal.

Reliving the past exhausted her and residing in the present held no charm. She collapsed onto the couch. She wasn't depressed. She didn't inherit that gene, or belief system, as she thought of it, from her father. He believed he could outfox life. He was in competition with everything, and whenever problems arose he took them personally. She wasn't so egotistical. He said she had a peasant's fatalism, just like her mother. She considered it realism, a point of view rather than an emotional state. She tried not to expect more than the sunrise and the sunset. Nonetheless, she was tired. Even though it was evening, she reached into her purse, retrieved a few narrow, dried leaves from a paper bag and put them into her mouth.

Marta sighed as the coca leaves stimulated the release of her saliva and the two began their chemical dance. This ancient habit of her mother's people had been demonized by the very devils who had transformed this sacrament into a drug. For centuries, Andean peasants like her grandparents had grown and chewed coca leaves for the stimulation it afforded them as they planted and harvested throughout the year. Their medicine people, the shamans and curanderos, had developed ways to strengthen the effect, to extract the essence from the leaves, this gift from Pachamama, Mother Earth. That essence was reserved for communicating with the gods in rituals and empowering runners to travel through the rugged Andes to deliver messages. It had been a sacred gift, until it left the mountains and jungle and emerged in the cities of the conquistadors as cocaine. They treated it like the gold they had stolen centuries earlier from the burial chambers and temples across their land. Once removed from the Andean culture, the coca turned into a hungry, chaotic power that destroyed those who created and consumed it.

The leaves softened and slowly began to set loose the mild stimulant, the daily companion of the farmers as they kept pace with the regenerative force of nature. Marta stood and walked to the window and peered out the front past the four different kinds of banana plants that she had kept alive all these years. Untended for nearly three months, along with the bay laurel and other herbal and medicinal trees, they were beginning to overrun the place, even for her taste. She had intentionally kept the front looking disorganized and uninteresting so people would not be drawn to the house. Over the years, few had recognized the pharmacopoeia that existed before their eyes.

Feeling stronger, she made her way to a window looking out the back of the house, flicked on two outside floodlights and viewed the devastation her father had rendered when she left. Near the back of the lot, a long, narrow hothouse tilted away from her at a crazy angle. Her mother had fashioned it out of found lumber, doors and windows. Adrian had taken a chain saw to the 4x4 posts that supported it and then tried to push it over on itself, but various vines that grew on it—tambor wasca, ajo sacha and ahahuasca, all powerful medicines and vision plants—had resisted the complete flattening. Evidently, Adrian's rage had then turned to yanking out the plants and bushes that were the source of the potions and poultices that had curbed his rheumatism, dissolved his depression and migraines and stabilized his diabetes. He even tore out the flowering, sun-loving annuals that she had planted to make the garden look "normal" in case anyone wandered into the back. It looked as if wild pigs, javalenas, had attacked this legacy begun by her mother and continued by her.

Adrian knew that it was the garden that ensured that Marta would never go far from him, just like it had secured Cerfina's undying gratitude and service. Cerfina had been in Los Angeles less than a year when her new husband, Nate Greening, the dashing pilot who had convinced her that they could create their own fates in faraway America, crashed and died in the mountains of her homeland. Stranded with her young son, the gods had seen fit to cross the path of this exotic beauty with a photographer who turned the image of her and Frank into magazine covers and calendars, then wooed her and offered her a place to literally grow roots. It was a love born of necessity, but Cerfina never spoke badly of Adrian, no matter how he paled in comparison with her first love. Instead, her mother often told Marta how blessed she felt that Adrian had given her a piece of earth to plant the seeds she'd brought with her from Peru. Having ventured far from her biological mother, unheard of for a peasant girl at that time, Cerfina had reconnected to the mother of us all, Pachamama. With a garden, she knew she was back in her mother's arms and would not lose her soul in this strange land. Growing up in that garden, Marta had absorbed the same knowledge and belief.

Marta flicked off the outside lights, leaving the dead plants to reside in her mind's eye as she stared unblinking into the darkness. She understood her mother completely, for Marta had stayed for similar reasons. Still, when she had told her father she was no longer going to take care of him, that she was, in fact, moving out because he had sold the land, she had felt a certain elation. But the liberation or whatever it was hadn't really set in before her father was pushed under that bus. She hadn't actually pushed him, but she might as well have. She had left him vulnerable to the many evil spirits that roam this land. She was sure that greed was what had killed Adrian, but she hadn't yet become aware of whose greed. She trusted she would get the message, and when she did, she knew she would have to take revenge on those responsible. She resisted this conclusion. It frightened her, what it might make her do. But in her bones, she had always known that she was linked to that ancient tradition, as old as the plants, which had followed her mother's people out of the jungle. In the meantime, she accepted responsibility for letting it happen. She had already confessed to it several times. Each time, a priest told her it had been an accident, that no forgiveness was necessary. But she knew how everything was connected in ways most priests would disdainfully call superstitious, and she wasn't afraid to face the truth.

Bereft but resolute, she walked slowly down the hall and stood in the shadows before her parents' bedroom. She opened the door and peered into a ghost-laden gloom. She could feel her heart pounding, threatening to come apart. She grabbed her arms and pinched herself until it hurt. The physical pain interrupted her grieving for a way of life destroyed and her yearning to change what couldn't be changed. She turned away and shuffled down the hall.

She had folded and sorted and ironed and cleaned and polished and dusted every inch of this place for too many years. It had begun with a solemn pledge she had made to her dying mother many years before. "M'ija, promise me you'll take care of Papa," her mother had pleaded. "He needs his medicines, and you know he'll forget to eat without someone to look after him." She hadn't mentioned caring for the garden. It wasn't necessary.

Marta had given Adrian nearly the same number of years as her mother had given him. It had killed her mother, and he might have outlived Marta, too, if she hadn't finally left. It had been like a divorce, and both her father and God were making her pay for it. Tears threatened again, but she choked them back: She had one last task.

Marta had anticipated that her father would be enraged. She also anticipated that he might turn violent, and she had tried to thwart him from hurting himself or anyone else. She walked into her old room, empty now except for a bed, a straight-back chair and a bureau. She dragged the chair into her empty closet and shakily stepped up on the seat. Bracing herself, she pushed at the wooden ceiling until a piece fourteen inches square popped up into the attic space. On her tiptoes now, she stretched her hand up into the darkness and found the shoebox she had hidden. Carefully, she brought it down and hugged it to her chest as she stepped off the chair. She didn't bother to replace the wooden square. Frank had arranged for church volunteers to pick up the furniture and anything else of value. Then the house belonged to the wreckers. Soon enough, the whole place would be in splinters.

She opened the box and removed a worn Santa Monica YMCA towel, feeling the weight of Adrian's gun through the towel. At the time she hid it, she was embarrassed over her presumption that he might go on a rampage just because she was leaving. He'd never been violent with her or Cerfina, but he was very all-American when it came to guns. More to the point, he believed in revenge. It was one of the few issues they agreed on. But she doubted he'd ever do anything to her physically, even though he had made vague threats when she had told him she was moving out. Nothing was said directly, of course, just enough to let her know that she was responsible for anything bad that might happen. She figured that if he didn't have an easy way, he'd never do anything too crazy. He never asked her where the gun was.

She tossed the box on the bed and scurried back to the doorway, suddenly cold. She must not sleep here again. She'd always suffered nightmares, but the worst was when she and Frank had stayed here the night of the funeral. She couldn't tell him, because he'd have repeated with unctuous sympathy that she was the saint of the family. When anyone noticed her at all, it was to suffocate her with hollow compliments. Even her father could be nice when he wanted something. But he couldn't sugarcoat the sale of the house. When he had told her about it, she had been forced to confront her life.

She had always told herself that she was ready to become someone, anyone else, when the time was right. Indeed, moving out was invigorating. She had cut her hair from waist length to shoulder length and hennaed it. She had joined a few co-workers for a "girls only" weekend in Las Vegas. It was challenging to create a life for herself after living it with, and, she had to admit, for her father. Even so, she thought that she was beginning to get a glimpse of a different, more alive person deep inside. Then he was killed, and her emancipation collapsed.

In the dim hall light, she saw the many rectangles on the wall where pictures of her mother and the family had hung. Adrian had tried to get rid of all photos with Frank in them long ago, but Cerfina had stood up to him. She wouldn't allow her past to be erased. Marta had taken all the family photos when she moved. Adrian hadn't wanted them, claimed he didn't care. But Marta cherished remembrances of those years when they had been all together. Now she wanted to throw them out, but she doubted she would have the nerve. She longed to change, but she was afraid that her habits had become her personality.

Marta hurried back to the living room. She placed the gun in the same canvas bag that held the statue. Whatever she had to pay to God and her conscience for her actions, she wasn't going to do it here. With a false vigor, she put on her overcoat, shouldered the heavy bag and slammed the scarred oak door behind her.

9

WEDNESDAY, FEBRUARY 9, 2005

FRANK WAS IN LOVE'S grip, and there was no ignoring its potency. During the various long stretches of celibacy that he both enjoyed and endured, he would forget why there were so many songs written about love. But now he was in awe of its power. It was more than wonderful and rare; love was chemical. And it was good for Frank. For one thing, he had not only kept the weight off, but had dropped a few more pounds. It was crazy to fall in love, but it was a fine madness.

Other than taking boxes of Adrian's files back to his own house, Frank had put off going through Adrian's papers, not wanting to give up any moment he might be able to share with Salvatore. Finally, after spending five nights in a row together, Sal had kissed him and pushed him out the door of his apartment, reminding Frank that he had to begin to deal with his stepfather's estate or he would draw attention to himself.

Frank had been honest with Sal about his fear of being discovered. Even though Frank wasn't a parish priest, his privacy was at risk. As a result of the sex abuse scandals, all priests were supposed to avoid clerical isolation. It had been his good fortune that the Cardinal hadn't insisted that he move into the housing at the new cathedral. He was considered low risk because he wasn't in contact with children. Nonetheless, the bottom line was that priests were supposed to watch each other and intervene if one of the brethren was acting differently.

Frank let himself into his little house furnished with a hodge-podge of castoffs from many parishes. Just down the block from a local parish church, it was one of hundreds of buildings that had been donated to the Archdiocese over the years. These tax-free "gifts" were but a portion of the Church's extensive real estate and helped account for why the Archdiocese's worth stretched into the billions.

He sat perched on an old wicker couch and stared at the boxes he and Sal had brought over. Adrian's filing system consisted of stuffing papers into a carton until it would take no more, writing the date on the front and then finding another container. Thank God he wasn't a true packrat, or his place would have been overrun. As it was, Frank was faced with over a dozen boxes that held the evidence of Adrian's worldly affairs. Frank didn't anticipate finding secrets. It had always seemed that anything Adrian did or liked or disliked had always been in plain view. He had made life look simple.

Frank began with the oldest, most tattered box. When he came across Adrian and his mom's marriage certificate, he realized he should ask Marta to join him on this trip down memory lane. He called her, and once she got over her indignation that he had even considered beginning without her, she agreed to come over.

Frank sat back and, as he waited for her, assessed how vulnerable his affair made him. He believed that no matter how alarming and embarrassing the pedophile scandal was, the old truth that the Church didn't want to catch its priests breaking the rules still prevailed. One's personal relationship with God was at the core of the Catholic Church. Sinning was a wake-up call to look at yourself more closely. It was judged harshly, but punishment came from within. This was where the bishops had screwed up. They wanted pedophiles to change from within. Even if they sent the errant priest away for counseling, most of them considered sexual abuse of children to ultimately be a spiritual malady instead of a psychological illness. They were naïve; they thought priests would outgrow it or overcome it through prayer and stern warnings. While they waited for God's grace, they'd forgotten about the kids. Now he and the other 97.5 percent of innocent priests were paying for that naïveté and blind faith by living in conditions that at times resembled a police state.

He accepted that huge mistakes had been made, but he missed the old atmosphere. Priests weren't meant to be cops, and until recently it had been an unspoken assumption that a good priest in the confessional was simply a conduit between man and God, a human link for contact with the divine. Most priests instantly forgot what had been confessed by anyone, but particularly their fellow priests. He'd heard the confession of many priests who admitted to sexual affairs with adults. Some went on for years, but he never felt it was his responsibility to intervene. He still didn't. At worst, it was a weakness to be overcome by the grace of God. He'd overcome it himself several times. In the past, if they slipped, it was to be confessed and forgiven until the temptation was eventually overcome. Eventually.

For the last twenty years, because the Pope demanded blind obedience, these discussions about problems with celibacy had to be conducted with discretion. But there were always other priests, friends, whom he could talk to. Now, things had changed. Frank was afraid to bring up his affair in confession. He was isolated, cut off from God and his fellow priests, the only ones he felt could really understand him. That was the worst part.

Frank's wrestling with his frustration and guilty conscience was cut short by a knock.

"You cut your hair!" he exclaimed when his half-sister came through the door.

"I trimmed it again a few days ago, but I cut it off to my shoulders when I moved out. You just never noticed."

"I was too caught up in the new color. Anyway, I love it short like this," he said. When she smiled, he added, "You look younger."

"I wasn't keeping my hair a secret," she responded. "You could have seen it sooner if you'd come for dinner last Sunday. You've never been to my apartment, you know."

And bring Salvatore along to spice up the conversation, he thought. "I've been very busy, Marta. I told you." He kissed her on her thickly powdered cheek. She carried a slightly overwhelming but poignant scent into the room, the same perfume their mother had worn.

"I suppose it was unrealistic to expect that we would come together more in this time of death," she said as she sank into the couch. "It would be too much out of character for us."

Frank resisted the guilt he was supposed to feel and tried to be compassionate. "It has been rather overwhelming," he lied and sat down next to her. "What's it like for you with your father gone so suddenly?" he asked awkwardly.

"He's no longer your father now?" she snapped.

Frank's jaw tightened. "Come on, Marta. Just because Adrian took Mother and me in didn't make him my father, to him or to me. And just because he's dead, let's not ignore that he ran me out of the house when I was fourteen."

"I know, I know. You had it the roughest with Dad, but somehow you were his favorite."

"Adrian's favorite was whomever he needed for something. I think he made up with me two years ago because he wanted to get right with God, and I was God's most obvious spokesman. So he apologized. I knew he was using me, but I didn't see that denying him forgiveness was going to prove anything. Besides,

I welcomed the truce. I admit it."

"So you stepped back into the family, and I was pushed aside after looking after him since Mom died."

"If you were pushed, it was by Adrian, not me."

"Forget it, Paco!" She leaned forward and pulled some papers out of the first box. "I had to care for Dad for twenty years, but you never did anything wrong. That's what I'll tell them when they come to interview me for your canonization."

Frank started to laugh. "You obviously weren't listening to Adrian all those years. He could never resist reminding me of my failings whenever he had the chance."

"And he could never resist telling me how I couldn't compare to you. But you never cared how I was affected. You just left until Dad started being nice to you."

Frank wanted to argue, but he knew it was true. Mutually frustrated, they began to leaf through the paper trail of Adrian's life. Now and then, photographs of the family brought forth a memory that soothed some of the bitterness. Frank pulled out a picture of Marta in her first-communion dress and handed it to her. She was the picture of innocence. "That may have been the happiest day of my life," she said, welling up. She turned it over. Adrian's careful script had yellowed, but was still legible: "M'ija angélica a seis años." Marta began to cry.

"My little six-year-old angel," Frank read as he squeezed her hand. "I guess he couldn't tell anyone that he loved them."

"Oh, he told me, whenever he needed something," she replied, pulling her hand away and wiping her tears.

Most of what Adrian had saved was papers and receipts pertaining to the house. There were a few letters, lists of things that had to be done and occasional clippings from *The Evening Outlook*, an old Santa Monica newspaper. In the tenth box, Frank came across a manila envelope with paperwork that related to Adrian's deal with TMF and Associates. The police had found the actual agreement in a file on Adrian's desk and had interviewed the people at TMF looking for leads, just like Peter Winston had suggested. But nothing came of it. Frank opened the envelope. It had papers dating back to 1993, shortly after Adrian had contacted him demanding financial help. Adrian had claimed that Frank owed him for all the years that Adrian had supported him. Frank had refused, but, realizing that the old man was impoverished except for the house, he had offered to help him sell it. Adrian was incensed and said he'd never leave his home. Two years ago, when they began to talk again, Adrian ignored Frank's questions concerning his finances except to tell him not to worry.

Frank turned back to the file. In 1994, TMF had paid Adrian $795,000 for the house, with exchange of title to occur upon his death. He turned to Marta. "Did you know Adrian received almost $800,000 for the house?"

Marta looked up, ashen. "Not until this moment," she gasped. She looked at a year-end statement from a brokerage house. "Last year he received $27,110, tax free."

"What?"

"He had it all invested in bonds. It says right here." She shook the paper violently. "He lied to me, Frank. He was crying poor, but he must have been saving some of that every year." She began to breathe in short gasps. "I thought he was almost destitute. It was one of the reasons I didn't leave sooner. I worried about him every day." Marta began to laugh in high, staccato squeaks. "He got me to pay the utilities and buy our groceries. He lied, he lied."

Frank sat speechless, then reached out and patted her hand. Marta stared into space and continued her strangled laugh as she spoke. "Isn't it odd that he finally told me he'd sold the house, Frank? I think that's odd. I'm sure he thought I'd never leave him no matter what he did." She choked back tears. "But, I did, didn't I?"

"Yes, Marta, you finally got out."

"I'll bet he still didn't spend much. He probably just doubled up on the free lunches at the Senior Center." She turned to him. "Did I tell you that some woman from there called me and had the nerve to ask me to repay a gambling debt that Adrian owed her?" Her tears rolled through the makeup on her cheeks.

"I'm sorry, Marta," Frank said, afraid and embarrassed for her. They sat in silence before they each turned back to a file.

Frank's file was stuffed with notes Adrian had written to himself as the house sale had progressed. Most were memos bragging about not needing a business degree to out-bargain some hotshot lawyers. Frank read a note scribbled in Adrian's hand. "Ray Thomas finally caved in. Okay the deal."

"Ray Thomas!" he blurted out. "Sweet Jesus! Marta, I know the man whom Adrian sold to. Ray is one of the mainstays of the Church's financial well-being in Southern California."

"Why didn't you recognize his company when the police told us who bought it?"

"I'd never heard of TMF," Frank said. "I mean, I know Ray very well, but," he hesitated, "he operates out of many different corporate fronts. He's a developer and a financier," he coughed, "a complicated man."

"But wouldn't he have known who Adrian was to you?"

"How? We have different last names. There's no reason to connect Adrian to me. The real question is how Ray got involved with this deal." Frank looked wonderingly at Marta. "Adrian could have found out that Ray Thomas was an associate of mine by getting the list of the members of the Archdiocese Financial Advisory Board. I'll bet Adrian sought out Ray to make a deal after I told him I couldn't give him money back in '93." Frank sank back into the couch in amazement. "My God, that Adrian was something. He decided to keep me out of his negotiations, but have it right in front of me at the same time. This is a real slap in my face, his way of proving that he didn't need me."

"Well, I obviously didn't know he was selling the house,

but I did know he was furious at you for not helping him out financially. He called it your third betrayal."

"The third! What in God's name were my first two?"

"He wouldn't say directly, but I'm sure one was that even though he had legally adopted you as a baby, you changed back to your father's name when you became a priest. That hurt him deeply."

"Like I wanted it to," Frank snapped. "Do you remember what he used to call me whenever he wanted to get to me?"

"Si, Paco. He called you a maricón."

"Or buggarón! Why would I want to keep the same last name of a man who teased me since I was eight years old about being a homosexual and a sodomite? And why would he even want me to keep his name? I never understood that."

"I think being gay was your first betrayal," Marta said. "Dad wanted you to become a priest because he thought it would control your sickness. He hoped your faith would be stronger than your sexual needs."

Frank held himself tightly as an old rage flooded through him. Though she appeared to tolerate his homosexuality, he was convinced that Marta felt the same way as Adrian had. She forgave him only because she assumed he was under control. Like a host of anxious Catholics, she saw homosexuality as a deadly flaw, a germ that was to be repressed by the antibiotic of prayer. He hated that he was surrounded by people who had only a conditional acceptance of something he knew he'd been born with.

He took a deep breath and forced himself once again to try to be compassionate. "I really am sorry that you got trapped into caring for Adrian. I avoided thinking how bad it was for you. I wish…"

"What would you have done?" Marta interrupted. "You should have stepped in when Mother died. But even if you had, I doubt I would have listened to you." The thought seemed to soothe her.

They returned to picking through Adrian's files. Frank took a thin folder from the last box. He controlled his reaction as he realized it was the will. It was simple and to the point and exactly what Adrian had told him three months earlier. Marta looked up. It wasn't a good time to deal with this, but there would never be a good time. "Did you ever see Adrian's will?"

"I didn't know he had one. He hated lawyers…among others." She looked at him warily. "So? Let me see."

He handed the document to her. "He left everything to me."

Marta looked away from Frank, her head jerking slightly. She glanced at the document briefly, then put it aside and sat muttering to herself. At first it was unintelligible to Frank, but gradually he could make out phrases of the Hail Mary prayer: "Holy Mary, mother of God, pray for our sinners" surfaced, then dropped back into a low rumble. Abruptly, she asked, "Why do you need it? You're taken care of by your, your brotherhood. Poor Catholics across the city already pay for your health insurance and silk suits and that obscene car."

"Look!" he blurted out. "I'll give you some, but you've got to realize that it's not actually going to me. It really amounts to a donation to the Church, and you have no idea how badly the Archdiocese needs money."

Marta emitted a loud, keening wail, and her eyes bugged out. Then she retreated into another silent prayer, rocking and holding herself. After several moments, she declared icily, "Well, I shouldn't be surprised," then added, "I stayed too long and he warned me that I'd regret it if I left."

"What are you saying?"

"I kept him alive, Frank, just like Mother did. She tended to his body and his spirit with her plants. She taught me about them so I could continue as she had done. We had plants for his arthritis, his heart palpitations and for depression. On my own,

I figured out how to treat his diabetes."

"That stuff is junk!" Frank erupted. "Mom tried to give me her herbal crap for everything. She almost killed me when I was nine and had appendicitis. She poured foul-tasting teas down my throat for two days until Adrian dragged me to the hospital."

"But she was usually right. She was very wise. She was a healer, a third-generation curandera."

"Marta, as much as I loved Mother, I also know that she was a witch, a Peruvian witch!"

She stared at him in smoldering silence. Then, in a low, controlled voice, she intoned, "That's right, your own mother is a witch. And you are the Inquisition!" Her face twitched. "But that's not all, Paco. You are the mestizo, the one of mixed race, the result of the conquest of the old, native ways by the new, modern ways. You are the one willing to destroy his past to make way for what? Progress and a new, better God? Isn't it interesting that people like our mother and her family could welcome Jesus, the god of love and forgiveness, into their hearts and their world to live in harmony with all the other gods there, but Christians still can't find enough love and forgiveness to accept the native world."

"It's the First Commandment," he responded.

"An unforgiving demand from a jealous, old God."

"Okay, Marta, you think I represent 2,000 years of cultural genocide, and you are purity and Mother Nature. What does this have to do with Adrian's death?"

"I kept Adrian alive for at least the last ten years in spite of all his ailments. As angry as I was, I warned and pleaded with him not to, but I'm sure he quit taking everything after I moved out. I think he got weaker and decided to die."

"You mean he became depressed?"

"A psychiatrist might have said so, but he would have been wrong. It was a spiritual illness. It was more like sadism, though that's still not quite the right term. Father was always doing things to make me suffer: little things like putting salt into my food if I left the table for something or turning up the TV or his record player when I was sleeping, usually that horrible Louie Prima and Keely Smith. He was a mean person." She turned to him with a twisted smile, a teacher explaining the ways of the world to her student. "We both know how mean he could be, but he also had to be in control. I think he may have committed suicide."

"Marta, no. You can't really believe that you, that Adrian…"

"Since he died, I've begun to remember things I knew, but hadn't been willing to recall." Marta sighed, and her voice took on a solemn, detached quality. "Two or three times a year, there are other slipstream accidents. That's what they are called. Just a few months ago, an old woman was pulled underneath a bus in Los Angeles on Beverly Boulevard near Fairfax."

"But that doesn't mean…"

Marta continued, "Dad would pick out the accounts to read to me from the newspaper. He was fascinated. It all came back to me very clearly just yesterday."

"But why? Even after you left, he had plenty of money. Why would he? It doesn't make sense."

"He didn't care about money, Frank. He was disgusted with people, and finally he didn't have any reason to hold on."

"Marta, please, you can't believe that."

"Paco, you of all people shouldn't be surprised. You know how far he went to hurt you each time he thought you betrayed him. Whether it was because you loved men or rejected his name or refused him financial support. He sent you away as a boy and cut you off completely until he had use for you again. He was cruel, but he was consistent."

"But you're saying he committed suicide to get back at you!"

"It was his way of saying 'F--- you' to the world, especially to me."

"Because you finally moved out?" Frank was incredulous.

"The fact that he gave all his money to you only proves how angry he was, and manipulative. He bought his way into heaven." Marta smiled vacantly at Frank. "It's not like I didn't know what he was capable of. I never told you that I hid his gun and ammunition when I left. I thought that would be enough. I still have it. But he found another way."

"But that's crazy!" Frank cut in, trying to surmount the tidal wave of her grief-driven logic.

"Human beings are often crazy, Paco. Craziness begins with us."

Frank composed himself and made his voice go gentle. "Marta, I understand you are upset. Adrian was mean, cruel— sadistic even. But he wasn't masochistic. He would never have risked his own suffering. He was too self-centered. He wasn't the kind of person who would kill himself."

Marta's confidence and energy abandoned her, and she slumped. After a few moments she nodded her agreement.

Frank continued, "And, you didn't kill him, directly or indirectly."

Marta shrugged a mild disagreement and Frank added, "In fact, as you said, you kept him alive for years." At this, some color returned to her cheeks, and she straightened up.

Encouraged by the shift in mood in the room, Frank sat back and continued, "I'm frustrated that we don't know for sure how Adrian died. I wish Peter Winston had caught someone. But until we figure it out, we have to stay calm and reasonable."

"With all the money you're getting, you can take a nice, long vacation."

Frank glared at Marta. When Adrian kicked him out of the house as a boy he had turned his back on his family and thrown in his lot with the Church. A little voice inside him said to be generous, to give her at least half of the money and save his half-sister from her father's spite. But he knew where his obligations lay. "I don't want the money to come between us, Marta. And since that's about all I'll get from this, I'd be happy to give you money for a vacation, too."

"A vacation!" She giggled strangely. "I was going to quit my job, and now I'm lucky to get a cruise to Ensenada. Paco, I'm going to have to work for the rest of my life, just to have a place to live. And how will I ever have a garden?" She gazed at him, but all affect was gone. She had retreated to where she could no longer be hurt.

10

Thursday, February 10, 2005

THE PHONE WAS RINGING when Peter and Samantha got home Thursday evening. Peter's stomach flipped as soon as he heard a man introduce himself as his father's surgeon.

"I'm afraid I've got some discouraging news, Mr. Winston." Peter felt the walls closing in. He resisted the impulse to hang up as the doctor continued. "Even though the hip surgery was successful, your father can't be rehabilitated."

"Why not, Doctor Yew?" Peter's voice didn't sound like it belonged to him.

"Basically, your father isn't able to grasp the concept of getting better."

"So?"

"If he doesn't understand why he has to go through the pain and effort of rehabilitation, then there's no way to motivate him to try to walk."

"Can't you just give him morphine?"

"He's under palliative care, but pain is only part of the

problem. Patients won't try to get better unless they can grasp cause and effect. We're never sure it's a problem until we try rehab, and that's why we didn't mention it to your wife. Anyway, rehab's no longer possible for your dad given the stage of his dementia. Basically, he's stuck in the present. He can't hold onto the idea of the future. It's very unfortunate, especially with someone who is otherwise in relatively good health."

Peter wished for a massive earthquake, anything to disrupt this moment. "So, that's it?"

"What do you mean, Mr. Winston?"

"That's it," Peter said louder, then caught himself. "That's the end of Dad's being able to get around. He's going to be bedridden, right?"

"Not exactly. I'm sure he'll be able to use a wheelchair."

That's supposed to be reassuring, Peter thought. "Okay, Doctor, thank you for calling, I guess." He hung up and immediately dialed Karen, a thirteen-year-old neighbor, who agreed to baby-sit. Not hungry himself, he fed Sam leftovers and, ignoring her protestations, left for the hospital like a man going to his own execution.

Peter stood at the hospital bed alone, the impact of the news still reverberating. Martin's frail, sedated body was barely visible beneath the slight rise and fall of the covers. Peter caressed the taut, yellowed skin of his father's skull. It was flaking, incredibly fragile. His father didn't stir, and it seemed like there was only the thinnest membrane of life that he would have to pass through in order to find his release. Peter knew with certainty that his father would will himself out of this life if he could. But his will had died first.

Peter looked at the hospital door. There was no lock. Whatever was to happen, he wanted privacy. He went to the door and jammed the top of a chair under the knob. Sweat broke out on his forehead as he turned back. Within two steps, his legs were like seaweed. He grabbed the metal railing at the side of the bed and sagged to his knees.

"Jesus Christ," he lamented, embarrassed at his weakness. He leaned his head against the cool metal bars and prayed, "God, take me out of this nightmare, please. Let my dad die or recover and give me a hard time for talking to a figment of my imagination." Peter brought his head up and looked forlornly at the passionate atheist who had ranted so often against Peter's faith. But Martin remained still, his disintegrating mind invalidating all but his very being.

A smell of disinfectant invaded Peter's senses, and he was glad that his dad wasn't aware any longer. He would hate this. Ironically, the only saving grace to this whole mess was that he no longer knew his own fate. Even though his long-term memory switched on at times, he rarely completed a thought. Essentially, he was stuck in a world beyond time and knowing.

Peter's head throbbed with his father's voice: "I will not be reduced to some vegetative state, and if I can't do something about it, you have to promise me that you will take care of it."

Peter had argued with him, but the biology professor had been adamant. For years, they had discussed this. Philosophically, Peter believed in free choice and accepted the principle of euthanasia. But as a concrete action, as something he was supposed to do if necessary, he resisted. His old man, forever the rational atheist, had been resolute. "You are as bad as your mother was. You hide behind your God, and your emotions rule your logic. Don't you see you are confusing love with sentimentality? Without my mind, I'm just molecules and atoms."

Peter glared at his father and silently addressed him. *You didn't need God because you thought you had everything figured out. You thought your intellect was redemption itself, but it abandoned you.* Anger pulsed through him, but he knew it was a cover for how weak and deficient he felt in the face of his father's demand. It would be so much easier if the old guy could walk out on an ice floe and be eaten by a polar bear like the Eskimos did when they became a burden to the group. At least, they used to do that. He must have read about it in those *National Geographics* that his father had given him as a kid. Polar bears and bare-breasted women. Peter smiled. Now bare-breasted women are a dime a dozen, but the only polar bear around was Jack Kevorkian, and he was in prison.

His dad had liked Kevorkian because he was unsentimental and unafraid to take on the government. *But tell me, Dad, why were you so family oriented when it came to death? Why wouldn't you consider going to a stranger to help you die?* Peter recalled that when he had tried to talk to him about this, his father had chided him. "Peter, in business you were tough! You wiped out corporations that were as good as dead. You thought that was healthy. So do the same for me. If it ever comes to where I can no longer think, help me die, please."

Another time, after one more debate, his father had said, "Surely, you aren't incapable of euthanasia. I just hope it's not because you have some religious qualms over hastening the inevitable. Remember," he intoned, "this Catholic God that you inherited from your mother, and that you still insist on honoring, he killed his own son. This is just a chance for you to get back, on behalf of all the Christian sons of the world."

Peter smiled ruefully. That crack was vintage Martin Winston: irreverent, outrageous and cloaked with enough insight that Peter couldn't dismiss him. *But, dammit, he thought, he expected me to do it because he was too cowardly to do it himself when he still had his wits.*

Peter grabbed the metal slats at the side of the bed and shifted his weight. His knees hurt, but he had to decide, once and for all, because his dad was about to be put into what he had always called "hell on earth."

"I will not be stuck in some goddamn nursing home to rot," he repeated over and over when they first, were told that his forgetfulness was Alzheimer's disease. "I'll kill myself first and if

I can't, you'd better." He had already joined the Hemlock Society and researched how to take his life. But he sensed he might need help, and he'd been unrelenting until Peter finally pledged to do something about it "when it was time." He had even made Peter shake hands on it. His father knew him well: that his son kept his word no matter what the cost.

Peter wanted to believe that his dad would have killed himself, except that his descent was so gradual. It was like the riddle he'd told him as a boy about how to cook a frog in a pot of water without the frog jumping out. The trick was to heat the water so slowly that the frog was enervated before he knew it. Alzheimer's had enervated Martin Winston, and turning up the heat was left to Peter.

But, Peter argued back to his guilty conscience, *I tried to do what he wanted. Three years ago I didn't allow any life support system after he had a small stroke. But he kept fighting back. Even in a hospital with all the tubes removed and no "extraordinary measures" allowed, he fought back. It wasn't in his nature to give up.* That was one of the things Peter used to admire about him.

Peter listened as the breath hissed from his father's parched lips. *Dad, you believed that humans had learned how to control nature, but you were betrayed by your own biological will or spirit or whatever the life force is. And you got the one thing you didn't want, more life. I'm sure you would have some brilliant theory to explain it all. But, you can't, and now I'm supposed to do what you never got around to.* Once again, Peter implored God to give him guidance. But, no sign came.

Hopeless and forlorn, his knees screaming, he gave up and began to slowly make the sign of the cross. *In the name of the Father*—Peter's hand stopped at his forehead, interrupting the automatic movement. *Yes, I am acting in the name of both fathers. God takes away life without sentiment, and that's what Martin wants. That's what I'm supposed to do, in both their names.* The hair on his neck rose from equal parts fear and excitement. What he was considering might seem audacious, but it was natural. Some would argue that it was arrogant, but it could also be seen as humble. He no longer felt the throbbing in his knees. *And, in the name of the Father, I will obey; I will do what he has demanded of me.*

His hand dropped down to his pounding heart. *And of the Son. Yes, I must do as Jesus did, obedient to the Father and as clear in my mission as He was. And, like Jesus, I do this in the name of love.* Warmth spread from the center of his chest.

Slowly, as he moved his hand from his left shoulder to his right, Peter felt as though his whole being was illuminated. *And of the Holy Ghost. Yes, even the taking of life can be done in the spirit of love and compassion.*

Peter clasped his hands. *Amen. Ah, men. How difficult we humans make life.* His hands began to shake, threatening his hold on his sacred mission until he grasped the bars, stood and thought no more. He took the pillow from behind his father's head and placed it over his withered face. For a long moment, there was stillness, but soon the body began to squirm, and then his father started to arch convulsively against the bed sheets. Horrified, Peter began to weep, and his tears scattered about the pillow, but he didn't release the pressure, and the carefully-tucked-in sheets restrained his father as he twisted. Though to Peter it seemed like forever, in less than a minute the struggle ebbed, and suddenly, in a heartbeat, the writhing stopped.

The absence of struggle was so different, so surprising, that Peter released his pressure on the pillow. In that moment, he was cast back into the dialogue he'd had with his father for his whole life: Why did Mom die? Is there a God? What is the reason for consciousness, for my life, for your life? In that moment of reunion, he knew he wasn't ready to end his father's life, even if his father disagreed. In a single movement, Peter withdrew the pillow, leaned over and breathed into his father's mouth. The old man began to stir again as Peter filled him with his own essence.

In the next moment, the sound of the door handle turning filled the room. The door easily slid the chair aside, and a nurse entered to see Peter resuscitating his father from what came to be called his nearly fatal choking episode. When Peter finally stepped back from the bed, he was a hero. Instead of the prison sentence he had feared, he received accolades as a dutiful and resourceful son.

SOMEHOW, PETER DROVE HIMSELF home. Judith was back from her business dinner. Sam was still up. His child swarmed his knees, joyfully crying out, "Daddy! Daddy! Daddy!" as if he were the only father in the world.

Judith gave him a kiss. "Karen said you had to go see Martin?" Peter nodded. "I'm glad you finally visited him, but why tonight all of a sudden?"

"The surgeon called to say that Martin wasn't going to get better, ever." Judith looked confused. "He can't be rehabbed, rehabilitated," he stammered, "and I can't talk about it anymore." Peter went to the liquor cabinet and pulled down a bottle of Arette Handcrafted Blanco Suave and withdrew into his office. One shot, two shots. He didn't know how to explain what he had done, or hadn't done, but he knew it wasn't over. Three shots, four shots. He was appalled: embarrassed for trying and unnerved for failing. Judith opened the door. "I need to be alone," he told her. She fixed him with an inquiring look, and he immediately repeated himself. She shrugged and went to bed. Five shots. The argument began all over. Defending and feeling both sides left him dazed. Six shots. He read the label, "100% de Agave." He'd paid one dollar for every goddamn percent. But it was puro tequila, no hangover. Seven shots. He silently insisted that he wasn't guilty to the bookshelves, themselves brimming with histories of murder for all reasons. Eight shots. At long last, the alcohol began to disarm his inner war of words. Nine shots. It was between him and Martin, and Martin was beyond reasoning. With the tenth shot, that's where Peter finally ended up.

11

Friday, February 11, 2005

PETER TAUGHT HIS CLASSES, though he couldn't remember anything about them. If he felt anything, it was occasional surges of a nameless emotion that quickly evaporated back into a mute, numb confusion. That night, he avoided Judith, just grunting and nodding enough to get by. But he knew she was watching him, trying to figure out what it was this time that had him so preoccupied. He kept his resolve not to binge again. He knew the problems that came with that kind of excess. But two glasses of his favorite Bordeaux wine had little effect, and he barely slept. As Saturday dawned, he intuited that she going to bore into him soon, probably that morning. She would want to know what was going on, so once he heard her in the shower he rushed out of the house, leaving a note. He scribbled that he had forgotten his license that he exchanged for the Camera Obscura key, and it was vitally important to retrieve it. Then, he wrote, he had some research to do for school.

His excuse gave him somewhere to go. Driving there, he concentrated on the radio blaring reports of more violence in

Iraq. The world was filled with people who killed on principle: terrorists, presidents. They all acted in the name of God, but how did they manage afterward? No answers came to him. He parked, and then, with his hand extended toward the car-door handle, he stopped motionless, like a fly in amber. He had accomplished nothing. Worse, saving Martin's life seemed to negate whatever reasons Peter had to end his life in the first place. What now? Thoughts and their implications short-circuited until his mind tumbled into the cold comfort of an argument with Judith. There was no way he could make her understand what he'd been driven to do. Saying that helping Martin to die came out of love and obligation was brushed aside with her sneering riposte: "I will care for him if you won't!" Even though Peter had ultimately made that same choice, it seemed self-serving. It was as if trying to kill Martin as well as saving his life—what he considered to be acts of love—took place because he was selfish. *Maybe*, he thought, *all love is about making oneself feel good*. What was certain is that nothing he had done had helped either Martin or him feel better.

Peter opened the door to the Camera Obscura. He didn't recall walking up the stairs. But there he was again. He must be in shock. That was it. Shock. Naming it helped.

Inside, several tourists conversed in German as one of them slowly rotated the wheel. The room felt warm to Peter. He took off his suede baseball jacket and watched the table as the view to the north of the building bled into the Santa Monica Mountains and Malibu to the west. Gradually the ocean, seen through the palms on the palisades, filled up the entire table until the pier came into view. The Germans chattered on as they turned the mirror toward the east. It halted where the bus stop and Ocean Avenue were once again in the middle of the table. Peter stared vacantly at the scene until he realized that his mind was on Adrian. It was a relief. He followed the tourists out of the room.

He made his way down the stairs into the Senior Center. He

surveyed the room and approached one of the elderly men who had been out on the sidewalk the day of the murder. He asked if he had talked to Adrian Montero's family. The man looked up from his game of dominoes and pointed to a woman nearby. "Mildred called them."

Peter recognized Mildred as the one who had said she'd been playing cards with Montero. He introduced himself and explained he'd seen her the day of the accident.

"I called Adrian's place, but nobody was there, so I called his daughter. The police had just reached her, poor dear. She didn't live with him anymore, but she had for years, looked after him even though he wasn't the easiest person to get along with, as I knew only too well." A woman sitting next to her patted her arm.

"You were close to him?" Peter asked.

"In a manner of speaking, but I don't like to say anything against the dead." She turned away as if to end the conversation.

"Sounds like he was a bit difficult," Peter said.

"A cheap S.O.B. is more like it," the other woman said.

"Cheap?" Peter asked.

"Wouldn't pay his debts," she added.

"Shush, Alice!" Mildred said, then turned back to Peter, blue eyes flashing beneath her white hair. "You're not with the police, are you?"

"Absolutely not," Peter responded.

Mildred leaned forward and whispered loud enough for them all to hear, "It's water under the bridge now, but Adrian Montero owed me 242 dollars and thirty cents. Gin rummy. Almost daily for a year." Her eyes gleamed and she added snappishly, "He always had some damn excuse for not paying me. I mentioned it to Marta when I called her, but on that issue she acted like she wasn't related to him. Then, earlier this week, she showed up."

Alice added furtively, "They don't allow gambling in here."

"Your secret is safe with me," Peter whispered back to Mildred.

"You must be a heck of a card player."

Mildred peered at him. "I get better when the bet is a nickel a point. Adrian knew what he was getting into. Besides, it's not like he was starving."

"He wanted people to think he was poor, but he couldn't stop bragging about his retirement plan," Alice chipped in. "He was rich."

Peter pulled over an empty chair and asked, "May I?"

Mildred nodded. "What did you say your name was?"

"Peter Winston," he answered as he sat.

"Winston, Winston," Mildred repeated as she scrutinized him, then said to her companion, "He looks a bit like Martin Winston, doesn't he, Alice?" To Peter, she added, "But you're chubby. Martin wasn't; he was a health nut."

"I don't recall him, Millie," Alice chimed in.

"Of course you do. You were here two years ago. Martin always wore a maroon cardigan and had a nose like a hawk. Very scientific. He wouldn't play cards, though." She turned back to Peter. "This is what's so maddening about this place: No one can remember a damn thing except me."

"Mildred is eighty-seven," Alice said.

Peter finally spoke. "Martin was my father."

"Oh, dear, I didn't know he was dead," Mildred said.

Peter blanched. "He's not dead," he said quickly, "but, he's, he's miserable."

Mildred pursed her lips and said briskly, "Well, I'm sorry, but it's like Bette Davis said: 'Growing old ain't for sissies.'"

"Adrian always bragged about how he had it figured out, and now see what's happened," Alice said.

Relieved to get back to Adrian, Peter asked, "What was this 'retirement plan' that you mentioned?"

Mildred cut in. "Alice never really understood it, because she wasn't a working girl like me. But I was in real estate for thirty years. Before I decided to take up cards," she added slyly. "I knew exactly what Adrian was up to."

"Which was?" Peter inquired.

"Estate for life."

"What's that?" he asked.

"It's an answer to the problem of having valuable property, but no cash, which is what Adrian was faced with over ten years ago. His house was leaky and run down, but the lot alone was worth close to a million. Now, of course, it's more like three or four million. Anyway, around 1993, he told me his stepson wanted to sell the place and put him in some retirement joint. But Adrian was cagey. I told him about this life estate business, and he put together a beautiful deal, not that I got anything out of it except a measly dinner."

"So he sold the place, got the money and was able to live there until he died?" Peter asked.

"Yep," Mildred said. "Called himself the king of the palisades."

"Pretty smart," Peter said.

"Smart, yes, but it sure didn't make Marta happy," Mildred said.

"Why not?" Alice asked.

"I told you, Alice," and she shook her head in frustration. "Marta showed up with him once in a while. She never said anything, but I could tell that she was ready for Adrian to kick the bucket so she could get her life back, if she ever had one. He complained about her when he didn't have anything else to gripe about, called her boring and worse. I never understood why she put up with that sour old butt."

"Mildred," Alice said, with her lips puckering. Then she looked at Peter. "Well, like we always say, it's never too late to make something out of your life."

"Marta finally got tired of the whole thing and skedaddled out of there several months ago. Made Adrian none too happy, I'll tell you," Mildred said, raising her eyebrows. "I'm sure she'll

get a nasty shock when she discovers he left her out of his will."
Mildred leaned toward Peter. "Adrian told me he gave it all to
the priest." She paused, overwhelmed by the audacity. "I knew
he was cheap, but I never would have guessed he could be that
vindictive."

"Are you sure? How long ago?"

Mildred looked at him with a smile, enjoying the effect of
good gossip. "About fifteen minutes after Marta left, from the
way he told it."

"Do you think that Marta knew?" Peter asked.

"She might have guessed. Adrian never forgot if someone
crossed him." She pointed to a man leaning on a cane, playing
dominoes. "He thought poor Jerry over there had cheated on
their score, and he made his life miserable. That's why I made
Adrian keep score when we started playing gin rummy."

"But do you think that Marta really could have known?" Peter
interrupted.

Mildred peered at him over her glasses, refusing to be rushed.
"When Adrian had good cards, he'd get humorous. As soon as
the bad jokes started I knew to dump all my high cards, before
he could go out. That's why I beat him over the long run: I never
lost big. Good fortune comes to those who pay attention, young
man."

Peter forced himself to wait a moment before he blurted out,
"So you think Marta picked up on what he was up to?"

"Well, something's got her in a snit. She marched in here a
few days ago and thrust every last penny of her father's debt in
my lap and left without a word. Rude as can be, as if it were my
fault." Mildred's lips drew tight.

The click in Peter's brain was so loud that it seemed like the
old ladies must have heard it. Crazy Marta wasn't innocent. It
was all an act. Her father had betrayed her, so she got her revenge.
She had even told him how she did it. She was a fucking genius.
She was hiding in plain sight.

Mildred carried on. "Adrian should have paid off his debts in a timely fashion. It's not like I have a rent-free estate and money to burn."

Alice patted Mildred's arm.

He thanked the two women effusively. He strode out of the Senior Center and headed up the parkway. Things seemed clear and sparkly, as if he had just woken up after sleeping for several days. Like the day of the murder, tourists and elderly people mingled as they sidestepped clumps of homeless people scattered on the benches and lawn. A well-dressed woman was feeding popcorn to the pigeons, talking to them in earnest, cooing tones tinged with longing. Another woman with a dirt-streaked face sat in the sun against a palm tree laughing to herself, and a man wearing several jackets and no shoes drifted past, a glazed look in his eye. There were many levels of madness here if you were willing to see them. It was scary unless you trusted that most people had learned to control their own brand of craziness. It usually didn't spill out on strangers.

That must have been what had happened to Marta: She had lost control. Adrian Montero was self-serving and mean, and she'd been stuck with him for all her life until she finally got the courage to move out. When she discovered she'd been screwed, she decided on revenge and got some bum to kill him. Peter's heart raced. It seemed farfetched. But he reminded himself that he believed in original sin precisely because people weren't born good: They had to work at it. He shouldn't be shocked at the existence of evil. Marta wasn't crazy, and she hadn't just snapped in a moment of rage. She had planned and brought in another person to help her. This wasn't a crime of passion. She had been methodical—obsessed, maybe—but not a psychopath.

Peter had read too many mystery books that ended up with the murderer being someone with no conscience. Psychopaths were capable of anything, because they couldn't experience another person's feelings. They had no empathy except as a means to get what they wanted. That wasn't evil; that was madness. Evil was when someone decided to destroy a person or a group knowing the pain it would cause. She went ahead anyway, because she believed that the end justified the means. Real evil was rational and done by moral, feeling people, like Marta.

Peter came to a stop. Across the street was the building he had chased the killer into. Who was that guy? He had a history, a story. He was someone's son. Maybe he did act on his own. But who would try to kill a stranger unless he was a psychopath or getting paid to do it? Either Adrian was in the wrong place when someone's madness spilled out, or this Mad Max character was so desperate that he was willing to kill for some payoff.

Marta could be behind it. She could have set it up. But killing someone, as he was learning, was a very complicated matter. Peter resisted letting his thoughts return to his own drama. His eyes roamed the face of the unfinished building until they settled on the placard announcing the developers: Thomas, McKenzie and Frankel Construction—TMF, the same company that had bought out Montero. Peter punched his right fist into the air. "You bastards!" he yelled at the building.

Maybe his first instinct was right, and Father Greening was wrong. TMF had bought Adrian Montero's place, acceding to his demand to live there until he died because he was practically dead. Peter knew from his research that it had projects all over Southern California. The principals in the partnership appeared to be real power brokers, on the boards of directors of many organizations and causes, especially Catholic ones. No doubt, they were used to getting their way, and they must have been real pissed off that Adrian lived on and on, costing them a bundle. Finally, they ran out of patience and decided to get rid of him. They paid off some lowlife bastard to kill Montero so business could proceed as usual. And it had worked, except the amateur assassin, in a panic at the scene he had created, ran back into a TMF building project to report to the contact person who set this up. The fact that Peter couldn't find him was no surprise. They would have hustled Max out of there on the double and maybe disposed of him, too. There certainly wouldn't be many questions asked about some homeless bum turning up in the surf; no way to guess that he had sold his soul to the devil.

This theory made more sense to Peter than Marta hiring someone. This was about greed. His years as an investment banker had taught him firsthand what greed could make people do. He was suddenly ravenous. He wanted to celebrate, so he quickly made his way to an outside table at a cafe. The waitress appeared, and he ordered an omelet with cheddar cheese, avocado, bacon bits and salsa, along with a mimosa: champagne with orange juice. He couldn't remember eating that day or the day before. That was very unusual. He liked to eat and eat well. He leaned back in his chair and picked up a local paper left by the folks at the next table.

The article on the impending demolition of one of the oldest remaining homes on the palisades was on the sixth page. He didn't find it until he was halfway through his meal. "Progress Threatens Another Landmark" said everything Peter had just figured out—except, of course, that Montero's death wasn't an accident. But it told how TMF and Associates hadn't been able to develop the property for over a decade and were going to raze it and begin construction of condominiums as soon as possible. The Historical Society vowed to stop it.

He should call Father Greening and tell him about this connection between TMF and the murderer. But TMF's role in the business affairs of the Archdiocese meant the murder plot could be connected somehow to the priest's interests. Peter needed to know more about Father Greening and, it hit him again, he had to prove there had been a murder before he could solve it. He was nowhere until he found Mad Max.

His appetite disappeared, and he gestured to the waitress to bring the bill. He felt chilled, but when he went to put on his jacket, he realized he forgotten it, probably at the Camera Obscura. When he opened his wallet, he saw that he'd also forgotten to retrieve his license once again. His mind spinning and his stomach churning, he ran across the street to the Senior Center. Mildred and Alice were gone. He let himself into the Camera Obscura room, but it was empty of everybody and everything, including his jacket. Dashing downstairs, he found a muscular young man at the office window. He was probably a student at Santa Monica High, but with over 3,000 students, who knew?

"Did anyone turn in a chocolate suede baseball jacket?" he demanded.

"What team?" the kid responded.

"No team, wiseass. Just an expensive suede jacket!"

"Nope," he shook his head apathetically.

"God dammit," Peter swore, beginning to leave. Then he remembered the key in his hand. "I want my driver's license back," Peter said as he pushed the key toward him.

The kid had to rummage through a drawer. "You're supposed to turn the key in right after you finish, you know," he said with a nonchalant arrogance.

Peter bristled. "You're probably too young to realize, but they only started locking the room a few years ago."

"Those must have been the good old days," the boy responded glibly, then he added, "Anyway, it's not my fault," He laid Peter's license on the counter.

Peter seethed, "So that means no one is responsible, right?" He grabbed his license.

The boy rolled his eyes and shrugged. "Except you."

"Fuck you!" Peter spat the words out and stormed off.

12

SATURDAY, FEBRUARY 12, 2005

CRADLING THE WARM TEA Sal had brought him, Frank watched the day awaken through one of Adrian's front windows. Across the avenue, a thick, ancient cypress twisted out of the earth. It sat coiled next to a towering eucalyptus and two giant palm trees. In the distance, a lone sailboat searched for a puff of wind on a flat, pale ocean. It wasn't yet eight o'clock on a Saturday, but the narrow park was coming to life with power walkers and joggers who wove between the few hardy souls who were settling onto the park benches, impervious to the chilly morning air.

The cliffs, piece by piece, pebble by rock, were in a continual state of collapse. Over forty feet had fallen away since Frank was young. That was almost a foot a year. And yet, this lot that was now worth millions and would soon be covered by multimillion-dollar condos was only about 120 feet from the edge. Why did anyone think that this deterioration was going to stop? Most Americans—maybe most people everywhere—lived for the moment and the immediate future. Live! Spend! Fuck! was the marketing message. He understood that mentality—he had been raised on it—but being stationed at the Vatican had taught him to think in terms of centuries, not decades. Shortly after he returned to Los Angeles, he had begun to put that long view of things into practice. To begin with, he had to prepare financially for a crisis that had gotten away from the American leadership. The local hierarchy knew that he'd been sent by Rome, so no one directly challenged him or wanted to know too much about his methods. The Cardinal, like the Pope in other circumstances, needed to maintain a discreet distance from his "fundraising" in order to maintain deniability. While he didn't officially speak for the Pope, it was known that Frank had his blessing.

Frank opened the window a crack and was rewarded with the bracing, green scent of eucalyptus. God's abundance was everywhere he looked. He'd grown up with this view. He'd taken it for granted then, and it didn't mean much to him now, except that it was worth a lot of money and he'd be getting it. He didn't think it hubris to feel self-satisfied that he'd been so successful. He'd keep only twenty or thirty thousand dollars for his own needs, a vacation to Italy with Sal maybe, and something for Marta. But the rest of it would go into the Saints Preserve Us fund he'd been building since coming to Los Angeles.

He was dedicated to the long haul and trusted that his work would ensure him a place in eternity. Nonetheless, it was challenging to live for a heavenly future, and he often yearned for the "now" in eternity. Worldly pleasures, like forgetting himself during sex with Sal, wouldn't last. Sal couldn't promise eternity. But since he was a boy, Frank had, on rare occasions, experienced brief periods of transcendence—"experiential seizures," doctors had called them. The episodes lasted only a few seconds, but the rapture of oneness with God was absolutely real, a gift that formed the bedrock of his faith.

Frank's job was to work for the glory of God. It just happened that he was responsible for defending the material well-being of the Church, and the price kept going up astronomically. The pedophile scandals that threatened every archdiocese in the United States were just one example of how things could get out of control. A settlement of over twenty-five million dollars in Louisville, Kentucky, had been one of the first hard figures to emerge in 2003. It was emblematic of the general problem. That amount was over sixty percent of the total worth of that archdiocese and little of it was covered by insurance. The bill in Boston was eighty-five million, and they were closing down one out of five parishes. The price of peace in Orange County came to over a hundred million. The bill in L.A. could end up being over ten times that.

From the beginning, Frank and others had known that this would create a financial crisis. But what they hadn't anticipated was that archdioceses, beginning with Portland, Oregon and Phoenix, would declare bankruptcy. It meant that their records would be opened up to the authorities, beginning with their personnel files. Filing for bankruptcy was a shortsighted, stupid thing to do. It handed the government and the public more reason to treat churches like any other corporation. Eventually it could lead to an end of their tax-exempt status. The breeze from the window was suddenly irritating, and he closed it, sending a flurry of old paint chips off the windowsill.

He cast an eye around the house. It was falling apart faster than Marta. He didn't want to be mean, but she could never have survived in this place alone. He was afraid for her sanity and worried that he might become responsible for her. If he had to institutionalize her, it would use up the financial windfall the Archdiocese was supposed to get from this estate, unless he placed her in a convent somewhere to be cared for.

Money always brought problems. The only thing worse was not having any. It was embarrassing, but he had to admit he had gloated over getting the estate when Adrian told him. He had imagined himself catching a touchdown pass and then strutting around the end zone, taunting homophobes the world over. Adrian may have driven him out when he was a boy, but time and concern over his own soul had scared the old man into some sort of turnaround. Not that he had apologized outright. That wasn't Adrian's way. But he had come as close to admitting his cruelties as he could, and Frank felt vindicated. His first and oldest critic had capitulated and his inheritance, though he knew it was guilt money, felt like he was finally getting his revenge. It was an odd experience for someone who had foresworn personal wealth.

The water pipes squealed and groaned. Salvatore was braving the shower in Adrian's bathroom. Frank felt the urge to join him, but he had a golf game at nine-thirty. To others, it looked like fun, but the golf course was where he did his best work for the Saints Preserve Us fund. The Cardinal had made it clear that Frank should take time off for family matters, but Frank had decided it was better for him to keep busy. He couldn't afford to rest as long as the enemies of the Church were hammering lawsuits on its door. Besides, this evening he and Sal would indulge in a special dinner before returning for a second night in Adrian's dilapidated estate. Other than Sal's tiny apartment, Adrian's seemed the safest and cheapest hideaway available. His own house was out of the question for sleepovers.

In two days, Monday, it would be Valentine's Day, not a favorite holiday of priests. Frank didn't want to draw attention to himself by dining out with his lover on that day, so he had made reservations for this night at his favorite restaurant: the esoteric Saddle Peak Lodge, nestled away in the Santa Monica Mountains. Nothing seemed more appropriate to him than to celebrate his rekindled sexual wildness with feasting on the venison and wild bird that were their specialties. It was expensive, an extravagance, but he felt he deserved to enjoy his good fortune. He'd been lucky in love, and financially it was like he'd won the lottery. He patted his dwindling belly and smiled: Wild game was low fat, and this much sex was great exercise. He glanced at his watch and went to dress.

As he drove down Wilshire Boulevard, his cell phone rang. "Monsignor, it's Reverend James Guttierez from the End of Time Temple. We met two years ago at the Martin Luther King, Jr., breakfast."

"Yes, Reverend, I remember." He recalled the man as an offensive evangelical salesman, yet undeniably charismatic.

"I've heard that you were the man who could green-light the sale of one of your properties across from us on South La Cienega. We've outgrown ourselves twice, and we're busting at the seams again. Do you know the building I'm talking about?"

"Yes, and I know your church. You've become hard to miss in that part of town," Frank said.

"Twelve thousand folks squeeze in twice every Sunday, praise the Lord, and more keep on coming, so we need space. The Archdiocese owns that two-story office building, and it's over half empty. Only a few insurance agencies and an herbal product outfit in there, near as I can see."

"And you wish to buy that property?"

"Well, actually, I'd prefer to lease it, but I assumed you'd rather sell."

"Why lease?"

"It's in our name, Monsignor. Not to put too fine a point on it, since I understand we work on a different sort of calendar than you Catholics, but our reading of the Bible indicates that Jesus is coming soon, and we'd rather not invest in this material world any more than is necessary." A cadence started to develop in the man's voice, the preacher overcoming the businessman's demeanor.

"Even though it would be more expensive for a while."

"Cash isn't a problem, I'm humbled to say. I know what your rental rates are. You figure out what you'd get with the building full and we'll sign a contract as soon as you can clear the place out."

"You work fast, Reverend."

"I don't mean to be brusque, but there are souls begging for our message, and time is short. Can we work out a deal?"

Frank assured the man that he would get to work on it and hung up. The advantages of the deal were significant, but were overshadowed by the proof that the Evangelicals were gobbling up dissatisfied souls, including many ex-Catholics, faster than you could say Armageddon. He shook off his concern as he pulled into the Pacific Golf Club, an undulating carpet of green that had long ago been carved out of the chaparral of the Santa Monica Mountains. He put a smile on his face as he approached his carefully chosen guests, Cyrus Dance, Dennis Riley and Kevin Gardner, not a priest among them. This was business, and Frank only played with other priests for fun. Frank hadn't been in Los Angeles long before he realized that the golf course was like an old-fashioned Internet. This was where insider information masqueraded as gossip or casual conversation. If you had the mind and nerves for it, and he did, that information could be parlayed into significant wealth.

Sean O'Leary, the suntanned, splotchy-faced veteran scheduler, waved them over with a twinkle in his eye and a brogue that thickened whenever a priest was nearby. "Say your prayers, boys, the new Monsignor is on the course, and the green fees to play at the Pearly Gates have just gone up."

Frank's friendship with the alcoholic dated back to when Frank first arrived from Rome. Many years of eavesdropping had furnished Sean with a wealth of clubhouse secrets. The devout Catholic was a valuable ally, and all he needed in return was someone to put in a good word for him with God. Nonetheless, it was like Sean to make sport of Frank's recently announced promotion. It was the standard male way of congratulating someone by ribbing him. Frank turned to the rest of his foursome. "Sean's so worried about his soul that he's trying to save himself by returning his empty bottles of Wild Turkey to his church. It seems he's a tad confused about redemption."

Sean O'Leary laughed heartily at the retort. His drinking was well known, and the good priest had stood him several rounds at the club bar. "That's why we keep tithing, Father. We need the priests to keep us sinners from total confusion."

Frank looked out at the rolling expanse and sent his drive only 120 yards down the first fairway.

"Uh-oh," Cyrus Dance exclaimed, "it looks like Father Frank lost some of his firepower when he dropped all those pounds. We better get him lifting some weights."

Men are so predictable, Frank mused as he stepped off the tee. *Particularly straight men*. So many found teasing to be the only form of intimacy they were comfortable with, especially with other men. As a result, being able to handle teasing became proof of one's manhood. For a priest, the challenge was somewhat muted. In the eyes of most laymen, celibacy meant there wasn't the usual competition over who had the biggest dick. But there was still money to compete over, and Frank was a master in that regard. Like many good businessmen, he didn't personally need to win every skirmish. He simply had to come out ahead at the end. So Frank offered no retort. He wanted Cyrus to feel like the top dog. He quietly watched Cyrus as he loosened up his muscular chest and back with a few practice swings. He was one of the Church's great success stories from the African-American community. When his football career at USC had been cut short by a shattered knee, he had fallen prey to drugs and despair, until he found God in a small parish church in Compton. Several years of hard work and a few key connections found him running his own air conditioning company at the age of thirty-two. When Frank had met him, he immediately recognized him as a prime candidate for helping out the Church. As a reformed sinner, Cyrus felt beholden to the Church. As a businessman, he was more than happy to give back a certain percentage to Frank's Preservation Fund in exchange for an exclusive service contract from the Archdiocese. And, as a Catholic, he was relieved at the thought he could get a little closer to heaven by helping the Church.

Frank accepted that many people would be critical of kickbacks on service contracts and find it illegal. It was a little like buying indulgences, the same thing that had so enraged Martin Luther. That's why secrecy was tantamount. But, especially in a society as materialistic as the United States, he found that most people expected that there was a price tag on salvation. Under his guidance, this system was applied to all the Archdiocese's chronic needs, from repaving parking lots to mortuary services. Kickbacks had become a slow and steady way to build the invisible cash reserves that the Archdiocese needed. Being invited for the occasional golf game sweetened the deal for these sole contractors, while, at the same time, Frank could carry on with other forms of fundraising.

As Frank exchanged small talk with Dennis Riley, a banker who had been on his financial advisory board for over ten years, he became aware that none of these men had mentioned Adrian's death. It didn't bother him exactly, but it underscored that few people, other than the Cardinal and some old friends from seminary, knew his family history.

Walking onto the third green, Kevin Gardner began laying out some ideas for recruiting new priests. He had the cockiness of new money. He'd been a surfer who'd made a fortune in the glory days of the dot-com era, donated a million dollars to the new Cathedral and raised even more. He seemed to enjoy being the youngest member of Frank's advisory board. He waited until Frank was about to putt before bringing up the sex abuse scandal. "What happens to the Archdiocese if the courts find that the bishops were negligent by not reporting the abusive priests?"

Frank stood over his ball. "Some insurance companies have already tried to back out. To the extent they succeed, we're screwed." Frank missed his seven-foot putt. "We've already paid out many millions and anticipate much more. We'll be fighting civil suits for years." He tapped the ball in.

Dennis Riley left his third putt two feet from the hole, and the others offered him a "gimme" to end his frustration. Frank was sharing a cart with Dennis, and they took off down the course. "I've got a pretty good idea, but how badly screwed would the Archdiocese be?" Dennis asked as they flew over the grass.

"Let me put it this way. The drop in the stock market in 2001 closed down many of the Church's outreach functions. That was unfortunate, but this could force the sale of land, close schools and parishes and generally cripple us for decades."

"I don't mind telling you, I don't like this tension between you and the insurance boys," Dennis said, running his hand through his thinning white hair. "The subject came up at a dinner party last week, and it got very uncomfortable. I don't like having to choose between capitalism and Catholicism."

"All relationships have their rough spots," Frank said and looked over at his friend. "It'll work out," he added soothingly.

"It better," Dennis harrumphed, his jowls shaking. The two men fell silent as a cool breeze rolled over them. From the open expanse of the golf course, they could see the dark ridges of the Santa Monica Mountains against the misty sky. Hanging above the range, two turkey vultures circled round and round.

"Death," Frank said to himself as he pulled up next to where Dennis' ball lay. Dennis gave him a curious look, and Frank continued as if he'd meant to be heard, "Something's always dying."

Dennis pointed to the vultures with his 6-iron as he got out of the golf cart. "And there's always something around to take advantage of it," he chuckled. "That reminds me," he said as he appraised his shot, "there's an outfit named Dove Toys that's borrowed money from a number of sources in a desperate way and appears to be falling into its own death spiral. Sad, really;

my granddaughter loved their stuff."

That's how it goes, Frank mused to himself. Little tidbits of information bubbled forth during these games or in the sweat room after that turned out to be invaluable if one was ready to act on them. He'd research that company and probably sell that stock short to take advantage of its approaching demise. Dennis' last tip made the Fund $52,000.

Kevin chipped onto the next green and continued his bent. "I'm sure that the Cardinal, to say nothing of the Pope, has been keeping an eye on this scandal for years. And, Frank, you don't seem to be the type to let anything take you by surprise."

Frank smiled. "Eternal vigilance maximizes solvency."

"So what have you done?"

Frank leaned forward and putted. The ten-footer hooked the edge of the cup and dropped in. He smiled at Kevin. "We're doing what anyone would do, making contingency plans."

Dennis chimed in, "Extraordinary times demand extraordinary measures."

"The Pope knows about extraordinary measures," Kevin said to Dennis. "Like in the case of Roberto Calvi. What was he called? Oh, yeah, God's banker. Sounds like a great honor, but he ended up getting killed for his efforts. Hey, Frank, how much did the Vatican finally pay to the defrauded investors of that multibillion-dollar investment scam that Calvi ran?"

"Without admitting any guilt, Pope John Paul II and Archbishop Marcinkus paid out over $250 million in 1984," Frank answered. "It was a mess."

"You were stationed at the Vatican at that time, weren't you?" Kevin asked.

Frank coolly appraised Kevin. He was typical of certain Catholics who seemed to enjoy how fallible the Church was. His kind experienced their belief in God as a sort of dependency, a weakness, and wanted to take it out on God's representatives. Still, Kevin demanded to be taken seriously. He was a man who did his homework. "Right. I was part of the effort to untangle it."

Kevin looked at him with deference. "Well, you guys did an impressive job of damage control, because I think the Pope got off easy. There was evidence that the Church was in bed with the Mafia and P2, that anti-communist, Masonic secret society that damn near orchestrated a coup in Italy."

Frank shrugged. "Nothing was ever proven."

Frank and Cyrus both ended up in the sand trap a few holes later. As they gingerly stepped onto the sand, Cyrus asked, "How did this abuse thing get so far out of hand, Frank? Do you think it's because of celibacy or some sort of homosexual cabal? Or did the people in charge simply stick their heads in the sand?"

Frank ignored the prejudice involved in the question. "I don't think it's any of those. I think it's a rule of group psychology that you take care of your own if there's a threat from outside."

"You mean if my brother picks a fight with an outsider, I'm going to help him with that battle before I pull him back inside our house and beat the stuffing out of him for being such a fool?"

"Exactly. Fighting for your survival is a given. It's a question of where your primary allegiance is."

"But aren't the parishioners part of your family, too?"

"Of course! Starting in the mid-eighties, the Church intervened with prayers and psychotherapy for the victims, along with a reasonable level of financial restitution. But things change if the victims become part of a class-action suit and threaten to destroy the Church."

Cyrus swung at his half-buried ball, and it lifted onto the green in a cloud of white sand. "Enter the lawyers."

"Right. Lawyers by definition have no allegiance except to those who pay them. They're rogue warriors."

From the green, Kevin spoke up. "It's more than just lawyers who say that the Church didn't follow the law."

"I'm not saying the attitude was right, but the Catholic Church wasn't unique," Frank responded. "You have to remember that our whole society was quite ignorant and naïve about sexual abuse well into the 1980s. Most everyone—doctors, therapists, teachers and priests—was looking the other way, and when society decided to see what was happening, it took time to adjust to the extent of the problem. By the 1990s, a sophisticated psychological intervention program for the pedophile priests was implemented in Los Angeles."

"I don't mean to be difficult," Kevin argued, "but good intentions are what the road to hell is paved with. Dioceses throughout the country are in trouble, because they tried to function outside the rules. In too many cases, the priests weren't turned over to the authorities."

"At the time, there weren't enough in the Church who thought it was a mistake." Frank blasted at his ball but caught mostly sand, and the ball hopped just a few feet. He stepped over to the ball and spoke as he stared at it. "I personally argued that the perpetrators should have been handed over to the district attorney from the beginning. Still," he looked over at Kevin, "whether we call it ignorance or arrogance, it's understandable that the bishops placed their allegiance in their Church rather than the government. We have a very long history of looking after our own." He focused again on his ball, and this time it lifted gently onto the green and rolled to within two feet of the hole. "Regardless, it's my job to see that the Catholic Church can pay for its mistakes and come out stronger than ever."

"You sound like we're at war," Cyrus suggested.

Frank smiled at him. He appreciated the pronoun he had used. "We can take great solace that the Church has been winning battles like this for 2,000 years."

"Yeah," Cyrus added ominously, "but this battle doesn't make us look like the good guys."

Maybe it was the fact that he hadn't had a lot of sleep since

Sal had appeared on the scene, but Frank was tired of people's myopic focus on the abuse scandal. He turned and addressed his audience. "You all have children, right?" They nodded, and Kevin cracked, "It wouldn't work out if everyone were a priest, Frank."

Frank ignored the comment. "And you are all dedicated to providing for them, your grandkids, your great-grandkids and on into the future, right?"

Kevin responded with a touch of impatience, "Obviously, Frank, but what…?"

"That means you don't consider the Second Coming of Jesus as a factor in your worldview. You are not Fundamentalists. You believe in a future here on earth. You probably care about clean air and water and preserving whales and trees because of that faith. That's not what a lot of other people believe, many of whom are either in positions of political power or are terrorists. That, my friends, is serious."

"What about within the Catholic Church?" Cyrus asked.

"Every institution has its fundamentalists, and we are in a conservative phase currently. But, regardless of our doctrinal struggles, few of us read the Bible in such a way that rationalizes ignoring the future."

"I've read the works of a few journalists who raise this issue, but you think this is a real danger?" Kevin asked tentatively. "It seems pretty far out to me."

"It is far out, but it's part of my job to be prepared for tomorrow's news." Frank putted his ball into the hole. "That's why I'm so sure we will weather this abuse scandal."

The implications of Frank's statement left everyone momentarily speechless, and they turned their attention back to the game. On the eighteenth green, Kevin asked Frank if he thought he was in line for being made a bishop.

"I doubt it. There aren't many 'prelatos d'onore,' as bishops without a diocese are called. And religious institutions don't tend to advance their financial experts to the highest positions. It's unseemly for a spiritual institution to appear too interested in material wealth."

"But they need you."

"There are many good men to lead the Church. What is in short supply are priests who know business. The best example isn't a priest but a layman, Bernardino Nogara, who was the Vatican's finance manager and director from 1929 until he retired in 1956. He grew ninety million dollars into one billion in ten years. In short, he made the Holy See independent financially."

"I'd say you are the best hope to be the next Nogara, Frank," Kevin said. "Only, in this situation, it seems like you don't have to make a fortune, but avoid losing the one we have."

"Gentlemen, gentlemen," Dennis burst in, "the good father has enough pressure just trying to get the ball in the hole."

Frank had tired of the game and decided that he wanted to win. He proceeded to drop in a long, breaking twenty-footer. Cyrus reviewed their scorecards. "Well, I guess the Church will survive after all. Frank managed to skunk the rest of us." Frank collected twenty dollars from each, delighted that his Saturday-night date was now partially paid for.

13

SUNDAY, FEBRUARY 13, 2005

SUNDAY MORNING, FRANK'S CELL phone woke him from a deep slumber. "Are you okay?" Marta asked breathlessly.

"I'm barely awake, but I'm—"

"I had a dream that you died in a fire in the house. It was horrible."

"I'm fine, Marta," he exclaimed, shaken that she somehow knew he was at Adrian's with Sal.

"Thank God! It was so real. Where are you now?"

"At my place, of course."

Marta asked tentatively, "Is it okay to go back to the house? I mean, they haven't started tearing it down, have they?" She didn't wait for an answer. "It really doesn't make any difference, I guess. I just want to salvage a few more plants from the garden."

"It's still muddy out there from last week's rain," he said. "When are you coming, I mean, going over to Adrian's?" he asked, looking at his watch.

"After Mass, or maybe I'll go over now. I don't know." She

sighed. "Where are you saying Mass this morning?"

Frank shook Sal to wake him up. Sal reached out to him sleepily and said, "Buon giorno."

"Who's that?" Marta asked.

"My clock radio just went off," Frank said, motioning to Sal to be quiet. "Why don't I meet you at Adrian's late this afternoon. I could help you."

"No, I need to go alone." She hung up.

Frank and Sal gathered all evidence of their weekend tryst and hurried out.

Across the street, Peter scrunched down in his car seat as the two men, laughing conspiratorially, rushed from the Montero place. They didn't notice him, but he was chagrined; he had gone from investigating a murder into spying on people's private lives. Thirty minutes earlier, while driving to Mass, he hadn't been able to decide if he should confess his attempt at euthanasia, or patricide—as the voices in his head called it—so he had come here instead. In his pursuit of doing the right thing, he sensed he had crossed a line

Slow down, the historian in him cautioned. *Don't let your personal crisis unhinge your moral compass. Just because you don't know what to do or understand something doesn't mean you won't. Be patient...and watchful.*

Peter waited low in his seat, hidden. He had seen enough to come to a singular and undeniable conclusion: Father Frank Greening was in love. It shouldn't have been important, but it was. A minute after the monsignor's black BMW receded in his rearview mirror, Peter got out of his car and slipped around the side of the Montero house.

He peeked around the corner into the backyard. The upheaval there made him gasp. Wherever he looked, plants of all sorts, large bushes and small trees had been hacked and ripped from the trampled soil. An extensive garden had been violently, yet meticulously strewn about. It lay shriveled in the clear morning sunlight. Near the back, a greenhouse sagged askew, held partly upright by thick vines. Great effort had been spent to ravage and destroy, like a battlefield where all the killing and mayhem had been done hand to hand. A memory flooded his mind: the trip he had made to Gettysburg when he was in high school. The long night he camped out in those haunted yet beautiful fields of Pennsylvania had hooked him on becoming a historian. He had absorbed the fears and frantic courage of the 52,000 men who had slaughtered each other over three days in 1863. Nearly as many Americans were killed as would die in the Vietnam War over a ten-year period. Until then, he hadn't appreciated the high price that standing up for principles can extract. Fifty-two thousand dead in three days was just part of the cost of confronting the horror of slavery. Those fields said to him that if you don't stand up for what's right, you are shaped by events: You are a victim.

Remembering those twenty-four hours he had spent in Gettysburg helped Peter understand, or maybe it was accept, why he was so drawn into the murder of Adrian Montero. On one level, there was no comparison. Adrian's demise, maybe his whole life, was of little significance. But part of what Peter learned from that immersion into Civil War history was that each soldier at Gettysburg had a story. As overwhelming as it felt at times, there are no small lives, only small minds. Peter was free to ignore what had happened to Montero, but if he did he would become enslaved to a lesser life; he would join Montero in his irrelevance.

Peter stepped into the yard and became aware of a soundtrack to this devastation: guttural rumblings intermixed with muted screeches. A chill raced up his neck as he tried to find the source of this foreboding mélange of sounds. His eyes settled on a fifteen-foot tree on the far side of the yard. Its outer leaves were pulsating, a sheath of green driven from within by an unseen source. As he stared, some leaves near the top parted and a swatch of lime green fluttered behind the darker leaves. As other spaces in the leaf cover opened and closed, he was able to glimpse into the middle of the tree, where at least a dozen green parrots were feasting with boisterous glee. Holding on with one claw, some hanging upside down, each bird grasped a yellow fruit with the other claw and voraciously ripped it apart with its menacing beak. Loquats! As a boy, he had picked and eaten them himself on his way home from school. But he'd never seen anything like this exultant aviary feasting.

His fear dissipated as he watched. Satisfied that they couldn't care less about him, he stepped up on the porch and peered into the house. It looked cold and worn and nearly empty. From the front of the house, he heard a door slam. He slipped out of sight. Then, peeking in, he saw Marta come into the kitchen, her head down, looking as tired as the house. Quietly, he dropped off the porch and scooted around the side of the house, back to his car.

THE NEXT MORNING, PETER stood in front of his Advanced Placement history class. He adjusted his wig so that the faux ponytail fell outside the black eighteenth-century gentleman's jacket and didn't tickle his neck. He gazed imperiously through wire-rimmed spectacles, scanning the attentive teenagers until his eyes settled again on a girl in the front row. "I meant, Madame, exactly what I wrote." He raised a document and pointed to it. "We hold these truths to be self-evident, that all men are created equal."

Appearing shortly before President's Day in the second semester as Thomas Jefferson had become a tradition in Peter's history classes. While he was hardly in the mood for it this year, he usually looked forward to the students' delight and attention. In this costume, he held an authority that was difficult to maintain the rest of the time. The kids, often hard to reach and prone to boredom, were his to mold, because, for all their posturing, they were still children at heart and therefore unable to resist the magic of pretending. In the past, he had loved it. Today, unsure of himself or where his life was heading, to disappear into another identity was, at best, a dicey proposition.

"But, Mr....?" the girl hesitated.

"Jefferson, Madame, Thomas Jefferson," and he bowed low to a round of giggles.

"Mr. Jefferson," she continued, leaning forward earnestly, "what about women?"

"Indeed," Peter said, beginning to pace in his long black riding boots, "what about women?"

"I mean," she frowned, "do you really think that only men are created equal?" A couple of female students applauded the question.

"Yes, thank God," he sniffed indignantly. "My colleagues and I are in quite general agreement that women are not to be considered equal to men because they are, in most regards, quite superior." He looked out into the classroom in a haughty fashion as the students contended with the implications of his statement.

"Then why aren't they mentioned in the Declaration of Independence?" another student asked.

"It simply wasn't necessary. It was irrelevant, since everyone knew that we were trying to establish political laws to govern society, which," he paused for effect, "is not the natural domain of women." Speaking now over some low boos and hisses mixed with muffled hoots of agreement, Peter continued, "Had we been concerned with the affairs of the home and children, then the document would have been quite different."

"That's really sexist," said the girl who had asked the question.

"That word isn't in our vocabulary, Denise. But I think I understand what you mean, and yes," he nodded, "there were a number of ladies who felt that women were being treated with, how shall I say, a certain prejudice."

"Like who?" asked another student.

"Like whom, I believe you mean, my dear girl. Well, there was Abigail Adams, the wife of John Adams, the second president of our new government, whom I succeeded," he added smugly, "as I'm sure you all remember."

"What about Abigail Adams, Mr. Winston?" the girl pushed.

"The name is Jefferson. I don't know this fellow Winston." Two boys in the back snickered. "Abigail Adams, a close friend of mine, by the way, was as outspoken in her thoughts about the rights of women as she was concerning the colonies' right to revolt." He continued, "Her letters to her husband would provide the basis for an interesting term paper, which I've heard you are obliged to write."

Several students wrote down the suggestion. As they made their way through the Declaration of Independence, they were provoked and thoughtful. Their questions became more and more pointed as they realized that their dreams for themselves had much in common with this document from the past. At times, they appeared upset with him rather than with the issues he presented.

"Yes, it's true," Peter said in response to a question. "Many of us who signed the Declaration of Independence were slave holders. However, you should remember that this was quite legal." A murmur of disgust passed through the room.

A girl spoke up angrily, "Mr. Jefferson, my mother told me that DNA tests proved that you had a slave woman as your mistress and that you had several children with her. That's like she was a slave twice," she insisted.

"How is that, Chandra?" Peter asked.

She didn't hesitate. "Because she was both a working slave and a sexual one. She didn't have a choice about being with you or not."

"Well, you raise a very interesting point. Given the recent proof, I am finally free to say that your mother is correct. Sally Hemmings and I had four children over a period of many years. And that situation provides the basis for another fascinating term paper. You'd need to research carefully, and you might want to consider if that situation was different from the affairs of other presidents. What makes this a scandal? Is it the sex or the slavery? For example, what if she came to me of her own free will?" Peter added, "Out of love?"

"If someone is a slave, there's no such thing as free will," Chandra came back angrily. "Choice is an illusion under those circumstances, Mr. Winston. That's just some racist fantasy." A wave of tension swept through the class.

"Mr. Winston will be back tomorrow," Peter said pointedly. "I'm Thomas Jefferson, one of the fathers of this country."

"Did you have a lot of slaves, Mr. Jefferson?" asked a tall, thin boy.

"Indeed I did." Peter's adrenaline stirred. They were entering a true wilderness zone, a wilderness of moral ambiguity made all the more confusing because there appeared to be such a clear map of it that none of the students recognized they were about to become lost. "However, I also believed in the abolition of slavery." Energized by their confusion, he added, "In fact, my fellow countrymen and I gained fuel for our revolutionary views because we saw that the English government with its taxes was, as George Washington said, and I quote, 'endeavoring by every piece of art and despotism to fix the shackles of slavery upon us.'"

"But that still doesn't make it right to own slaves yourself," another student rang out.

"Guilty as charged, my young man. Nonetheless, I am also the most famous champion of individual rights and religious freedom of my time. I represent a paradox, a contradictory union of opposites, made understandable only by its context.

I abhorred slavery, yet took no immediate steps to stop it." The students rumbled their dissent, and Peter raised his voice to be heard. "The reason is quite simple. By maintaining slavery and shrouding my real feelings about it, I guaranteed my election as president, where I could ensure that this nation would be forever bound to the notion of individual rights. About sixty years later, those ideas, personified by Abraham Lincoln, whom I inspired, were strong enough in this country to go to war over and put an end to the horrors of slavery."

A sea of hands waved urgently. One boy slammed his history book and shouted, "That's just plain racist, Mr. Winston."

"Well, young man, if by that you mean that I thought that the Negro was unequal or lesser than a white, then you would be mistaken. However—and this is the basis for another interesting paper—if you mean that I protected the institution of slavery for the political and economic advantage of the Southern states, you would be correct."

Their outrage and repugnance washed over him. Peter watched their contorted faces and silently considered how little teaching had to do with facts. It was about training the mind to be able to handle the contradictions and paradoxes that life presented. It was his job to challenge those who wanted to see things one way. But it could be a painful, unpopular process. He taught moral imagination. It was the basis for empathy and respect. It was the single most convincing sign of higher consciousness that he knew. He was convinced that imagination and compassion were what made democracy work. It meant you could put yourself in another person's place whether you agreed with him or not. *Otherwise,* he thought to himself, *we would simply vote for our side and outlaw or kill the other side.*

He pointed at a Native American face in a poster on the classroom wall. "It's easy to walk a mile in the moccasins of Chief Seattle because he seems so pure. But you balk at stepping into Jefferson's shoes because his dilemmas are more like ours today."

"How could you go along with something you didn't believe in?" a girl's probing question rose above the hubbub. A rumble of assent followed her question, and she added sarcastically, "You're a hypocrite!"

"A hypocrite?" he repeated. "If you were living in my time, you might not be so judgmental."

"I don't think there's any excuse for preaching one thing and doing another," she said, getting stronger. "It's what makes us kids so sick of the adult world. It's why nobody respects politicians or anybody in power."

"Ah," he said, sniffing the air, trying to lighten the mood, "I am getting a scent of moral superiority."

"Well, your attitude stinks, Mr. Winston," said a boy in the back, just loud enough for a few other kids to hear and laugh at.

"Enough!" Peter bristled. His nerves were stretched too thin to be instigating this sort of confrontation. All the pent-up frustration he had recently endured surged through him. Struggling for self-control, he took off Thomas Jefferson's granny glasses and cleaned them meticulously. He adopted a deceptively casual tone. "A historian recently wrote about Thomas Jefferson, 'Privilege is addictive.' It could also apply to you students." He put his glasses back on. "Through the magic of time travel, I have some information about your society's current problems, and I'd like to ask you a question." The students barely listened as they roiled with indignation.

"Americans make up only four percent of the world's population, yet you use twenty-five percent of the world's energy. You live well, while most in the world are enslaved by poverty. How do you reconcile that?"

"Mr. Jefferson, that's how it is these days," said a voice from the back. "Everybody wants to be rich. That's why so many people are trying to get into the United States."

"That may be," Peter said, "but don't you have a responsibility to address that imbalance? If you don't take individual responsibility to address this problem in some way, you are hypocritically benefiting from it." The faces staring at him showed that he was losing them. It was getting too abstract.

"How many of you recycle?" All but three raised their hands.

"Good. How many of you have done anything around your home to conserve energy?"

Four hands went up, tentatively.

"Well, there's a problem."

The students looked nervously around. Finally, one said, "We're just kids."

"A weak excuse, Bill; in fact, it's pathetic. But let's make it more immediate. How many of you drive a car?"

Half the hands went up.

"And how many of the rest of you plan to buy one when you can?"

All the hands went up.

"How many of you have protested the lack of efficient mass transit in Los Angeles?"

A blank silence greeted the question.

"Okay, how many of you have spoken out about global warming and the extent it is caused by the U.S.?"

Three hands.

"Why not? Overwhelming scientific evidence indicates that the United States is the main source of a pattern of global warming that is heating up the earth and may eventually cause the deaths of billions of people, including some of you." He paused. "So, isn't driving a car and doing nothing about this nation's energy use hypocritical and immoral on several levels?"

A strained silence followed. Finally, one boy said, "You can't blame us. That's not fair."

"Why not, Alex?" he asked

"Because we didn't have anything to do with it."

"And, I, Thomas Jefferson, didn't invent slavery." Peter said bluntly.

"But there's nothing I can do to stop it." The boy was frustrated, his face reddening. "Giving up my car isn't going to help some kid in Africa."

"Maybe, maybe not," Peter nodded, "but now, the situation has changed significantly. Instead of pleading ignorance, you are now beginning to bear witness to a terrifying dilemma. If you don't stand up for what you believe in, you are, as the saying goes, part of the problem. What makes me, Thomas Jefferson, noteworthy and famous, is that I didn't let the sense of powerlessness in the face of the British or slavery stop me. You have no idea what courage and determination it took to stand up to power. I am famous for good reason, but I am not without faults." Peter's voice rose. "You need to understand me, or you will be seen by the rest of the world as hypocrites with no claim to greatness." The bell rang. Peter put up his hand to stop their exit. "For tomorrow, read the Bill of Rights. Again, I hope. Put as much energy into thinking about them as you would some stupid video game or TV show. If you do, you might get off your butts and do something about today's problems. And," he added, "you will be ready for a quiz."

Several students glared at him as the classroom cleared of agitated, debating young people. Peter pulled off his wig and paced. He hadn't done that time travel bit before, had never turned their youthful arrogance back on them, but they deserved it. Once more, a cloud of anger descended over him. He banged his desk with his clenched fist. Pain broke through his outburst, and as he rubbed his hand he submitted to what he'd been trying to avoid.

Jefferson was a hypocrite. The kids were right. They had good instincts, but they didn't appreciate how hard it was to be true to your ideals. Jefferson was against slavery, yet he went along with that evil by telling himself that he was serving a greater good. But was he just kidding himself? Did his compromises allow slavery to be extended another three or four generations?

Peter ran his sore hand through his damp hair. He went to a window and opened it to get away from the rank smell of tired running shoes and adolescent ferment in the classroom. As his lungs filled with fresh air, it became clear that this had everything to do with Frank Greening. That priest was compromised: Peter had known it as soon as he had seen him bounding out of Adrian's house the day before like a giddy teenager. The way Greening straightened out as soon as they hit the sidewalk made it clear that this was a dangerous secret, but how dangerous? Of course a priest would want to keep his sex life discreet, but what if someone threatened to expose him or was blackmailing him? Was Frank so vulnerable that he could be forced to help kill Adrian? It was a stretch, but it was possible. Peter wanted to not care, to say, "Fuck it!" to the problems that didn't concern him directly, but if he did, he was a hypocrite, too. He closed the window.

He knew the truth about what had happened to Adrian Montero, but what difference did that make if he wasn't willing to stand up for it? And, so far, he had failed at being true to his word to Martin. Maybe everyone is a hypocrite. Maybe we all understand this at some level, and that's why religious heroes like Gandhi, Jesus and Buddha still have such a magnetic pull on human hearts and minds: They lived their values.

Once, long ago, Peter had been idealistic. He had marched against a war that he considered illegal and unnecessary. And that protest had eventually been effective. He had become a Marxist. He promoted the coming socialist revolution because he believed so fervently in the eventual communistic stage of society where fairness and equality would prevail. But the movement had been co-opted, and all that was left was the sexual revolution that was then exploited to market things. By the time Reagan became president in 1980, Peter had been turned off from trying to directly change society. He decided that if he couldn't destroy capitalism, he'd use it. He was like Jerry Rubin, one of the founders of the Yippies, who became a stockbroker. Peter figured that the only answer was to become rich enough that social problems didn't drag him down. And he had. He had made millions in less than ten years. Soon after, he quit the money game and turned back to history. But, in returning to what he loved, he had been seduced into trying to improve the state of the world.

He looked down at his wingtip Belgrado loafers. The cherry calfskin was splattered with mud from tramping around Montero's garden the day before. He still liked fine things: 460 bucks, and he was ruining them. Disgusted with himself and everybody else, he slipped his wig on as the next class clamored in.

14

LATER: MONDAY, FEBRUARY 14, 2005

MARTA CAME HOME AFTER work on Monday in a black mood: Gossip could do that to her. She had faithfully served the city of Santa Monica for over twenty years, yet she sensed that people were talking behind her back. She didn't know how, but she was sure they'd heard she'd been left out of the will. She shouldn't have told anyone that she had considered quitting once the estate was settled. It enraged her to think of the insinuations and outright lies being told about Adrian, about Frank, about her. She knew how cruel people could be. Many of the other women who worked with her called themselves Christian, but she had often observed how two-faced and mean-spirited they could be.

She threw the deadbolt of her front door. Quitting might not be an option, but she no longer felt obliged to prove her worth. She had told them not to expect her tomorrow; she was taking some personal time. Except those rare days when she had stayed home to care for Adrian when he was sick, she'd never missed a day.

She removed her clothes, carefully hanging up her blouse and folding her slip and returning it to its place in her bureau. Her neatness was calming. She'd learned not to expect much from life, had made a virtue out of it. She'd made a virtue out of virtue. She had paid off that woman at the Senior Center so no one would speak badly of the family. She resented it, but it was a manner of honor, even if Adrian hadn't cared enough to pay his own debts.

She was modest and religious, unlike so many other women today. At work, they probably thought she was still a virgin. She wished she was, but she had ruined that, too. She slipped off her panties and chastised herself for wanting to be thought of as better than others. She had given herself to only two men, and both times they had ended up deserting her. *Pendéjos*, she thought, and immediately her head was ringing with her mother's admonishment. She was always right there when Marta thought in Spanish. That was the language they had used when they were together, without the men. Adrian spoke Spanish only when he swore, which was fairly often. Paco left it behind when he became Frank, when he left the family. Now he pretended he didn't understand some words, but he knew. To forget one's childhood language was to nullify and deny who you were, like swallowing one's own tongue.

Her cell phone rang, but she ignored it, not wanting to contend with the malevolence at the other end. It never spoke, and, even if she didn't answer, it would leave a message of heavy breathing or strange noises. She had called the telephone company to check out the numbers that appeared, but they were always from a pay phone. She wanted to believe it was some stupid teenagers, except that it was no coincidence that these calls without a caller had begun not long after Adrian died. She imagined it was her father reminding her of her faults, except that his spirit didn't need a telephone to communicate with her.

Naked, Marta walked into her small bathroom and flicked on

the light. She looked into the mirror and forced herself to smile, to expose her gleaming white teeth: a small vanity. She had the dentist bleach them; otherwise, she knew she would never smile at all, and people would know how unhappy she was.

Her smile disappeared when she looked at her short-cropped hair. She had continued cutting it after that devastating evening with Frank, and at least another two inches were gone. Until she left her father, she had kept it down to her waist. It was her large vanity and a link to her mother and her long, black mane. Except for leaving her garden, she thought that cutting and dyeing her hair was the most dramatic thing she had ever done.

She tugged at the short tufts, barely an inch long. It hadn't been pure black for years, and now some of the gray was tipped with a purplish haze. Her head appeared to be covered with errant stalks of moldy hay. More than ever, she looked like an espantapájaros, a scarecrow, just liked Adrian had chided her when she was an adolescent. She had inherited his body, not her mother's short, rounded Indian stature. What was even worse was that she had never outgrown her tall, skinny, gawky phase. When she withdrew further into herself, Adrian had added espantadizo espantapájaros: a timid scarecrow. How he had laughed at his cleverness while her mother scowled, but, like Marta, she remained silent.

She continued scrutinizing herself. The rings under her eyes were, if anything, more prominent: tan became yellow, which yielded to a moldy chocolate color. She hated her skin. Her eyes followed to her turkey neck, una papada guacolote that seemed to unfold down her chest to small sagging breasts. Creases of skin dropped to her soft, little stomach that sagged between her hips until it all disappeared into the nether region below. Her gaze stopped at the thick tangle of pubic hair. She never understood why she had been given so much hair there. It was excessive and had always bothered her. She opened up the cabinet and pulled out scissors. At least it could be neat and hew to a triangular shape. She began to trim around the edges on the top and down the sides. She spread her legs wide to clip at the bottom. It had to be done right, even if no one else would ever see. But each time she stopped, she'd see more that was out of balance: too long here, too short there.

She cropped the entire patch down to half an inch. She stared at the floor, the pink and blue tiles barely visible beneath the pile. She stared at her vagina, her taco, her father called it when she was little. For the first time in over thirty years, she saw it clearly since it had disappeared beneath the black tangle. Whatever pleasure it was purported to offer had passed her by. It was as if she had been given a clitoridectomy like those poor little girls in Africa.

She put the scissors away and dabbed herself with perfume. But she began to feel cheap and stepped into the shower to scrub herself clean. Just because she loved scents didn't make her a puta, she had argued to her mother. Other women obviously loved perfumes, but it seemed like she was the only one who got into trouble. Several years before, a so-called friend from work had insisted that yoga would change her life. She had finally gone to a class, only to have the instructor pointedly mention, "No perfumes or scented creams, please" and glare at her. She had been so embarrassed that she had never tried it again. That left walking as her sole exercise, if you didn't count shopping and cooking and cleaning and sewing and ironing for Adrian until recently.

Marta turned off the shower and dried herself. Using the towel to sweep the pubic hair into one big pile, she then put it in the wastebasket carefully, getting every last strand. She shook out the towel in the shower and washed the remnants down the drain. She put on her robe and wandered around her apartment. After a while, she reached for her phone and punched in a number.

"Paco," she said when he answered, "did you try to call me a while ago?"

"No, did…?"

She interrupted, "Mother told me there's something not right about those people who took Dad's house."

"What do you mean, 'told you'?" he asked.

"Well, it's like talking."

"Do you mean talking to you, like you're hearing voices, Marta?"

Marta frowned. She resented having to translate one cultural tradition into another, especially to someone who should understand. "It's like praying," she finally explained.

"Oh," the edge came off of Frank's voice, "like praying."

"Yes. That's what it's like," she answered. "I have Mother's picture next to the statue of the Virgin that I took from the house."

"You carried that statue to your apartment by yourself? It must weigh a ton."

"I'm not weak."

"And you've made a sort of shrine?" Frank asked haltingly.

"I had to bring her to my apartment. It wasn't right, leaving her there. She was lonely, and I couldn't hear her."

"What do you mean?"

"I talk to Mom, and sometimes the Virgin Mary answers." She laughed nervously. "Mother told me to tell you this business with the house isn't right. There's something wrong about it." She paused, listening, though he was silent. "I think the Virgin agrees."

"Just what is wrong with it, Marta? Did they tell you that?"

Marta smiled, happy to be taken seriously. "No, not yet, anyway."

"Marta, I have to go. I have an important meeting."

She frowned. "Of course you do, Paco. I'll pray for you."

She knelt at her shrine. A picture of her mother was next to the statue of the Virgin, along with some flowers she'd picked at the house the day before. She lit several votive candles. She prayed silently for a long time, invoking spirits and saints, gods and God, a powerful mlange of her two traditions.

When she was ready, she took a bottle that was on the altar and carefully poured some of its contents into a ceramic cup. She hadn't had meat, alcohol or spicy food for three days and, of course, no sex. That was easy. She had cooked the husk of the ayahuasca vine for several hours the night before like her mother had taught her, mixing it with the leaves of the chacruna bush. The Indians of South America had imbibed ayahuasca for millennia, and drinking it ceremonially was a common element of the Andean culture. This time, Marta hoped to receive information that might reveal who killed her father and what she should do about it. Marta drank much of the brown, bitter liquid from a ceramic cup, settled into the pillows she had arranged in front of her altar and remembered her mother. As always, there lingered in her mind the old question her mother had struggled with: How do I honor my people and maintain my rightful place in the natural order as I make my way through this modern world?

Cerfina's journey had begun as a teenager, when she realized that she had to leave her pueblo. Among her people, women could become shamans, but it was rare and discouraged, because learning the medicines was an arduous and dangerous process that could cause miscarriages. Becoming a shaman was possible only for females with imposing gifts and the most powerful magic. Cerfina was very bright and she had the gift of healing and was fearless in her soul traveling, but her visions had been confusing to the villagers. She told them of seeing a giant silver bird that exploded into the blinding sun. It was horrific and beautiful, and she was both frightened and intrigued. But the images were foreign. The bird had no ring around its neck. It wasn't the condor, one of the three central icons of the Andean culture along with the anaconda and the jaguar. And her sun didn't appear to be the source of life, but something that devoured life. It was clear that she was gifted as her grandfather had been, but her visions didn't tell a story that anyone understood. The people of her pueblo were unsure of her, and without their full support, a girl would not be allowed to mature into a full-fledged shaman.

It was in the mercado in Cuzco, where 17-year-old Cerfina sold coca leaves, that she was wooed by a handsome American, Nate Greening, only 5 years her senior. He kept showing up at her stall every few weeks. When she learned he was a commercial pilot, she understood what the silver bird was, and she accepted that her fate was to fly off and be devoured in a crash. She was partially right. She fell in love and flew away, but it was her new husband who later died in a ball of flame. So instead of a Peruvian shaman, her mother had become a pioneer in America, an Andean wise woman who brought her earth-based wisdom into a culture intent on conquering nature. Cerfina found herself in a society that maligned and outlawed the vision plants of the earth. She learned quickly to keep her knowledge hidden to all but a very few of the Americans she came to know. So while over the last forty years psychedelic mushrooms, mescaline and marijuana had all been condemned, ayahuasca was still little known.

It was surprising to Marta that Adrian had remained ignorant of the true nature of what was in the garden. But people only see what they want to see, and her father was arrogant enough to be blind to many things. Despite his Mexican parentage, he held an unrepentant belief that it was a good thing that for over 200 years Americans had been damming rivers, cutting down virgin forests and eradicating native peoples and other species without regret. He identified with that. As far as he was concerned, he was Spanish, a conquistador.

Cerfina had taught Marta everything she knew once she realized how eager her daughter was to learn. It was satisfying to her mother, because Frank hadn't shown any interest in the plants. Nonetheless, Cerfina no longer considered herself a true curandera after she came to America because she had no village to share her information with. She could travel to the non-human world, the real and eternal world, and bring back news and information. But to be developed, her knowledge had to be shared. Without the pueblo, the gifts of a shaman were never fully unwrapped. When she left Peru, she had hoped that, if she survived, she would find a village where she could share her gifts. But, over the years, all she found in America were a variety of friends who appreciated her for the potions and lotions she provided for their aches and pains. They were never more than a group of individuals who had her in common. They couldn't support her, much less truly understand her.

If anything, Marta was more isolated than her mother had been. She didn't have the same confidence in her knowledge that her mother had had. From the very first time her mother had given her ayahuasca when she was fourteen and had begun her flow, the visions and messages had seemed to complicate her life, no matter how true they were. Experiences of overwhelming beauty made it difficult to return to her classes at St. Monica's and tell her friends what she'd done that weekend. "I talked with god," wasn't an acceptable answer when god was a huge snake or a giant bird. And, as often happened, when these gods were fierce and demanding there was only her mother to remind her to embrace the god, not the fear.

Her mother's death had forced Marta to become stronger and accept her own relationship with the plants. She had learned that fear of how to deal with the world was to be expected. Now, even without the solace of her garden and home, she still had to believe that she was in her rightful place. Sitting in her apartment at the edge of a city that sprawled forty miles in almost every direction, she still had the huge wilderness of the ocean, the original source of life, close at hand. Pachamama was here amidst freeways and high rises. Marta had only to be open to the messages sent by "the tendril of the soul" as ayahuasca was known. She had to remain patient and humble. She took a few more sips and leaned back again.

Experience told her that a sort of death awaited her as the price of communion with the spirit plant, a death of the identity each human usually holds onto so protectively. Ayahuasca was the portal into the wisdom of the natural world, a world of oneness, a continuum of being where nothing was in opposition, but simply another aspect of the universe.

A stream of energy flowed behind her eyes and Marta felt herself approaching the threshold. Part of her resisted and she leaned to her side and retched into a bowl she had placed there. It wasn't sickness she expelled but attachment to this world. As difficult as she found it to live and thrive in this environment she was nonetheless a part of it. Her mother had been wonderful in helping her to understand this. There was no judgment. We were all seduced by the realm we were born to because, following our birth, we gradually came to experience ourselves as separate from our human mother. This was natural and necessary even as it introduced the illusion of duality. Ayahuasca brought us back to oneness.

Marta retched again then slowly sat up and began to rhythmically shake a gourd. Brilliantly colored hallucinations streamed into her mind's eye and for what seemed like forever she rode the tail of a plumed bird that transformed into a three-headed serpent. Time became circular and she could predict what was going to happen because it felt like it was happening again. Yet, it was always different.

The colors and images went on playing a game of cosmic tag across the heavens of her mind until she was no longer watching it, but had become it. She was a parrot, a green, Amazon parrot.

She understood what ayahuasca was saying. Green Amazon parrots had escaped the cages of their careless owners and become naturalized citizens of Los Angeles. Like slaves captured in the jungles of Brazil and Peru and brought here for the pleasure of the locals, they had escaped and begun to take over the skies of Venice and Santa Monica, driving away the other birds that lacked their formidable beaks and claws. Marta found herself in a shrieking, green cloud of parrots, free to scream louder than car horns and sirens, fitting easily into the preening cacophony of the international city. The flock descended out of nowhere over the palisades and landed in a small grove of guava and loquat trees, themselves immigrants from Peru and other southern lands. Other tropical birds, iridescent scarlet macaws and elegant cockatoos, ripped the soft fruit from the branches and the parrots joined in the feeding frenzy.

As Marta merged into the foliage, ayahuasca's rhythm changed and the sensation of flying became the cadence of running and leaping. She was suddenly looking out of the eyes of a large jaguar with a speckled orange and black coat. She bounded down a rocky cliff through green trees and arced through the air toward a blazing hoop. As she sailed toward the burning circle she saw what was incinerating: a family portrait of Adrian, Cerfina, Frank and little Marta, all with melting smiles. Terrified, but helpless to stop, she plummeted through the flames toward a sandy beach where her front claws eviscerated a body that disintegrated beneath her. In its place was a blackened X, burned into the sand. It looked like a crucifixion, but as she came closer it was a bird on its back, wings out and its sharp beaked head lolling to the side, a sacrifice.

Marta regained a sense of time. From past experience she assumed a few hours had passed. She thought she may have been singing, even yelling, but she couldn't be sure. She hoped not, or, at least, that her neighbors weren't home. She lay exhausted from the exertion. Birds and other animals cooed and spoke gently to her. Any fear or concern she felt abated, even as the jaguar she'd been inside of came and lay next to her purring. Cradled in their love she was released into a sweet, deep sleep, at peace and at one with all.

15

Tuesday, February 15, 2005

P ETER SQUINTED THROUGH DENSE fog to the Camera Obscura building forty feet away. It was shrouded in a tangled cobweb of opaque strands, as if a giant spider had entrapped it. A car slid past him through the clouds. From the farthest end of the Santa Monica Pier, a foghorn bleated its plaintive warnings. Even bundled up in his car, he could feel the damp chill that had chased the pedestrians off of Ocean Avenue. There was little that was reminiscent of that sunny afternoon seventeen days before.

It wasn't reasonable to be here, he knew that, but he was determined to figure out this mystery, and this was one of the few places where he could think. He wanted more information: What were other business projects of TMF? How did they overlap the holdings of the Archdiocese? Already, these questions had led him to try to uncover the Archdiocese's assets on the Internet. But everyone from *Time Magazine* to the *LA Times* had found that it was impossible to know the true extent of its real estate, businesses and investments. He had talked to some of the reporters, and they all said the same thing: The financial holdings of the Archdiocese were a house of mirrors. He couldn't even hire someone to get to the bottom of it. He wished he could turn the search into some kind of cause or challenge to bloggers on the Internet and get hundreds or thousands of people working on it. Given the abuse scandal it shouldn't be that hard to get going. But he had no sense of how to spark such a movement.

By keeping its wealth a secret, the Archdiocese was abrogating its responsibility to model the moral and ethical path for other institutions and individuals of wealth. It was outrageous to Peter that when it came to having money, the Catholic Church dropped its role as a spiritual and moral leader. It was a profound, corrosive mistake. He knew too well the amorality of money.

Nonetheless, until he found Max, he was dependent on research to get new leads. He had already decided to take a half-day off from school to check out Los Angeles County records. He pushed the button that illuminated his digital watch: 7:37 p.m., 2/15/05. Yesterday was Valentine's Day and he'd forgotten. *I was too fucking busy being Thomas Jefferson!*, a voice in his head argued. It had never been a big deal between them, but still, Judith was hurt, then she got mad. She claimed his absentmindedness came from being obsessed with the murder of Adrian Montero. *Stupid argument!* He didn't try to smooth it all out, because it made it easier to avoid talking with her about his dad. *I knew how that conversation would go.* Years ago, she had been part of a discussion between him and Martin about euthanasia. She disagreed with both of them. At the time, it had seemed like an abstract problem, a philosophical debate that made little difference in their lives. But, like Alzheimer's itself, it had crept up on them.

Just two days earlier, without telling her what had happened in the hospital, he had tried again to explain his agreement with his father. Judith had managed to be both supportive and dismissive. "If you don't want to care for your father, I will," she had said. *Like I was complaining about it being too much work.* She didn't think people had a right to die whenever they wanted. She thought we each had an obligation to live fully and care for those who were dying as best we could. She wasn't without experience. She'd spent years as an oncology nurse. Ironically, that time had convinced her that cancer was one of the best ways to go, because it gave everyone a chance to come to terms with dying. "People get to complete their relationships, and many, many people get to leave this world surrounded by love. It's never easy, but dying consciously is a gift." *But she couldn't explain how Alzheimer's was a gift.*

Again, he was on his own. There was no one he trusted to understand what he had attempted, and what he was obliged to try again. To make things worse, in spite of his pleading to handle it without him, Judith continued to report on Martin. Getting him settled was second nature for her.

That evening, to avoid another blowup, he had told her he had to get some air and would find dinner on his own. She hadn't complained. She was probably glad to have him out of the house. He accepted that he'd been difficult to live with. But he missed his connection with her, and he was worried about them. He hadn't heard her laugh for a long time. Her laugh was the first part of her he had fallen in love with, and now it seemed to be gone. *Along with my fucking patience.*

He pulled a snapshot of them out of his wallet. She was stunning in a revealing black cocktail dress, laughing at something he'd just said. Barefoot, she was about five foot nine, like him. With her three-inch heels, he was in over his head. Her green eyes, like the eyes of a cheetah, were hypnotic. Her only flaw, a minor one, was that her eyes were a little close together. She knew it and sometimes ran her fingers through her short, silky hair to fluff it out. That gesture broadened her face and softened her look. But rarely did she lose the self-confidence in her eyes. She could live with her flaws. *The question is, can she live with mine?*

By hiding his attempt and commitment to euthanize Martin and his efforts to solve this murder, he was building a secret life, like an affair, only he wasn't getting off. He knew Judith would be more than surprised to hear that he was on a stakeout. *Just because I'm . . .* The voice in his head started to argue with her, but there was so much he hadn't told her that he shut it down.

He hoped that Mad Max was going as nuts as he was. Of course, he might be dead or a long way from LA, but Peter had to do something. *And sitting out here freezing my ass off is a whole lot better than nothing.* The police had come up with no new witnesses and no leads after the article ran in the paper. He had pestered Sergeant Jones every day of the week after the murder, but last week he only called him twice. Peter didn't want to let Jones forget, but he also didn't want to piss him off any further.

He finished a glazed donut. He picked his teeth and burped. Remnants of Chinese takeout in a Styrofoam container congealed in the chilly air on the seat next to him. The sweet and sour sauce looked like rubber cement. He began whistling "Bridge on the River Kwai." He jiggled the carton, but the squeaking of the Styrofoam interrupted his whistling. He stopped everything and stared into the murky night, until Judith's warning that Martin's care was going to be expensive, as much as $6,000 or $7,000 a month, entered his mind. She wanted Peter to "figure out" Martin's finances. *Fuck!* He could feel himself being drawn into the compromise he'd sworn he would avoid. The money was the least of it.

Peter was financially comfortable, but he was no longer rich. That embarrassed him, considering that from 1979 to 1989 he had made millions. As an investment banker, he'd had a hell of a wild ride playing with the big boys in the adrenaline-charged world of junk bonds and unfriendly takeovers. He'd spent, snorted and made more than most guys earn in a lifetime. But he'd gotten caught holding a wad of bonds that had proven to really be junk after Michael Milken went down.

Peter twisted in the car seat uncomfortably. He could still feel that hollow sense of disbelief that had overtaken him when he'd discovered his demise. It reminded him, once again, why he wasn't going to return to the wheeling and dealing world of leveraged buyouts. No one knew better than he did that making deals was more addictive than cocaine, than sex, than anything. It was a whole way of thinking and being that he had quit. Since then, he'd avoided the dot-com madness that had followed junk bonds, and he was convinced he could resist the next sure thing.

He shrugged and stretched his neck. He didn't have to prove anything anymore, though some part of him still missed the excitement. A hostile takeover was simple and, unless you had a romantic view of human nature, natural, like wolves culling the weak and old caribou from the herd. In order to finance the buyout of a vulnerable company, something mismanaged or that had fallen out of favor, you sold bonds. Then, to pay back the new debt, that company was forced to sell off its assets to create a lean, competitive business in its place. And it worked. The junk bond market of the '80s was a revolution that put the '60s to shame. *We helped remake America. We pushed out the old corporate elite and made room for entrepreneurs with balls: anyone with courage and vision. It was a lot more class-conscious than that new left/hippie bullshit. Michael Milken took over where Marx failed, and the gospel according to Milken was clear: We made money for a lot of smart people of any race or background, plus we made American industry competitive. Of course, some people got hurt, but it was only because they weren't paying attention. It was a homegrown revolution, fucking capitalistic populism.*

The intermittent yelp of a siren yanked Peter's mind from its whirling sales pitch. Flashing lights penetrated the fog as an ambulance passed by. Vaporous walls of shimmering emerald greens and cardinal reds lit up Peter's little world like a discotheque or a cathedral. It disappeared quickly, along with the myth he was spinning. It was bullshit, and he recognized it too well. He had worked with a cabal of insiders that had sold going into debt like there was no tomorrow. But the whole damn thing had ultimately amounted to no more than a con game. *A fucking pyramid scheme!* Junk bonds proved to be junk more than Milken or any of the rest of them had been willing to admit. The game had gone on for years by creating new and different bonds to cover the many companies that were defaulting, but eventually, and inevitably, the pyramid had crumbled. Only those at the very top had survived with their billions intact. Milken had paid out hundreds of millions in fines, but it was a pittance of what he'd been able to squeeze from his deals. For him and a few others, like Greek gods hanging out on Mount Olympus, tomorrow had yet to come.

Peter admitted that he had become sloppy. His edge had been dulled from living too big for too long. When it came time to bail, he wasn't paying attention. He was sure his old left-wing cohorts from college had savored his comeuppance. And they were right; he had sold his soul to the devil. *But it wasn't about greed!* He'd gone into banking when he'd concluded that socialism was hopeless, staid and corrupt. Strangely enough, he did it because he agreed with the *Communist Manifesto*, in which Marx and Engels foresaw that capitalism was destined to steamroll national, religious and cultural boundaries. He'd been looking for a way to manage the invincible market economy in order to create a humanistic version of capitalism.

It wasn't even about the fucking money. He got out because he finally accepted that he couldn't control things that he felt responsible for. The core of the business world is incorporation, and incorporation creates a monster, a Frankenstein with no personal responsibility. *That's why I got out!*

Peter nodded in agreement with himself. Ultimately, he couldn't accept that paradigm: It erased the soul of business. That was why he was so upset by the financial secrecy of the Church leaders. They made a big deal out of helping the poor, but they avoided demonstrating how to be rich. If the Church couldn't model a responsible, transparent way to manage wealth, then greed and exploitation would always rule from the shadows.

The faces of the proud but desperate couple who had confronted him one afternoon were still emblazoned in his mind. They had taken the bus a thousand miles to ask if he personally understood the impact that corporate "restructuring" had on people. They described the demise of their town in Ohio once the company had been decimated. They wanted to know if he cared that he had destroyed people's lives. The truth was, he had never put a face on it.

Peter rubbed his numb thighs and turned on the engine to get some heat. He knew that he had done nothing wrong legally, but that didn't mean he wasn't responsible, and being responsible was the basis of his personal philosophy. So, in 1990, he quit the investment world and New York, took his remaining money and came back to Los Angeles and graduate school at UCLA. He was ready to pursue his first dream, teaching history.

Returning to school served him in many ways. First, he loved studying and debating the form and meaning of human experience as shown through history. He was happier than he'd ever been as he got his doctorate and began teaching. He could have worked at a college, but he chose to teach in a high school filled with every social problem imaginable. He fed off the challenge. Certain friends and neighbors saw his career as almost heroic, but Peter knew it had helped him regain a sense of meaning and control. He also knew that that sense was, once again, slipping away. *But this time quitting my job won't change a damn thing.*

Three homeless people, thickly wrapped in layers, appeared from behind the Camera Obscura building and drifted across the street in the thick fog. Peter turned on his windshield wipers to see them more clearly. They looked like mummies and moved like ghosts, but none of them moved like Big Bird, now known as Mad Max. Mummies and ghosts: Peter smiled in spite of himself at such anthropomorphic fantasies of what life after death looks like. When he had picked up Sam from nursery school, Sandy had told him that a rash of new siblings had changed the kids' chatter from death to birth. To the rhythm of the windshield wipers, Peter sang a Beatles song very slowly, like a dirge: "Obla dee, obla da, life goes on, yeah, la la la la life goes on." *Yes, it does, but it has to mean something.*

The top of the Camera Obscura building momentarily appeared through the fog. The impact of that technology was at least as revolutionary as the Internet today. Vermeer and Michelangelo, among others, changed the way humans saw themselves. But once we could replicate nature, we humans took a huge and dangerous step and assumed control over it. We played at being God, and now we were paying for our brilliance and arrogance. Global warming was reinforcing how potentially insignificant the 200,000-year evolution of Homo sapiens was in the four-and-a-half-billion-year-old earth. *Shut up with your fucking historical analysis and do something!*, a voice bellowed in his head.

He turned off the engine and groped his way across the dark street to a phone booth he knew was there. He dropped in fifty cents and dialed. Marta's voice delivered a terse message that he'd memorized. It didn't matter; his response was the same whether she answered or not. He lowered the phone to his thigh and jangled the change and keys in his pocket. Marta was some kind of crazy, or at least was keeping secrets. If she got scared that someone knew what she'd done, she might reveal it somehow. After a few seconds, he hung up and stared out of the phone booth, shivering. He felt a chill that wasn't from the cold. He was keeping secrets. And he was feeling crazier and crazier.

Trees, cars, the Camera Obscura and everything else had

disappeared from view. The foghorn moaned louder and louder. He yanked open the squeaky aluminum door of the phone booth and was enveloped by a solid wall of fog. Fighting a rising panic, he charged blindly across the street. "Fuck!" he shouted as he stumbled over the curb and crashed onto the wet grass. Ignoring a throbbing toe, he pulled himself up and inched his way along the curb until his car took shape in the gray a few feet ahead. Panting with relief, Peter climbed into it, started the engine and began to quickly pull out. Just as quickly, he braked hard. *You're gonna fucking kill yourself!* He pulled back to the curb, put it into park and tried to settle down. After a few moments, Martin jumped into his mind. Peter told himself that if there were one positive thing to point to in the mess that his life had become, it was that he wouldn't have to explain this to his father. Martin had become an actor in an absurdist theater piece, his brain a blackboard continuously being erased. Even so, Peter felt like shit. His mind screamed: *It's not my fault! I didn't give him Alzheimer's.*

A full-blown argument erupted in his head. *But you are allowing him to suffer, even though you agreed to never let this happen.*

How do I know that he's even suffering? He doesn't know anything. The fog beaded thickly on the windows, but he didn't notice.

You know he never would have accepted this life, the voice retorted. *He was a proud man. He deserved better.*

But it's not a fair demand. There's nothing I can do. If I give him cyanide, I'll go to jail.

If you loved him, you would find a way. The voice was merciless. *There's the Hemlock Society, and people have been helping AIDS patients die for years now. You promised. You took responsibility. You promised, you promised.*

The sound of his own horn beeping over and over as he unconsciously pushed against the steering wheel brought Peter back to his senses. Ashamed and embarrassed, he peered out at the street, but he was trapped in a gray, dimensionless world.

He wanted Martin's Alzheimer's and Adrian's murder to be instructive, like the history that he taught. But he couldn't get any clarity. Tears collected but didn't spill over. He wiped his eyes and, slowly this time, began to drive through near-zero visibility. The fog thinned as he made his way inland. By the time he'd covered the mile to his home, it had lifted to a six-foot ceiling. He didn't go inside. Instead, he walked around trying to collect himself. Across from his house, he leaned against a sixty-foot pine tree. He peered around the thick rough trunk and looked into his own living room through the arched window with its leaded glass.

Samantha ran into the room. She dove onto the couch, then stood on it and began to bounce up and down like they'd told her not to. You'll squash the down feathers, he had said.

He heard a car start up a block away. He saw himself peeping in on his child, an outsider to his own life. He lost his balance and scraped his cheek on the bark. With shallow, rapid breaths, he scurried inside.

Peter slept very little that night and jolted awake at dawn. His toe hurt, and his finger probed the tender new scab on his cheek. His stomach roiled with anxiety. Judith was tucked into a corner of their king-sized bed, still asleep. They had barely spoken after he had gotten home. He couldn't bear to hear about his father, and he was sure she'd go ballistic if he mentioned his stakeout.

He shuddered and yawned, then got up and walked into his office. It occurred to him that the Camera Obscura represented the same dilemma for him now as it had historically. It had allowed him to see "reality," but that didn't mean he was in control. When other people were screwing up, he would tell them that the problem was that they weren't living according to any principle. They were just making up rules as they went along. He scrutinized the books and piles of magazines and pamphlets scattered about. An agenda for the Environmental Club jumped out at him from the mess. Word of Thomas

Jefferson's comparison between owning slaves and driving a car had circulated through the student body. As faculty advisor, he'd gone to a lunch meeting of the Environmental Club to prepare for the campus Earth Day observation in the spring. Several students had challenged him about what he was personally doing to reduce energy consumption, and he had been reduced to mumbling about recycling which, in Santa Monica especially, was as easy as getting a suntan. He was vulnerable to charges of hypocrisy.

Without thinking about it further, he decided to ride his bike to school. He had bought mountain bikes for Judith and himself about the same time Sam was conceived. Now they hung from hooks in their garage like desiccated carcasses of prehistoric animals. He figured he could even pick up Sam from her school with it. She'd love it.

In the shower, he looked with disgust at his soft stomach, then beat out a little rhythm on it. He was seriously out of shape, and the prospect of doing something physical while simultaneously proving his integrity was very attractive. Plus, he had to do something about feeling so down. His dad, the fitness freak, had always said it was impossible to be depressed with endorphins rolling around in one's brain. It couldn't hurt. With new resolve, he went into the bedroom and announced his decision to Judith. She was barely awake, but he could tell she thought it was a good thing for him to do. He inhaled a bagel and kissed the females in his life goodbye. By 7:20, he was pedaling west on a side street to the palisades. He joined the bike path on Ocean Avenue going south to the high school. It was still foggy, but nothing like the night before. It seemed providential that he passed both Montero's place and the Camera Obscura on the way. It made keeping an eye out for Mad Max seem as natural as riding with no hands: You just had to keep your balance.

16

Wednesday, February 16, 2005

THE POOL AT THE Beverly Hills Hotel was a power vortex, and Frank Greening was floating in the middle of it. Nearby on chaise longues lay dozens of people who were either very wealthy or pretending to be. Beyond them in the shadows of the cabañas rested the true power brokers, old money as well as new, who never stopped working even with a drink and a hundred-dollar cigar in hand. Frank wasn't one to gloat over how he'd ended up in this spot, but it was ironic, at the very least. He reminded himself that everyone who dealt with millions of dollars had an interesting story. He'd never met a rich man who didn't think he was unique in some way. But, as far as Frank knew, he was truly different. It wasn't that he lived simply; many rich men lived simply. Even more were thrifty. The big difference was that, while he managed an enterprise worth billions, he had accrued very little personal wealth. That changed the nature of the game, usually to his benefit. Of course, he still had to answer to God.

Prior to Adrian's death, Frank had been so busy defending

the Church that he had ignored his own connection with God. That was a mistake; it always was. Since Adrian's death, Frank had said Mass every day.

Frank raised his head from the inflated raft and took in his glistening body. He was enthralled by it. It was a novel experience to take his shirt off in public, to say nothing of arriving early for a meeting and lounging in the pool. His brown skin glowed like polished mahogany. He smiled to himself at the thought of the taunts he had received as a child. This "dirty Mexican" had done very well.

Peering through dark glasses, he considered the other guests around the shimmering, turquoise pool. In a matter of seconds, he counted nearly ten men either poolside or among the staff who, he was sure, were gay. It was so different now. One no longer had to lie or, at least, to live a lie. But when he was young, he had learned to conceal his true self. He hadn't wanted to be "queer," yet his sexual fantasies were different. For years Adrian had sensed that difference, and in the summer when Frank was fourteen, Adrian discovered his stepson naked with another boy. A few weeks later, Adrian drove Frank to the seminary. The academic discipline and moral rules certainly didn't put an end to his sex life, but they did put him on a path toward God. When he finally became a priest, it actually made his life a little easier because, for a long while, celibacy's promise of heaven triumphed over his sex drive.

Frank lay back and splashed himself with water to cool off. Everything became much more complicated during the times he wasn't celibate. He had to construct a credible outer life and conceal the truth about nearly everything. But it felt natural: He had learned secrecy as a child, and lying was second nature. He thought of it as discretion.

He glanced at his watch. Ray Thomas was late. That was unusual. Promptness was a trait they shared and appreciated in each other. Once again, Frank considered whether or not to mention his connection to Adrian Montero. It wasn't surprising that Ray didn't know that he and Adrian had been related. It confirmed how completely Frank's past had been erased. Someone might suggest he was lying about that, too. However, until Adrian's death and the inheritance, Frank considered his family history as something that had lost all relevance. He still didn't feel like explaining it to anyone.

Frank's cell phone played a gentle bit of Bach from the waterproof egg resting next to him on the raft. It was Ray Thomas, caught in traffic on Interstate 10 as he returned from Palm Springs. He promised Frank he would be there in thirty minutes. Frank assured him that he would keep their visitor happy.

A burst of sunlight reflected off the pool, around his sunglasses, and momentarily blinded Frank. With the space behind his eyes a shimmering void, Frank felt the disorientation that often portended an epileptic fit. He forced himself to breathe evenly and not to picture himself slipping helplessly to the bottom of the pool. Soon the fear and lightheadedness evaporated, and Frank peered through his dark glasses to the cabaña that Ray kept. It was empty except for a man in a brown suit sitting in the shadows nervously watching the gorgeous young women around the pool. Frank paddled over to the steps and, as he emerged from the water, the smiling pool boy approached him with a thick towel. The muscular young man knew Ray Thomas was a big tipper and treated his guests accordingly.

Sitting down, Frank explained in Spanish that their host would be a bit late and asked if the gentleman would like something stronger than the cola that he'd been sipping. The middle-aged Peruvian insisted he was fine, but his tapping foot revealed his nervousness. That was usual in these moments. Frank asked how their mutual friend, a prominent Latin American bishop, was doing. Many of the referrals of foreign businessmen who came to Frank for financial help began with their local bishops. It was an international network of clergy that Frank had developed over twenty-five years. Once Ray Thomas had made it clear that he had a nearly unlimited amount of money that he could lend, Frank had effortlessly slipped into the role of middleman. He didn't want to know where Ray got the money, and he didn't care to know how the borrowers would use it. In this instance, he was going to be a bit more involved, since the Peruvian didn't speak English well and he was needed to translate. As usual, he would forget the details just like he did when hearing confessions. They chatted for a while about the current state of politics in Peru, about the lasting effects of the near-fascist state that had developed under President Fujimori and the difficulty in establishing a stronger role for the Church. He kept the conversation to general topics and was spared the details of this man's financial problems. It made it easier to ignore any compromising aspects of the businesses he was aiding. After a few minutes, Frank excused himself to shower and change before Ray Thomas arrived.

With hot water massaging his shoulders, Frank pondered his situation. Like most priests, he was dependent on the Church for his spiritual as well as material needs. He understood that the Los Angeles Archdiocese might have to pay out as much as a billion dollars in damages. It could cripple the institution. Even with insurance and the millions he had amassed to deal with the problem, the Archdiocese would be hard pressed to protect the health insurance and retirement funds for the priests. But he had known this all along. It didn't change his allegiance. It simply meant that defending the Archdiocese was self-protection.

The only argument for keeping his $800,000 inheritance for himself was this: If his activities became known to the public, the Archdiocese might cut its ties with him in order to control a scandal. As Kevin Gardner had mentioned during Saturday's golf game, the Vatican had abandoned Roberto Calvi. It wasn't fair. Calvi had only been doing what was necessary when it appeared that the Vatican was going to have to pay taxes to the Italian government. He secretly invested Church monies in companies throughout Italy, even in a pharmaceutical company that manufactured condoms. Of course, when it came out, it was embarrassing, a worldwide laugh at the expense of the Pope. But what really raised eyebrows was evidence that Calvi had essentially laundered money from all sorts of deals, including the Mafia's heroin trade. The Pope had looked the other way as long as Calvi was making them billions, but eventually the fraud and other scams began to unravel. When it went bad, they hung him out to dry, literally, under Blackfriar's Bridge in London in 1982. Of course, it was never proven.

Frank faced the shower and shifted the handle to cold. In the end, the Vatican hadn't been able to trust Calvi. He was a banker. He wasn't one of them and ultimately couldn't be counted on to fall on his sword for the Church. Frank was different. His life and well-being were the same as the Church's. Separating his fortunes from the Church was a slippery slope he had to continue to avoid. Most important, in his own mind, he had to be impeccable, because the activities he oversaw to help the church, while already of dubious legality, would be considered immoral if done for personal profit. The bottom line was that all money he gathered for the Church, including his inheritance, had to go into its coffers. He really didn't have to consider the issue for long, because everything else in his life had been dedicated to God. Like the cut he'd take for arranging today's loan, Adrian's gift was helpful because neither he nor the Church would have to account for it. It would go directly into the Saints Preserve Us fund.

As he had many times over the years, Frank marveled at the position he occupied. The separation between church and state put him in a realm beyond normal laws and restraints. With the water cascading through his hair, Bob Dylan's sneering, nasal refrain, "To live outside the law, you must be honest," drifted through his head. This snippet from his youth made him chuckle, even though he didn't believe he lived outside of all law. He lived under his own law or, as he preferred to think of it, under God's law.

Frank began whistling "La Paloma," enjoying the resonance of the tiled shower.

"Hey, Padre, it that you whistling that damned mariachi music?" a voice echoed.

"Hello, Ray," Frank shouted as he fumbled to turn off the water and grab his towel. Suddenly, he was the late one.

"Some idiot dragging his big-ass boat up from the Colorado River scattered it all across the freeway. Stupid son of a bitch. Even my chauffeur couldn't find a way around that mess."

Frank wrapped his towel around his waist before he stepped out of the stall. He found Ray Thomas leaning against a tiled wall, holding a gin and tonic. He was a tanned, handsome seventy-year-old who looked about sixty, but thought he looked forty-five. "Well, Frank, maybe I just haven't seen you for a month or maybe because I caught you half-naked, but here's to the thin man." With his usual studied confidence, Ray Thomas raised his glass in a toast. "You look great, more than ready for that monsignor ceremony. It's Friday morning at ten, right?"

Frank blushed and nodded. He'd never had a compliment from a straight man about his body. He fumbled with a thank you, the moment threatening to become awkward until Ray brought the focus back to himself. "I'm going to have to step up my gym routine to keep pace with you."

Frank had an urge to ask Ray about TMF. He wanted to share his surprise at finding that Ray had known his father and had bought his family home. They were logical questions, especially to a friend, but they were tainted with the suspicion that Peter Winston had spread. Frank knew that he was the firewall between Ray and the Cardinal. If what Ray Thomas was involved in threatened the Archdiocese, Frank had to deal with it. To begin with, he had to determine what was true and what wasn't true without jeopardizing their relationship. It confused things that they really were friends, not just financially intimate. Ray was one of the few non-priests and the only business associate whose company Frank truly enjoyed. He didn't know if he could keep his emotions from clouding his decisions. "How are you doing, Ray?"

Ray Thomas looked up, touched by the intimate tone of the question. "Well, my friend, to be honest, it's been a little tough lately. Nothing financial, mind you, but staying ahead of the game means that certain decisions are more complicated than others. Whoever says that being a businessman is cushy just because we can enjoy first-class service is a punk. You need steel balls for this game—you know that as well as I do." He hoisted his glass toward Frank and took a big swallow.

"What decisions, Ray?"

"The oldest problem in the book, Frank: what to do about unproductive assets. But not to worry. It's nothing that affects you or our arrangements. Fact is, I wish my other business dealings went as smoothly as our little loan business." He toasted Frank again. "To us, Frank."

Reluctantly, Frank let it go and changed the subject. "Have you met Señor Alvarez?"

"Yeah, we traded 'buenas tardes,' but that about tapped out my Spanish, and he's a real fish out of agua when it comes to speaking English. I got him a drink and came to get you."

"Well, if you'll excuse me while I dress, I'll come out and see if we can't find a language that everyone understands."

Ray Thomas laughed. "Frank, I've always appreciated your one-track mind. I'll go order us something to eat. You hungry?"

Frank shook his head and treaded to his locker alone. He made himself acknowledge his worst fear: What if Ray Thomas had had Adrian killed? What would he do? The answer was immediate and as old as the Church: no outsiders, no police.

But then what? Frank wasn't a violent man. He was a financial expert, not a gangster.

Methodically, he buttoned his shirt and tucked it in. For the first time, he wondered what Peter Winston was up to. He was probably a harmless kook and had dropped his so-called theory when no one took it seriously. Sergeant Jones hadn't mentioned him, but it would be prudent to find out if Peter had turned up anything suspicious about Ray. There was no hurry, but when it came to church affairs, Frank was a very prudent man.

17

Monday, February 21, 2005

For the rest of the previous week, Peter had ridden his bike to and from school. Whether or not the students were impressed, his critics were silenced. He didn't invest in the whole biker costume. He was still too self-conscious to show himself in skin-tight shorts and a shirt. But he did put out $250 for a fine pair of M-frame glasses to give his efforts the hint of a Lance Armstrong look.

In the evenings, his Internet research on the activities of TMF led him to trying to unravel the Archdiocese's finances. Besides being a secretive empire that had always hidden its wealth, it was now scrambling to incorporate every little parish so the Archdiocese itself would be a less lucrative target for lawsuits. But, even though it was decentralizing itself on paper, Peter knew the Church had always been a strict, paternalistic hierarchy. Besides the Cardinal, someone, or some group, had to be at the center running the show. But their tracks were well hidden. The more he found, the more questions he had. All weekend, whenever he wasn't bicycling and Judith wasn't around, he did more research.

Monday was President's Day and no school. Peter explained to Judith that he was going for some serious exercise. He made himself a sandwich and headed out for a long ride in the Santa Monica Mountains. He found himself speeding down a fire road screaming obscenities at the top of his lungs. The release was fortifying. It tempered his nagging sense of impotence, and he figured it wasn't any crazier than yelling at bad drivers from behind the wheel of his car. He headed deeper into the wilderness. The tangled chaparral was in bloom with the tops of ten-foot-high ceanothus covered with millions of tiny blossoms: white, rose and ice blue. From certain angles, it looked like there was a light dusting of snow covering entire hillsides. Even as his heart was racing from exertion, he could feel himself quieting emotionally. He rested at the top of a ridge. The vast stain of Los Angeles spread out to the southeast while the Pacific Ocean twinkled between the hills to the west.

Peter coasted for several minutes down a fire road until he pulled up at a seasonal stream flowing down an arroyo. On an impulse, he hid his bike and followed the stream for fifteen minutes until he came to a large pool. Two cottonwood trees and some willows grew around the clear, greenish-gray water with grasses and ferns that he guessed would reappear along its banks every year. His quietude was broken when he spotted a large animal print in the mud. It was nearly four inches across. His gut tensed. A mountain lion had been here within a day or two. He was caught between the urge to run and the desire to celebrate. He told himself that he lion was a remnant of the grand, natural design of the Los Angeles basin. *Hell*, he thought, *even grizzlies had roamed these hills until the early twentieth century.* Peter decided to treat this as a positive sign, a return to normalcy. He needed to believe that.

After stretching in the warm sunlight, he pulled out his sandwich, munched a few bites, then put it down. He stripped off his clothes and stepped gingerly into the cold water. For a moment he stood hesitantly as his feet numbed. Then he cried, "Charge!" and dove into the water. With a noisy exhale, he came to the surface and quickly swam to the other side, climbed out, sat on a heated rock and closed his eyes.

Barking startled Peter out of his sunbath. He spotted a pack of dogs on the ridge of the little canyon. He figured he was no more than a mile or two from houses, so he wasn't too surprised. However, listening to them descend into the canyon, snarling at one another in the underbrush, he became concerned. He walked around the pool and across the stream toward his clothes and food. He was about twenty feet from his stuff when the dogs came raucously out of the chaparral. The first dog immediately headed for the sandwich. Peter yelled at it and it slowed, but another dog passed it to get to the food. Peter yelled louder and threw a rock that he had picked up. Amazingly, the rock hit the dog's shoulder, and it yelped and backed away. As Peter approached his food, he realized that the six animals had formed a loose circle around him and were growling ominously. Looking at these mongrels closely for the first time, Peter saw that they were skinny, with sores and raggedy coats. They weren't well-kept housedogs. They were discards or runaways, half-wild, maybe part coyote. Wishing he at least had shoes on, Peter reached down and picked up another rock. As one of the dogs darted in toward the food, another snuck in behind Peter. He yelled, threw the rock at the food bandit and tried to swat at the other one. The first one retreated, but the other clamped down on his wrist. Peter screamed and with his free hand grabbed its neck and tried to press its windpipe. As he did, another dog charged him. Peter saw it at the last moment and, using the dog that was clamped to his wrist like a bat, knocked it aside. The move made him stumble, and he fell to his bare knees. He could feel the dog's jaw shift, but it still held on. He raised it up and brought its head down on a rock, two, three times. As he did, another dog darted in, snatched the sandwich and sprinted away. In an instant, the rest of the dogs were off in a cacophonous chase, leaving their dead partner and Peter sitting in the bright sun among blood-spotted rocks in a vacuumed silence.

With a spasmodic jerk, Peter released his grip from the throat of the dog and pried his bloodied wrist from its jaws. He fell back, unbound from his attacker, as a gurgled roar emerged from his gut and split the newfound silence. It was a jumble of triumph and pain, disgust and relief, all bound together. A howl rose again that weakened into a broken cry. He stood and stumbled back into the creek, where he found a blessed numbing for his wounds.

As the frigid water washed off the blood and dirt that clung to his body, Peter examined his wrist. There were some deep gashes, but he could still move his fingers, though with great pain. He dried off using his T-shirt and tied it around his wrist to staunch the blood. He struggled to get his shorts and shoes on as a throbbing in his wrist began. His eyes passed over his shattered dark glasses that had flown off during the battle to the bloodied head of the dog already covered with flies. He felt no remorse, but he no longer felt triumphant. With a wave of disgust, he realized he'd have to carry the corpse back to be tested for rabies. Weak and disoriented, he made his way up the stream to his bike, tied the dog on with a bungee cord and pedaled out of the mountains onto the blacktop streets. It didn't occur to him to stop for help. With single-minded intensity, he headed for the emergency room at St. John's Hospital. He tried to ignore the pain by thinking about the mountain lion. There was something honorable, sacred even, about its presence in those hills, while the dogs were part of something evil and perverse, like a drive-by shooting. *Yet both are natural,* he reminded himself. *God is present in both. No!* the historian in him resisted. *One kills for food but the dogs kill for the hell of it. And humans are much more like the dogs than mountain lions. This is the reason humans like to think that God created man. It was and is the ultimate comfort: There had to be a higher purpose to all of the pain and suffering that we create. But what if God were just another story? After all, "In the beginning was the Word," and that acknowledged that consciousness began with storytelling. God didn't create man; man created God: someone in our image who understood, who had it all together.*

The doors opened automatically to the emergency room as he walked his bike in. A young gangbanger with a knife wound in his shoulder stopped his moaning and looked with surprise at the dead dog with its head bashed in. The two battered men locked eyes for a moment, both in shock from how easy it was to throw of the thin layer of domestication.

Judith picked him up from the emergency room, full of concern and sympathy. Spaced out from a painkiller, Peter carried on about some statistics the emergency-room doctor had told him: that over twenty Americans a year are killed in dog attacks while in the last century in California, only six people had died from encounters with mountain lions. She was unimpressed and when they got home, Judith expressed worry about more than his wounds. She argued that this incident was part of a pattern of odd behavior and unexplained absences. He laughed hysterically when she asked if he were having an affair. He finally revealed that he was researching TMF and staking out the Camera Obscura. It was hard to justify, especially the night visits.

Her voice cracking, Judith said, "I'm afraid, Peter. You seem to be obsessed by something no one else saw or knows exists."

Peter nodded silently: not just Montero's real murder, but his attempted one. He stared at her through glassy eyes. Even with the well-being of his marriage in the balance, he couldn't reveal his quandary with his dad.

Exhausted, he slept motionless until dawn. Rapid eye movements beneath his eyelids gave evidence of dreaming. A warm breeze flowed from the air conditioner he'd neglected to adjust the night before. It caressed him as he slept and was incorporated seamlessly into his dream. He was in the desert, a rifle in his hand. Sand crunched under his feet as he made his way up a wash through lavender smoke trees and creosote bushes. The first rays of the sunrise intensified the contrast of light and shadow. From beneath a bush he heard an unmistakable rattle, and he leapt to the side just as the snake lunged for his leg. The reptile landed close to him. His heart pounded wildly in his chest, but instead of running, Peter pressed the barrel of his gun behind its head. The snake couldn't strike, but Peter couldn't get away: a standoff. Without thinking, he grabbed it behind its head with one hand and near its tail with the other. He stood up, and a dance began: a writhing, twisting, sensuous dance. It couldn't bite him, but he couldn't let go of it. Their movements were synchronous, a rippling duet, their bodies spiraling like a double helix. When the snake threatened to break loose from Peter's grip, he tried to control it by squeezing tighter, but this made the serpent struggle more. He relaxed his hold the slightest bit and the snake relaxed, but it had gained a fraction of an inch and it angled closer and closer to Peter's hand with its gleaming fangs.

Peter's eyes snapped open. He sat up and looked around the room in the dim light, trying to neutralize the effects of the dream. Judith slumbered on the far side of their bed. Quietly, so as not to wake her, he put on a robe and hurried down the hall to the living room. He sat on the couch and replayed how he had repulsed the dog attack. Despite his throbbing wrist, he felt like a winner, virile and tough. *That's probably what the dream was about,* he thought. He generally ignored his dreams and rarely had such vivid ones. He leaned back, encased by the feeling in the dream and immediately knew it wasn't about the dogs in spite of the fangs being so similar. The feeling was the same he'd had before he picked up the pillow to satisfy Martin's demand.

Peter began to tremble. How could he let his dad suffer if he really loved him? He leaned over and wept copiously into a couch pillow.

"Daddy?"

He gagged on his tears, suddenly exposed.

Samantha stood at the edge of the room in her pajamas, clutching her teddy bear. "Daddy, whatsa matter?"

Her innocence and vulnerability accentuated his own weakness, and he instantly wanted to banish her and those feelings. Barely stifling an angry response, Peter pushed himself upright on the couch and said hoarsely, "I'm okay, Honey."

"Why are you crying?"

"I, uh, I had a nightmare and, uh… "

"That's why you're crying?"

"Not exactly."

"Why?"

"I was thinking about my dad."

"Oh." Samantha thought quietly for a moment. Satisfied, she said, "Daddy, I'm hungry."

"How about French toast?"

"Yummm!" Peter gathered her to him and kissed her forehead. Whatever else happened to him, he was determined to not take it out on his child. And he was equally committed to never putting her through a split-up. He knew what it felt like to lose your family.

Peter brought a cup of coffee into the bedroom as Judith was waking up. He quickly dressed for work as she sat up and took a sip. "Judith, I know things are weird," he began, then faltered.

"You're weird," she said. "And you are way past needing a haircut."

"I'm not having an affair. That's the last thing I need in my life."

Judith shrugged, not convinced either way, and took another sip.

"I don't know what to do about my dad."

"There's nothing to do, Peter. He's in a nursing home," Judith said matter-of-factly. "A good one. It's a sad sign of the times that there are more and more that specialize in patients with dementia to choose from." She put the coffee cup on the bedside table. Peter stared at his wife for a long time in spite of knowing that his silence had become a breeding ground for Judith's fears. He wheeled around and left.

In class that morning, Peter's wrist hurt so much that his writing on the blackboard looked liked chicken tracks instead of the neat, orderly outlines that he usually created to underscore his messages. The morning dragged on, with nothing in his explanation of the Electoral College system or the evolution of the Roman legal system sparking any interest in him or the students in the first two classes. In the fourth period, he was bored and disgusted with the shallow thinking being displayed during a conversation of current events. When a particularly cocky senior, in response to a court case about euthanasia, argued that the husband of a brain-dead patient shouldn't be allowed to remove feeding tubes, Peter's blood began to boil. He wanted to disappear, but there was nowhere to go. Oblivious to the impending eruption, the student, adorned with his letterman's jacket, pontificated that assisted suicide was the same as murder. Peter tried to restrain himself, explaining that since medicine was now able to extend life, it had to allow people to be able to choose death. Then he overflowed into a harangue: Free choice was central to human existence; we all had to ultimately take responsibility for our life. No one—no government, no institution, no religion—could remove the requirement for personal choice and responsibility. He ranted on and on.

A vast silence greeted his explosion, and he began to retreat from the middle of the room. Thirty-seven pairs of eyes followed him back to his desk, and just as his audience released its collective exhalation laced with smothered expletives and giggles, the bell rang and all that energy blew out the door into the hallway.

Peter sagged at his desk, chewing on his scraggly moustache

when the principal walked in. She said she came as a friend, but she'd had a few complaints the week before and was concerned about his "stress level." His reassurances sounded hollow, even to him.

He escaped the campus at lunchtime, fitfully jogging and walking into downtown Santa Monica as his mind whirled with thoughts and fears. In a sweat, he stopped outside a restaurant and tried to read the menu pasted on the window. Dazed and unsure if he was even hungry, his focus shifted to the view reflected in the glass: A haggard stranger with a two-day stubble and long matted hair stared back at him from the window. For the briefest of moments he didn't recognize the man. When he did, Peter's silk tie and monogrammed shirt couldn't hide the fact that he looked worse than Mad Max had on the day of the murder. Shrinking away, he turned only to see the Camera Obscura on the other side of Ocean Avenue. Mortified, he hurried over to a bench. He couldn't go on this way. Something had to change.

Trembling, he pulled a slip of paper from his wallet and punched in the numbers on his cell phone. "May I speak with Father Greening, please?" he asked. "Tell him it's Peter Winston. It's an emergency. I have some important information regarding his stepfather." Peter waited, staring at blood that had appeared on the bandage on his wrist.

"Hello, Mr. Winston," Frank said.

Relieved that the priest seemed to remember him, Peter blurted out, "Frank, I've got good news."

"You do?"

"I think I know who's behind your stepfather's murder."

"Really? Who?"

"Well, it's a little complicated. I mean, I've spent a long time on the Internet trying to track down the people behind it, and I've spent even more time here at the Camera Obscura."

"You're at the Camera Obscura?" Frank asked.

"I'm nearby. It's nearby, across the street."

"What did you mean about all the time you've spent looking for the people behind it? What people?" Frank asked.

Peter ignored the question and instead described how he'd been waiting for Mad Max to show up at the Camera Obscura. "I've always had a feeling, a real strong intuition that I would catch the guy, but I was starting to feel hopeless until I saw the mountain lion prints yesterday. That was reassuring. I knew that things were still somehow okay, that the whole world wasn't crazy. But right after that, some wild dogs attacked me, and I felt completely off-center again. You know, scared that anything could happen to anybody and there wasn't any logic or sense to it, to say nothing of fairness—like what happened to your stepfather, I guess, and what's happening to my dad."

"Which is?" Frank inquired.

"Uh…Alzheimer's."

"I'm sorry to hear that. But what's all this about a mountain lion and wild dogs?"

"I'm sorry. It sounds improbable, I know, but yesterday I rode my bike into the mountains because I was trying to forget about Adrian's murder, if only briefly. I found a big mountain lion print next to a stream and then I got attacked by a pack of dogs and ended up with stitches and antibiotics."

"But you're alright?"

Peter looked at the bandage. The blood spot hadn't increased. "I'm okay, I guess."

"Okay." Frank paused. "I'm surprised and, I suppose you could say, impressed with how seriously you seem to have taken this seemingly hopeless task." Frank cleared his throat. "Now, who do you think is behind this?"

"Right! Right! Okay." Peter tried to settle himself so that what he was going to say would sound reasonable. "After Mad Max—oh," Peter interrupted himself—"that's the nickname I gave the guy who pushed your stepfather. Anyway, after he attacked

Adrian, this guy ran into a building. I followed him in there, but he disappeared, like he was being helped. Two weeks later, I went back and discovered that the building is being built by TMF and Associates, the same group that bought your stepfather's place."

Frank felt a chill run down his spine and interrupted, "And I've discovered that TMF is a large company with lots of projects. What you're saying doesn't prove anything."

"No, but it ties the very guys who profit from getting your stepfather's place to the actual killer," Peter said.

Frank took a deep breath. "Not only is this a very weak link, but you should know that this supposedly diabolical company that you are suggesting had Adrian killed is largely owned by a man who is a major contributor to the Catholic Church."

"You're talking about Ray Thomas," Peter said with relief.

"How do you know about Ray Thomas?" Frank asked warily.

"I researched TMF and all the general partners. He stood out because he's so involved in the Archdiocese." Nervously, Peter forged ahead. "Then I discovered that you were head of the Archdiocese's finances, and I...well, I'm glad you brought up who Ray Thomas is to you."

"Mr. Winston, you sound like you are suggesting that you consider me a suspect in this intrigue of yours."

"Not really, at least not anymore. I mean, I wouldn't have called you if I thought you were involved, would I?"

"I'm not sure what to expect of you."

"Yeah. Well, I can appreciate that this seems pretty crazy. To be honest, it's been driving me a little crazy." Peter felt himself going off track. "What I really want to know is if you'd help me investigate the TMF part of it, because, to be honest, I could use some help."

Frank hesitated, unsure of how to play this situation. "Are you still trying to find this Max fellow?"

"Yeah, I am, I am," Peter stammered. He picked at a food stain on his shirt and laughed a hollow laugh. "But I don't think I've really figured out what I'd do if I caught him. I mean, I doubt the son of a bitch is going to admit anything, and if I call the police on him he'd probably just be set free, and then I'm sure he'd disappear for good. So," his voice picked up energy, "that's why I've also been coming at the situation from the other end, and that's where Ray Thomas becomes important."

"You seem quite committed to this…uh…cause," Frank stated.

"Committed, yes, getting close to obsessed, I'm afraid," Peter agreed.

"That could be a problem," Frank said, allowing himself to sound sympathetic and gaining time to consider what strategy to take with this man. The saying "Keep your friends close, but your enemies closer" rang in his head.

"My wife thinks I've gone off the deep end."

A silence built between them. Peter started to speak again, just to keep the conversation going, but he stopped as Frank said decisively, "Peter, I'd like to understand more about you and what you've discovered. Would you drive up to Ojai on Saturday? We are going to have a ceremony honoring Adrian, among others, at a ranch near there. You might find it beneficial, and we could talk after."

"Hell, yes!" Peter shouted with relief, then calmed down enough to write the directions.

18

Saturday, February 26, 2005

P ETER DROVE THROUGH RAIN to the quaintly hip town of Ojai. The two-lane highway continued east into the low mountains, and within ten minutes there were no houses around. The rain turned to drizzle that reflected the luminous afternoon light, beautiful but desolate. *Even emptier than the Santa Monica Mountains,* Peter thought, *but probably more mountain lions.* He glanced at his directions. "Get there a little before sundown," he had scribbled, "about a two-hour drive."

The car radio turned to static as the road entered a narrow canyon. He turned it off and resisted the urge to fill his head with music from a CD. Giant sycamores with mottled gray bark arched over the two narrow lanes covered with their fallen brown leaves. A muddy, rampaging creek paralleled the twisting blacktop. Peter barely noticed as his mind filled with thoughts of Judith. He knew that she was fed up with his obsession with Adrian Montero. When he told her he was going to a church retreat, she informed him that she had made an appointment with a therapist for the following week. Since he wouldn't talk to her, she said, the least he could do would be to show up and try to save their marriage.

Careening around the corners, Peter carried on in his head: *Great! Let's get advice from someone like Thatcher, my analyst friend who left his wife for a 25-year-old grad student. Or, there's that radio shrink who's been married four times.* He shook his head. Therapy wasn't the problem. He'd thought about doing it a few times over the years. Besides, even if he didn't want to tell her what had happened at the hospital, he was glad that she was fighting for them. He turned the radio back on and concentrated on finding a better station.

The rain stopped, and the road straightened out as the canyon opened into a valley. An oldies station filled the car with "He's a pinball wizard," and Peter sang along until his mind drifted. He wondered if Frank's lover would be there. He worried that he was about to try to get help from someone who couldn't even keep his vows. *Forget it,* he told himself, *it's not like I'm some model of consistency. Besides, I'm here to get help on solving a murder, not for spiritual or marital counseling.*

A moment later, he hit the brakes as he sped by a small, hand-carved sign near a dirt road. Nervous but excited, he backed up the highway and read "Henderson Ranch." He turned up a steep hill as the sun broke through the cumulous clouds on the western horizon. In less than a minute, he reached the crest and drove out on a plateau, surrounded by mountains on three sides. He followed the ruts toward a stand of large cottonwood trees. Beneath them, in the golden light, lay a ramshackle ranch house with several cars and pickups parked at random. A hundred yards past the house, he could see about ten or fifteen people standing near a hut of some kind. There appeared to be a fire pit near them. Peter slowly drove toward the house and stopped as he came to three children with dark brown eyes looking out from under straight black hair, each a half head shorter than the other like Russian dolls that could fit into each other. Peter lowered his window.

"Do you know where I can find Father Greening?" he asked. The littlest one pointed with one hand toward the house as the oldest one said, "Uncle is inside." Then they stared silently again. Peter felt naked under their gaze and mumbled "Thanks" as he hit the gas, spinning his tires in the gravel. The children took off in a flash in the other direction, running and jumping down toward a pen and shelter. In his rearview mirror, Peter saw several goats.

He pulled up under a tree and closed the car door, wondering if he should lock it. He was relieved to see Frank come out of the house. "I hope I'm not late," Peter said.

Frank shook his hand and replied, "You did fine, Peter. Besides, we're on Indian time up here." Frank had on jeans and a faded blue flannel shirt. His mouth was fixed with a welcoming smile.

"Indian time?"

"Things happen when they happen," Frank explained, "sometimes for reasons we aren't aware of."

"Then I've been on Indian time for four weeks," Peter said. "But what does that have to do with your stepfather? I thought he was Mexican and Catholic, like you."

"He was Mexican and Catholic, and I can assure you that we have had more Masses said and candles lit than if we were if Mexico. But my mother was Indian, from Peru, even though we never talked about it much."

"Why not?" Peter asked.

Though irked at the personal nature of the question, Frank only became more sincere. He'd already prepared himself that a certain intimacy and vulnerability were going to be necessary to accomplish his goal. "Adrian raised us to think of ourselves as Spanish, higher class, you know. One reason why I continue the old ways with these ceremonies and rituals is to counter that attitude."

Peter was a little embarrassed to be let in on a family secret. "Indian ceremonies? Is that what we're going to do now?"

"Yes, we're going to have what non-Indians call a sweat lodge. Did you bring your shorts?"

"Yeah." He grabbed his old gym bag from the car with everything that Frank had said to bring.

"Come in and change. I'm sure the stones are about ready."

As they walked toward the house, the children hurried by, carrying a pan of goat's milk. "These are your nephews and nieces?" Frank looked at Peter with confusion and Peter explained, "They referred to you as Uncle when I saw them earlier."

Frank held open the screen door of the adobe house for Peter. "We aren't related in any formal way, but we are all related in a larger sense. That's one of the reasons I invited you today. I realized that you were fiercely struggling with this question of how things relate."

Peter's eyes filled as he heard this. It was the first time he felt like someone might appreciate what he was going through. He wiped his eyes as he stepped through the doorway, intending to turn and say thanks. Before he could, he found himself staring into a living room aglow with the radiance of sunset, pulsing in a mellow orange light. Dust motes floated between two old couches. Throw rugs covered an uneven, scratched wooden floor, while broken bridles, stuffed birds, books and innumerable knickknacks of ranching life were scattered on and under heavy tables and chairs. The newness of everything had long been rubbed off. It was here because it was useful or told a story. On the other side of a door came the murmur of women's voices and Merle Haggard on the radio. A rich, pungent smell seeped out and mixed with the shimmering light in the room.

Enchanted, Peter stared at the far wall, where, tacked to the wood, was a pelt still connected to the head of a mountain lion. Frank closed the front door and observed Peter. "The Hendersons used to hunt them, when they ran cattle. Now the cattle and most of the cougars are gone."

"He seems to be following me," Peter said finally.

"Then why don't you bring him in with you? You could sit on his back." He went and took it down without waiting for a response.

They changed clothes and a few minutes later were walking toward the lodge. Peter cradled the mountain lion skin in his arms. He was in his swimming trunks and old sneakers feeling pale and flabby next to the tall, slim and brown Frank. The air was cooling fast, and Peter had goose bumps. Frank explained that on this occasion there was going to be a men's sweat and that the women were going to have a moon lodge later. They approached the men, about twelve in all. Frank introduced him to an older fellow who was going to lead the ceremony. Red Hawk offered Peter a pliant hand to shake. Three other men nodded a welcome and most smiled at him as they spoke and joked in small groups, warmed by a large fire pit of shimmering rocks. Some carried drums, and four had long braided hair. Dove calls floated up from the chaparral nearby, underscoring the hushed quality of the setting.

Frank exchanged warm, silent hugs with several of the men, but there was no attempt at further introductions. He then stood quietly observing Peter, who was looking around self-consciously. In a half-whisper Peter asked, "How does this connect to your stepfather?"

"We sweat to get rid of our impurities, both physical and mental," Frank answered as the color drained from the landscape in the waning light. "We give them over to our mother, the earth, and to all our relations who have gone before us."

"Kind of like an Indian twelve-step program," Peter cracked, but his eyes showed concern that Frank would take offense.

Frank smiled. "Yes, we do acknowledge our powerlessness. However, this is different in that this is seen as normal, not a result of despair or addiction. Every one of us has problems, but this is something we do simply to reaffirm our place in the natural order of things." He breathed in deeply and continued, "Tonight, we are especially honoring the spirits of Adrian and of Red Hawk's uncle, who have recently passed over to join the other grandfathers. Just as others, hopefully, will honor us."

"Doesn't this conflict with being a priest?" Peter asked. "I mean, isn't it praying to a different God?"

"The Church has had to make accommodations for the practices of the natives wherever it has preached the gospel," Frank chuckled. "It has changed in the twenty-five years since my ordination. So have I. I began as a parish priest barricaded behind statues and doctrine. Now I'm a clerical investment counselor, but I still pray to the same God. Just as the Church leadership has begun to reflect the cultural diversity of its members worldwide, so too has it tolerated the honoring of God in diverse settings."

At a signal from Red Hawk, the group began to line up in front of the small, domed lodge. It looked to Peter to be far too small to hold them all. At the front of the line, Red Hawk began drawing in the air around each man with a glowing, smoking, tightly bundled clump of leaves. "Smudging," Frank said over his shoulder, "with sage, for purification." Peter watched skeptically as Red Hawk erased, as it were, the invisible grit surrounding a heavily tattooed man.

After his smudging, each individual bent over and disappeared into the black hole of the lodge. Peter was next to last, behind Frank and followed by someone named Anton. When he stepped inside, he could barely see. After crawling only a few feet, he sensed Frank stop and settle down. Peter stopped, trying to leave some space between him and Frank, but Anton crowded in closely behind, bumping Peter's butt with his shoulder. Peter moved ahead until he ran into and recoiled from Frank. Then he felt Frank's hand on his arm, pulling him closer so that finally they sat cross-legged with knees overlapping and shoulders rubbing. Looking across the circle, he could make out that the others were as tightly packed.

Uncomfortable with the sudden intimacy, Peter worried that he'd been rash in coming. He remembered hearing another teacher talk about her experiences with Native American ceremonies. It had seemed hypocritical to use the rituals of a native people that your own ancestors had tried to exterminate. He had always felt judgmental of those neo-hippies who adorned themselves with leather and headbands. Spiritual vampires, he had called them. His mind raced with an inner tirade against his own foolishness.

Suddenly, through the opening came a large glowing rock carried on a shovel that was placed into a shallow pit in the middle. Peter tried to tip away from the intense heat. As he leaned back, his left hand landed on the skull of the mountain lion, his fingers curling into its mouth. Peter only partially stifled a yip of surprise. At the same time, he began to feel a sharp poking from the twigs and leaves he was sitting on. "Sit on him," he remembered Frank saying. He struggled to his knees and jerked the pelt forward. In the dim light coming through the open flap and from the rapidly growing pile of glowing rocks, Frank and Anton steadied Peter and helped him spread the pelt out beneath him. He sat again, feeling the fur rough and prickly as he moved one way, smooth and yielding the other. The fire-tender brought in a final rock, somehow squeezed into the lodge between Anton and Red Hawk and the flap was closed.

Peter's mind slowed its chatter as his eyes adjusted to the salmon-colored glow. The faces across from him began to shine. Some of his own sweat trickled down his ribs. It was hot, but not too uncomfortable. Red Hawk scattered something over the fire and the lodge filled with a pungent smell, like tree sap. With the first whiff, Peter remembered pulling open his father's sweater drawer and being hit with the sweet scent of cedar. He smiled at the memory until a rivulet of sweat made it into his left eye. He closed it and rubbed against the sting.

"Mitakuye oyasin," the men said. Frank leaned over and whispered that it meant "to all my relations." Red Hawk welcomed the spirits from six directions and asked for their blessings on this ceremony.

Still rubbing his eye, Peter barely noticed Red Hawk lean out over the rocks with a long ladle in his hand until he heard a rippling explosion. Suddenly he was overwhelmed with hot steam and ash. He recoiled as Red Hawk applied another crackling dose of water to the rocks. Peter could barely breathe. Claustrophobia gripped him, but he didn't want to be weak and quit. He tried to distract himself by counting to ten with each inhale and exhale so that the fear of suffocating wouldn't make breathing more difficult.

Red Hawk said something about suffering being part of living and to stay inside the lodge except for dire emergencies. But the more Peter tried to stifle it, the more it felt like a scream was about to wind its way up his throat. If he weren't so desperate for Frank's help he would have already bolted. In a last-ditch attempt to catch his breath and calm himself, he twisted away from the rocks and lay back on his side. To his relief, the air was cooler down lower. As his fears abated slightly, he opened his eyes again. He was curved around Frank, who remained upright. It was very intimate, yet perfectly natural. He sensed Anton on the ground behind him. Frank had said that in here one must simply accept what one is, not pretend to be what one thinks he should be.

As impossible as it was for Peter to imagine, Red Hawk began to sing and was soon joined by others as well as drums. Peter's breathing became less jerky, though the air was still stifling. He closed his eyes and concentrated on his breathing. The sweat continued to pour off of him as he felt the beat begin to carry him along. As the song ended, Red Hawk invited them to speak to the grandfathers, to give thanks and honor. Men began to share, simply, thoughtfully, one after another in no particular order. After an indeterminate amount of time, Frank began to talk, and Peter sat up.

"I would like to welcome the spirit of my stepfather, Adrian," Frank began. "Adrian married my mother when I was a baby, after my real dad died in an airplane accident. Even though Adrian adopted me and gave me his name, we were never close. My mom used to say he was jealous, that I reminded him of her past. Anyway, the older I got, the meaner he got." Frank paused, and several of the others made low, guttural sounds of understanding and reassurance. "By the time I was fourteen, I was glad to get away to seminary. As strict as it was, it was better than living at home, and I never really returned except to visit my mom and sister. Even though I took back my biological father's name before I was ordained, many years went by before I faced how much I hated Adrian and how that bitterness had become part of me. I prayed to be released from it. I told myself I didn't hate him, and finally I started to believe it. But it wasn't true. I just drove a hardness deeper inside of me where I couldn't notice it."

Frank paused, and several of the men murmured "Ho."

"Even after I was assigned to Los Angeles over twelve years ago, we rarely saw each other, but a couple of years ago he started coming to Masses that I was saying. One day he invited me back to his house, where I had grown up. He said he was sorry if he had been mean to me." Frank coughed, "A lot of venom surged up over that 'if,' and I was ready to write him off once more. Then he asked me to forgive him, and I could tell he meant it. Even though I wasn't sure if it was God's forgiveness or mine that he was asking for, I gave it." Frank sighed deeply. "That hard place that had taken up residence in my heart was dissolved." Frank was silent for a moment, and then added with a chuckle, "Which isn't to say that my new, softer heart hasn't created problems.

Still, his apology released me, and for that I am deeply thankful." He stared into the rocks and then finished with, "Ho, mitakuye oyasin," which the others repeated in a chorus of support.

A thick, comforting atmosphere filled the lodge. Peter interpreted the resonant grunts and nodding heads of the others as a sign that they believed that, despite everything, human affairs made sense. He held the lion's head in his hands, completely alienated from that sentiment, seeing it as a quaint yearning for order and meaning. He saw himself outside the lodge, wild, prowling through the hills. In the silence, he tried to clear his throat, but it came out like boulders shifting in a stream. The sound brought him back, and as he opened his eyes he saw a few men looking at him expectantly. He was the only one who hadn't spoken.

"Adrian was murdered!" His voice shredded the peaceful cloud that hung in the air. "I'm the only one who knows because I saw it happen." Peter's heart began to speed. "But I can't prove it." All eyes were on him. Red Hawk sat stony faced, rocking slightly. "What do the grandfathers say about that?" Peter declared into the murky darkness. The silence hung uncomfortably until he continued, "And, as far as passing over? Hell, I wish my father were dead. And so would he if he could still hold a thought in his head." Peter leaned forward, throat dry, voice cracking. "I've tried everything to end his misery. I fucking tried but it just goes on and on." He hesitated, afraid he'd revealed too much, then sensed that his admission sounded like normal filial duty. "So, ho, Adrian, you got killed and it's not fair. And ho, Dad, you're alive and that's not fair. And ho, ho, ho. It's just one big cosmic joke."

Peter sat rigidly in the heat, gripping the lion's head, silently challenging the men to contradict him. The group shifted, like a snake attempting to digest a rat. In the strained silence, Peter closed his eyes. As his breathing deepened and he settled back into himself, he heard Red Hawk intone, "Ho, mitakuye oyasin," and the others joined in. A moment later, the fire-tender pulled the flap of the lodge and the sweet night air flowed in, ending the first of the four segments of the ceremony.

19

SUNDAY, FEBRUARY 27, 2005

S TILL EXHAUSTED FROM THE night before, Peter
stood alone at the kitchen sink cutting strawberries into a
bowl of Corn Flakes. The Hendersons had left for Los Angeles
to pick up a daughter. The house was empty except for Frank
sleeping somewhere. Peter considered how he could get Frank's
help. He was still suspicious of him, though now he liked him.
He'd come to appreciate, even enjoy, "the sweat." He'd been
surprised that no one had offered advice after he'd poured out his
anger and anguish. There seemed to be an unspoken agreement
that when things got fucked up you just had to hang on. He had
ended up feeling stoned or, rather, ecstatic from sweating in the
searing heat mixed with drumming and chanting. Afterward, the
men had shared a hearty stew. By then, Peter was nodding off,
and Frank had insisted that he stay over.

Peter licked the vibrant red juice from his fingertips. He'd
called Judith the night before, and she'd made it clear that
staying over didn't endear him to her or help his claim that he
wasn't having an affair. The possibility that he'd found someone

to help him solve Montero's murder only upset her more. She was slightly mollified when he reiterated his willingness to see a therapist with her.

He sat down to his breakfast at the kitchen table thinking that he understood Frank's ambivalence toward his stepfather. Adrian Montero had been a difficult son of a bitch. Nonetheless, Frank was willing to forgive and honor Adrian. Peter liked that. He identified with someone who was willing to fulfill his obligations. If Frank could make peace with his own nemesis, Peter should be able to trust him to help find Adrian's killer. But he couldn't get over his doubts about Frank as a priest. How could he trust a man who was living a lie?

"Good morning, Peter," Frank said as he came through the swinging door. In contrast to Peter, he was dressed in an unwrinkled shirt and chinos, with his hair combed.

Caught between two impulses, Peter vamped, "You look as crisp as a new hundred dollar bill."

Frank ignored the compliment and headed for the coffee maker. "We need to talk about what happened to Adrian."

Peter hesitated. "Right, but first I have to ask you something."

Frank turned to face him.

"I'm sorry to spring this on you, but it's important to clear up. I know about you and your, what do you call him—lover, boyfriend or just plain Mortal Sin?"

Frank leaned back against the counter, face controlled but his stomach roiling. "What are...?"

"I'm the guy who knows things about you and your family that he has no business knowing, Frank."

Frank's eyes narrowed. "That's abundantly clear, but this is a new level of intrusion."

"I know it looks that way, but I want to trust you, and secrets make a man vulnerable to God knows what." Peter shrugged. "I'm only upset with the hypocrisy of your behavior, not the behavior itself."

"Hypocrisy?" Frank erupted, "I don't understand what you're talking about, but I can't have this conversation without a cup of coffee." He grabbed the coffeepot and set to work as a way to mask his rage and fear.

Peter waited a few moments before continuing, "I thought I could overlook your professional shortcomings when I came up here, but I was wrong. The Church is too important to me."

"You mean you're a Catholic?"

"On my mother's side. She arranged for me to receive the gift of faith. On my atheist father's side, I got the gift of scientific analysis. Which makes me a devout skeptic."

"Which leaves you where, exactly?" Frank asked.

"I choose to believe, to have faith, as a way to explain the mysteries of the universe and to create order in the human world. I go to church regularly and believe in the divinity of Jesus. But because I believe in the Church's capacity to lead people to a moral life, I know that priests like you make a travesty of my faith."

Frank looked up from the coffee grounds. "Because I've supposedly broken my vows?"

"Because you pretend not to," Peter responded. "I don't give a damn about what you do unless you lie about it."

Frank blinked. "Does this mean you plan to tell others about me?"

"Hell, no!" Peter said. "That's up to you. Besides, these days, with all the sexual abuse in the Church, this would hardly be noticed."

Frank flicked the coffee maker on. "Unlikely, but thank you for not going public with your suspicions."

"Look, Frank, I don't expect anyone to be a saint. In fact, I expect everyone to be human; just don't lie about it. For Chrissakes, it's not that difficult to understand. What I'm saying is that I believe in the power of confession. It forces us to confront ourselves."

Frank swung around. "Does that mean you don't have secrets, that you confess all?"

"Just a minute," Peter said. "You don't deny you're fucking around with that guy?"

Frank stared at the floor. He was seething. Few things got to him as easily and deeply as when cafeteria Catholics, the ones who picked and chose what they wanted to believe, accused clergy of inconsistency or hypocrisy. These liberal, deconstructed, postmodern wimps had the nerve to call Catholics who struggled to live by the rules of their faith hypocrites. It was outrageous. This man had no idea of the struggles Frank had. Yet he was willing to stand in judgment of him. Frank exhaled heavily and willed his pounding heart to slow. Not that he wanted Ray Thomas to actually be involved in Adrian's death, but the thought that he might be suffering this arrogant prick's crap for nothing was excruciating. Unfortunately, he didn't know, so he looked Peter in the eye and said, "I have a lover."

"Okay," Peter said. "Thank you." He hesitated. Frank's confession invited similar honesty and, after all, he was a priest. The problem was that Peter wasn't convinced his own action was a sin. At the same time, he knew he needed to talk about it with someone. "Well, I do have a secret. I kind of hinted at it last night, but…well, okay. Not too long ago, I tried to smother my crippled, demented father in the hospital in accordance with his demands."

Frank ran his hands slowly through his thick black and silver hair. "Christ have mercy," he murmured. A balance of damning information had been established. He relaxed somewhat and looked at Peter sympathetically. "Your father requested that you kill him when he got to this stage?"

"Requested, suggested, pleaded and demanded: all of the above many times when he was still coherent. And I agreed more than once."

"But you tried and failed?"

"I chickened out." Peter's voice dropped, and he mumbled, "Except for trying to figure out this morass with your stepfather, I haven't been able to stop thinking about it." He brushed an ant off the faded yellow Formica table. "It's not over. There will be other opportunities."

"Dios mio," Frank swore, and they both were silent as the coffee maker gurgled. Before it finished filtering, Frank poured himself a cup and sat down at the table, studying the rumpled, confused and edgy soul across from him. He had Peter wrong. He was only theologically a liberal Catholic. In his soul he was traditional, conservative and looking for someone to take control. Frank smiled inwardly. He knew about taking control. "What makes you think an individual could, or should, take on such a momentous task as deciding on life and death?" he asked.

Peter snapped out of his daydream like he'd been slapped. "You make it sound like I'm being dictatorial, but that's not it at all. It's compassion. I don't want my dad to suffer. I'm acting alone because I'm the one who made the agreement. Individuals have been deciding, as you put it, on life and death forever: warriors, doctors, mothers, fathers and sons. It's an age-old problem."

"Indeed it is. But when a life is taken as a result of a collective decision, as in the case of war and executions, it isn't murder. Murder usually is the act of an individual acting alone, not the collective."

"While our society is collectively trying to decide what to do about people with certain diseases and those who are kept alive by medical intervention, some individuals are forced by circumstances to take action. I could have taken a vote in the sweat lodge last night to see how many agreed with mercy killing, and I bet I would have found a big majority in favor. Intuitively, we know it's okay in certain situations. The question is, which situations and what's in the heart of the person deciding?"

"That's why institutions such as the Church have been created by humans, to help us with these difficult decisions."

"I would be more comfortable going to the Church with this if it weren't so keen on condemning those it disagreed with to hell. I'm a Catholic because of Jesus, not because of the Pope."

"That would make you a Protestant."

"It's obvious you disagree with the Pope, too," Peter shot back. "Does that make you a Protestant? Look, I know what the Church says about euthanasia, the same line as it takes on abortion: The sanctity of life is more important than the quality of life. But individuals have always been in front of the Church, forcing it to come around. Maybe you're one of those individuals, too."

Frank redirected the conversation. "You said you were motivated by compassion. Is it still compassion if your father is no longer suffering? It sounds like his mind is about gone. If he's no longer in pain or feeling upset or humiliated, what problem are you solving?"

Peter sagged at the table. "I'm not sure."

Frank got up. Arguing, even if he was right, wasn't going to help. It was time for sympathy. "I've got to eat something. You want toast?"

Peter shook his head no and pushed his bowl of cereal to the side.

Frank put bread into the toaster. "We're quite a pair, aren't we?" Peter looked up and Frank continued. "You're being forced by your sense of morality and ethics to do what you don't want to do, and I'm condemned by my church and my morality for doing the most natural thing in the world." He sat back at the table and took a sip of coffee. "It's quite challenging."

Eager to change the subject, Peter responded, "I understand my challenge, but I really don't see why you can't deal with your situation more openly. It's not like you're the first gay priest."

Frank's jaw tensed again. "And I don't see why it's any of your business."

"I need your help, but I've got to be able to trust you." Peter stood up and poured himself some coffee. "Look, you've already rejuvenated me by inviting me out here, and you certainly don't owe me anything, even though currently I seem to have dedicated myself to your family."

Frank looked askance at him, and Peter quickly added, "Okay, forget that, that's bullshit. What I'm trying to say is that I am trustworthy, I'm good with secrets. I may challenge you, but I won't betray you. I've always taken any responsibility seriously. That's what's got me in such a bind with my dad and now with Adrian."

Loath to have to prove himself to this man, Frank went to the toaster and lathered butter on his toast. He took a big bite, then declared forcefully, "I find it deeply offensive that you would presume to understand homosexuality." He swallowed and looked intently at Peter. "I was a gay baby. I've known my sexual orientation since I was a little boy. It wasn't a choice." He approached the table with his mouth full again. "You can say something if you want."

Peter started to speak, then shook his head and was quiet. Frank sat and continued. "After I was sent away to seminary as a horny and quite experienced boy of fourteen, I came to the opinion that the Church had a brilliant solution to sex and the difficulties it stirred up. I thought that the Church fathers knew that sex was so powerful that to give it up would go a long way to guaranteeing entry to heaven. I envisioned that the priests redirected their sexual energy and used it as some sort of spiritual rocket fuel. Unfortunately, many priests, both straight and gay, approached the challenge of celibacy by naïvely denying their sexuality. As the whole world now realizes, a few of them ended up so tightly wound that they leaked all over."

"A few?" Peter blurted out scornfully.

Frank tapped his spoon on the worn Formica of the tabletop. "Less than three percent of the priests in the U.S. have been charged with abusing young people. The Church made a monumental mistake in trying to hide the problem, but it's not as widespread as the anger and hysteria suggest. And it is complicated." Frank took a sip of his coffee. "Do you know that there were married popes and priests in the early centuries of the Church? And that the rule on celibacy was nearly changed forty years ago during Vatican ll, until Pope John the 23rd suddenly died?" He took a breath. "Celibacy is not a matter of scripture. It's not something God demanded. It's a product of Church politics."

"I know Church history, Frank. I know this scandal isn't about homosexuality. I also know that priests' taking sexual advantage of parishioners was a problem as early as the eleventh century. It was written about in the *Book of Gomorrah* by Saint Peter something, and the Church still hasn't responded to it in a meaningful way. But, like I said, this isn't about sex; it's about living up to one's word."

"St. Peter Damian," Frank said, appraising him anew. "I forgot you were a historian." He took a few moments to finish his toast. "Until a few months ago, with rare exception, I was sexually dormant. Then, I was informed that I was being made a Monsignor."

Peter lifted his brushy eyebrows. "Congratulations."

"Thank you, but it's a meaningless title. There's no power that goes with it, and it actually runs against current policy for this archdiocese. The Cardinal wanted to have more positive news to focus on within the community, to highlight the good priests." He allowed himself an ironic smile. "Anyway, as you seem to know, shortly before I became a Monsignor, just before Adrian," he hesitated, "before Adrian was killed, I fell in love for the first time in many years. And for the first time in an even longer while, it's sexual."

"Have you confessed it?"

"I wish I could, but because the Church didn't handle child abuse as a serious psychological disorder and a criminal act, other sexual sins that aren't criminal are being treated very seriously. I wouldn't be arrested, but it's unlikely I would be allowed to occupy the position of responsibility that I do now." Frank took a deep breath. "Hypocrisy doesn't have anything to do with it. I simply won't do anything to jeopardize my current obligations."

"Except take a lover," Peter stated quietly.

Frank glared at him. "I think your hatred of what you call my hypocrisy is basically a cry on your part for a world with set, black-and-white rules." Frank leaned forward. "I don't know what drives you to be so rigid, to be so hard on yourself and everybody else. It must be something very powerful, because many people I know would have little judgment about this crisis I'm going through. As you said yourself, it's not about sex. They might judge me as weak, but hypocritical? Hell, no! If the sexual abuse hadn't been so mishandled, even the Pope and others in leadership would be sympathetic. They would trust—that is to say, they would have faith—that I could work it out with God."

Peter cast a skeptical eye.

"Not anymore," Frank continued. "Now, it looks like they were too sympathetic to errant priests. In this climate, they'd intervene. They'd push me into counseling or even relieve me of my duties. But Peter, I'm weak—human, if you will—but I'm not sick. This isn't neurosis or pathology. I'm in love with another free-willed adult."

"But," Peter interrupted, "even you admit you haven't come to terms with what you are doing."

"What in God's name do you think I'm trying to do?" Frank blurted out. "I took this weekend off from the one person I want to be with more than anyone in order to think about what's going on in my life. And now I'm hashing it out with the right wing of the Church, you."

"Where is your lover this weekend?"

"My friends up here know I'm gay," Frank rubbed his face tiredly, "but even they might be uncomfortable at condoning a breach of celibacy."

"How do you condone it?" Peter asked automatically.

Frank drew himself together. "Do you use birth control?" he asked, and Peter nodded. "Do you confess it?"

"No, I don't consider it a sin."

"Does it bother you that you are in disagreement with the Pope on this?"

"Not at all. I believe in free will. My relationship with God isn't dependent on Rome."

"And yet, you go to communion and consider yourself a card-carrying Catholic?"

"Sure, but it's different for priests."

"Only if you wanted to advance under Pope John Paul II. There have been two keys to getting ahead: Oppose birth control and oppose female clergy. It's a loyalty test. I'd probably be a bishop by now if I hadn't spoken out for birth control years ago. But John Paul II ended all serious dialogue. It's forced many priests to shield their personal opinions and behaviors. In spite of this, I'm convinced that just as the Church got us out of the Dark Ages, it still stands between civilization and another Dark Age."

"Even though it rejects your sexuality," Peter interrupted.

"Even though it breaks my heart, it saves my soul," Frank declared passionately. "To believe that all priests agree with those doctrines is a fairytale, and to expect us to speak out officially, at the expense of our calling, is naïve. Nonetheless, I would die for the Church, because it is the best hope we have for a humane world."

Frank's speech left them both a bit dazed. They looked at their watches, and, in silence, they washed up the breakfast dishes and collected their stuff. Standing in the living room, Frank broke the tension. "Peter, you said you need my help, but then you attack me. I don't know what you want."

Without thinking, Peter blurted out, "I want a fucking answer!" He looked away, embarrassed by the rawness of his response, then tried to explain. "When I was a boy, if I was bad and didn't confess it, even if I had a bad thought, I was told I would end up in hell—forever. I took that real personally. The prospect of heaven provided hope, except I knew how hard it was to be good. It was a nerve-wracking situation, because I believed so completely. Then, a supposedly all-powerful God let my mom die. I never got a good answer for that, and I thought I gave up on believing."

"What do you mean?"

Peter leaned against a table. "In college, I really got into Marxism. Communism promised heaven on earth. How could I resist?" Peter tried to laugh. "I told myself I'd given up on religion, but eventually I realized that, for me, Marxism was just another fundamentalist belief system. After my revolutionary phase, I went through my raging capitalist phase: another extreme position. When that went bust and I began teaching, I thought I'd finally grown up and settled down. I was convinced I'd found a radical middle. I came back to religion, since my reading of history confirmed for me that the religious drive is at least as strong and basic in humans as the sex drive. But I figured I was liberated from my need for absolutes, from what I call my fundamentalist's fantasy. Maybe I'm kidding myself."

"When you're raised to believe in Eden and heaven, it's hard to come down to earth. Being gay has helped ground me, but I'm not sure how to help you when you are so rigid and judgmental." Frank sat down in an overstuffed chair and looked at Peter. "Do you still think I have something to hide?"

"I guess not." Peter hesitated. "I was worried that if you were too deeply in the closet, someone could blackmail you and, you know, force you to go along with whatever. Now that seems a little paranoid."

"It is," Frank agreed. "So, how can I help you?"

Peter sat on the couch. "Like I said on the phone, I've been researching TMF, and especially Ray Thomas. I figured you could find out more about him since he popped up on a lot of boards of directors that appear to be fronts for Church holdings."

"Fronts?" Frank stiffened.

"Come on, Frank." Peter's vulnerability peeled off. "I don't need to tell you that the Church is very secretive. I tried to find out what its holdings are and I couldn't. Hell, even *Time* magazine had an article about how impossible it is to determine how rich a diocese is. And if it looks like the Church has something to hide, it probably does. I mean, why aren't the Archdiocese's assets transparent? Why can't the average Catholic scroll down the Archdiocese website and see exactly what their spiritual leaders have invested in, what land they own and what businesses they are part of?"

"Well, if you want to be crass, it's because the Archdiocese is an empire worth billions of dollars, and it didn't get that way by letting outsiders decide how it should be run."

"Empire! Outsiders! Jesus, I left corporate life and returned to the Church because I wanted to be part of something that stood for morality and eternal values. I didn't think it was still an empire selling dispensations and salvation like in the Middle Ages."

"Are you so naïve, Peter? It's still about power. I don't need to tell you that everyone, from kings to dissidents, has tried to take down the Roman Catholic Church for 2,000 years. The Church is a survivor, and it must be doing something right, something vital, or it would have disappeared like hundreds of political regimes and religious movements. And it's not just in the past. More religious wars are coming, and we are going to be hit from both sides. One-third of American voters take the Bible literally, including a great number of politicians. These folks think the end of time is prophesized. They usually won't admit it, but they don't give a damn about the long-term future of the earth because they think Jesus is coming. And it's the same or worse in all the other major religions. The Catholic Church has to be tough. It's compromised and imperfect, but it's a beacon of hope and reflective of something humans need, or it wouldn't have lasted all these years."

"I wonder if that isn't just another fantasy."

"What other international organization speaks up for the poor, day in and day out, like the Catholic Church? Who else with our financial clout is spending money, time and energy on the well-being of the disenfranchised throughout the world? You can call it self-serving missionary work, but the truth is that no one else takes on poverty and inequality like we do."

"Okay, you are great social workers."

"More than that. We don't carry the baggage of nationalism or tribalism, and we aren't bogged down in politics like the U.N. We connect directly with people in any country on the basis of need. We may be self-serving as far as building the faith, but we aren't primarily motivated by money or prestige. We simply try to emulate Jesus Christ."

"A beautiful homily." Peter replied. "Really. It's what brought me back to the Church, that and a desire to redeem myself. But we're not talking about Christian charity and good works." Peter leaned forward, "I think that whoever set up Adrian's assassination did it out of greed. And who had something to gain? Well, you for one. You're going to get about $800,000."

Frank gestured helplessly toward Peter in amazement.

"Yes, I know about it. Adrian had a lot of secrets but he also left quite a trail down at the Senior Center. The thing is, I don't think you knew that Adrian had written you into his will until after he died, so you've never been at the top of my list. Then there's Marta. I'm not sure if she knows that she's getting nothing, but I'll bet she thought she had something to gain from Adrian's death at the time." Peter went silent as Frank lowered his head and began shaking. Then Frank reared back into the old cushions and unleashed a torrent of laughter.

"Marta?" he spewed after he caught his breath. "How can you know so much and still be so ignorant? When Marta was little, she wouldn't kill a mosquito even as it sucked on her arm." He laughed again, then turned serious. "Now, if a mosquito were biting her mother or even her father, that was another story."

Peter was chagrined, but was still determined to finish his list of suspects. "Okay, Frank, you had your laugh, and by discounting Marta the focus moves to Ray Thomas. Despite the half-assed investigation by the cops, I figure he had the strongest motive: He was wasting a lot of money because of his 'estate for life' agreement with Adrian. You could help here. He's a bigwig Church supporter. I don't know how that connects, maybe it's irrelevant, but…"

"It is!" Frank interrupted and stood up. "TMF is Ray Thomas, and he is an important Church supporter. So what? I was more shocked than anyone to discover that he bought Adrian's house eleven years ago. I still haven't mentioned it to Ray, because it's embarrassing to me that Adrian left me out of his business dealings. But again, so what? The police investigated and found nothing wrong. Maybe Ray had to wait years to collect, but there's nothing illegal about making 500 percent on an investment. The bottom line is that you have no real evidence connecting Ray Thomas or TMF to this," and he bowed to Peter to give him the benefit of the doubt, "this murder. Nothing, except your…what? Your intuition? Your fanatical desire for revenge for something that has nothing to do with you? I think you've placed yourself as the hero of an imaginary morality play. But there's nothing to be learned here except that life involves suffering."

Peter struggled up from the couch. "You think I'm crazy?"

"No, I think you're trying to forget your own problems." Frank's voice gentled. "I was impressed with your passion and with what I thought was integrity. But it now seems more like you've been obsessed and that you are becoming self-destructive. I told you about TMF at the cemetery a month ago. All you've done, besides spying on my life, is to link TMF to where your supposed killer ran after committing his nefarious deed. Nothing's changed."

"You don't believe that I saw someone push Adrian?"

Frank put his hand on Peter's shoulder. "Actually, I do. But I don't think it was a plot to get his money. It's part of the madness we all live in. There's another person out there in the world with blood on his hands. I don't like it any more than you do, but neither of us can change it. It's humbling, but, then, it takes humility to survive in that radical middle you described."

Peter faltered and Frank continued, "You're a good person, Peter, maybe too good for this world. You're an idealist, and I've seen a number of people like you self-destruct. Fortunately, you have a lot to live for. My advice to you is to forget Adrian and get on with what's right in front of you. Help make your father comfortable. Pay attention to your wife. Enjoy your little girl." He dropped his hand. "And trust in God."

They walked to Peter's car, where Frank hugged him. He watched the dusty green Saab drive slowly away, a look of grim satisfaction on his face. He was exhausted, but he shouldn't have been surprised at what it took to wrestle control over this situation. The Church was a master at offering intimacy while relieving people of their burdens. He'd been real with Peter: imperfect, yet realistic—just what all humans need to see in others in order to trust.

20

Friday, March 11, 2005

TWELVE DAYS LATER, FRANK entered the wood-paneled conference room of Imperial Bank at 11:10 a.m. Five other members of a subcommittee of the Archdiocesan Financial Council were already seated and chatting. "I apologize, gentlemen, for being late."

Dennis Riley waved away the apology. "I don't recall that happening before, Frank. It must be that Monsignor status going to your head." A hint of an Irish brogue crept in, as it did whenever he was kidding or drinking, both of which he did often.

"That's why I enjoy serving on this committee," said Howard Logan. "It gives me a chance to forgive a priest instead of vice versa."

"The difference, Howard, is that all Frank needs forgiveness for is being late. Our sins are far more serious," said Curtis Haynes, the lone African American among this august group of successful businessmen.

"And that's why we are here, gentlemen, to make amends

for our past and to pass along some of our good fortune to the Church," added the chairman, Ray Thomas.

And to receive some good fortune from the Church, Frank thought. Helping to guide the finances of the Archdiocese had been a reciprocal arrangement that had brought great wealth to many Catholic-run companies in Los Angeles for more than a hundred years. From the beginning, knowing where schools and churches were to be built meant more than simply getting the contracts for building them. It also gave a heads-up to these businessmen and their predecessors as to where development was going, giving them plenty of opportunities to pick up the surrounding land cheaply, as Los Angeles spread out from its original sleepy mission. At the same time, these men and their fathers, cousins and friends before them, gave the Church the benefit of their knowledge so that the Church had become one of the biggest property owners in the county. And it was all tax-free. Frank was aware that many people estimated that it was also the wealthiest institution, except for the government itself, in California, if not the whole United States. Nobody knew for sure, except the Cardinals and Bishops themselves and their financial advisors like him.

After Frank took his seat, Ray Thomas focused them with smooth efficiency on the list of items that they had to consider that month. There was nothing particularly thorny to deal with, nothing to compare with the arm-twisting and out-and-out threats that had marked the fundraising for the new cathedral several years before. In fifteen minutes, the meeting was over, and Dennis Riley, the bank president, pressed a hidden button. A solemn Filipino bartender slipped into the room and exposed a full wet bar from behind two sliding inlaid rosewood panels. He began taking orders for drinks as he handed the men their menu for the lunch that would be brought up from the elegant restaurant downstairs.

Frank sat back with his diet soda, reduced to an outsider in this group of hardy drinkers as a result of his ongoing effort to maintain his weight loss. Still, he loved his job of overseeing the investments, real estate and general financial well-being of this soul-saving enterprise. There was no way an impoverished institution could successfully represent the interests of the poor. One had to align with the powerful in order to wield power, just as one had to be at ease with great wealth in order to defend the Church's spiritual mission.

"So, Monsignor, how is life as a thin man?" Howard Logan turned to him with an affable smile and blotchy red skin glowing from his first scotch.

"I wouldn't be honest if I said it was easy, but…"

"I lost a lot of weight when I was about your age. You're forty-six?"

"Forty-nine."

"Right. It was after a small heart attack, and the doctors took away damn near every pleasure I had. Scared the bejesus out of me is what they did. In fact, I think it was about then that I finally got religion." Howard Logan laughed heartily and took a sip. "Shortly after that, I donated that new gymnasium to St. Benevides, and then Sally and I chaired the annual campaign a few years later."

Frank nodded. He knew all this only too well, but, like most men, Howard needed to talk about himself. It was what passed for conversation.

"Anyway, they let me have a few drinks now, twenty years later. I guess they figure it's going to take more than that to kill me." Howard laughed and turned to get the attention of the bartender for his second and last permitted drink.

"Ray, I hear your TMF group is ready to break ground on those condos in Santa Monica." Kevin Gardner, the most recent addition to the committee, addressed the dapper chairman.

"Well, it's a bit more complicated than that, Kevin," Ray said. "We've finally got the land. Now, we just have to help some of the local do-gooders see that just because a house is old and run-down doesn't mean it's a landmark or of historical significance. Hell, if getting old were what it took to be valuable, then we'd all be national treasures. Except for you and the Monsignor, or course. You both need a few decades of aging." The others had stopped their chitchat while the senior member of the group answered, and now they laughed.

"What took so long for you to get going on that property, anyway, Ray?" Howard asked.

Ray Thomas surveyed the eager listeners before him and, seduced by an opportunity to self-effacingly demonstrate his cleverness, began to speak. "Well, gentlemen, I made an arrangement that I had never done before and never will again. I'll tell you only to warn you away from any such foolishness. I bought that spot in 1994. The owner demanded cash up front plus he wanted to live out his days there. He wanted nothing to do with a reverse mortgage. My wife, bless her foolish heart, told me it was common in France—*un viager*, they call it—and my people here said it's not unheard of in the States. At the time, the owner had all sorts of ailments and wasn't expected to live for more than a year. But that SOB pulled off the longest damn recovery I've ever seen. I'll tell you, it really started to get under my craw."

Frank stared out of the windows at the view of Mount Baldy to the east as an acid reflux seared his throat. He was used to keeping secrets about his sexuality and the Church's money, but he had never suspected that hiding his family history would complicate his work relations.

"So, how'd you handle it?" Kevin Gardner asked eagerly.

Ray Thomas looked over his glasses, and with perfect comic timing, cracked, "Why, I had him bumped off, what do you think?"

The other men in the room erupted into laughter, but Frank was stunned. He knew Ray Thomas' sense of humor. It was always self-serving. As he had often admitted, Ray enjoyed fucking with people's minds. But he was telling the truth. The joke was that the truth was so outrageous that no one believed it.

Howard turned to Kevin and cracked, "Ray got a MBA from the IRA."

"Really, Ray," Kevin continued, "how did you make the guy go away?" Frank struggled with a wave of nausea even as he silently blessed Kevin for being so persistent.

"It's hard not to take it personally when someone is causing you to lose money." Ray scrutinized the new man. "I stewed over the wait, all the while trying to keep my banker happy." He nodded to Dennis Riley. "Finally, my prayers were answered. The old bastard staggered off the curb into the path of a city bus." His piercing blue eyes shined, and he chuckled.

"Seriously, the guy got killed?" Kevin asked.

"It was tragic, of course." Ray Thomas dropped his smile, though he couldn't stop adding, "But merde happens."

Frank breathed deeply and tried to calm down by imagining himself as a child in a safe place. To his horror, the image that sprang to mind was his old favorite hideout, the room at the Camera Obscura.

"Imperial Bank discounted the loan on it as long as we could, but I told Ray in the fall that we could hold on only until the spring," said Dennis Riley, the president. He toasted Ray Thomas. "He got lucky."

Ray Thomas raised his glass. "Luck of the Irish, Dennis. Never bet against it."

Howard Logan took a drink. "I trust you had a Mass said for the poor fellow, Ray."

"Of course, Howard. I underwrote a whole week of them at our lovely new cathedral."

Frank bolted halfway out the door before he threw up. Ashen-faced, he apologized profusely and assured them he could make it home on his own is spite of the sudden onset of what he insisted was no more than a nasty stomach flu.

As soon as he got to the privacy of his car, Frank left an urgent yet vague message on Peter's answering machine. He was too shaky to tackle the freeways, so he drove home via Wilshire Boulevard to wait for Peter's call. He vacillated between a zealous desire for justice and a cold fear of the ramifications of this situation. To focus himself, he set about reviewing Adrian's papers pertaining to his deal with Ray Thomas. He wanted to find a way to break their arrangement, but he found nothing except his stepfather's notes bragging that he'd got exactly what he wanted.

Marta left a message, wanting to talk about becoming a cloistered nun. She wanted to bow out of this world. He thought she was suicidal, constrained only because it was a mortal sin. But Peter didn't call. Exhausted, Frank finally phoned Sal to say he had had some important business come up and he wouldn't be back that night. Sal had no way to help with this problem. He was a simple man with an uncomplicated life. Frank had to protect him and the haven they had created together.

He dozed on the couch all night in a restless, apprehensive slumber. The sound of his front-door handle rattling woke him. He glanced at his wristwatch as his eyes opened. It was a little before 6 A.M. It was just like Peter to show up unannounced. Frank sat up, trying to decide how he would get Peter back into his obsessive private-eye mode without having to reveal any more about his connection with Ray. He rubbed his face. What if Ray was really speaking metaphorically yesterday? What if it was simply bad taste instead of murder? Frank cleared his throat as he stood. His gut knew that Ray hadn't been joking, even though he had been laughing. Frank opened his front door as the knocking got louder.

An irritatingly dry, warm morning breeze blew into the room from the desert a hundred miles away. In the doorway, back-lit by the rising sun, was Ray Thomas.

"I hope I'm not disturbing you, Father."

"What are you doing here?" Frank burst out.

Ray stepped in, forcing Frank to back up. "I was concerned about your health, Frank. Your illness seemed to come on so suddenly that I was forced to consider that it was related to something I had said."

Frank backed farther away, struck dumb at the brazenness of this man. The harsh light of the dawn turned the edges of Ray's cashmere sports coat translucent, like the shell of a giant scorpion.

Ray closed the door. "So I decided to do a little research into your family history. As you know, Father, I always do that with anyone I have business with. It's good to know whom one is dealing with, but, and here's the lesson for me, I never looked up your background." Ray casually looked around the small, modest room. Cold, blue eyes turned back to Frank. "I suppose it's a result of never having had reason to distrust you. Or, perhaps, it's a feeling I've had since I was a kid that once a person works for the Church, they cease to have a personal history. Blind faith, I suppose. Maybe there's no other kind. But then to find out that you, someone I considered a friend and one of my closest business advisors, had been raised by a man that I had done business with. I was appalled that I had missed the connection. To be honest, Frank, I was surprised you never told me."

Frank wavered, lightheadedness threatening him.

"I would have thought that you'd have been tickled at the connection. You know, helping each other out with a mutually advantageous arrangement like one big Christian family. I'll tell you, I feel tricked." Ray leaned over and picked up Adrian's copy of the contract from the coffee table. "I can't believe that you didn't know about this. Unless, of course, you want me to believe that your stepfather never told you about our arrangement. That doesn't speak well for your family relations, now does it?" He tossed the contract back. "Not that it will cause us any problem.

The police have looked into it and couldn't find any evidence of wrongdoing. Which is good for all of us, because you can imagine how upset the DA would be if something were to force me to reveal the undeclared millions you've collected for arranging loans between all sorts of unsavory characters. And, my dear friend, you better believe it would become a bargaining chip if I thought I were at risk of going to jail."

"You have just as much to lose in this as we do, Ray."

"More, I would say, when you include what happened to Mr. Montero. But we are getting ahead of ourselves. I'm a businessman, not a martyr."

Frank clenched and unclenched his fists until, in a low, hateful voice, he swore, "May God have mercy on your soul."

"Well, Father, God and I have a complicated relationship, but on balance I think He will forgive me my sins in exchange for extending His domain here on earth."

"You are evil," Frank sputtered.

Ray grimaced, then looked at Frank with mock compassion. "That's the problem right there, Monsignor. Up to this point, you've been quite willing to pimp loans for people who had, shall we say, a spotty credit history and take your finder's fee to build up your war chest so you can fend off angry parishioners and anybody else. We've all benefited tremendously from the many years of cleaning up my people's money. But I was afraid that you wouldn't be able to see the big picture in this situation. That's why I rushed over this morning before you did anything rash." He walked about the living room, looking around. "I understand your anger, I really do. If I had known your involvement, I would never have resolved my problem in the way I did. Or had my little fun at the meeting yesterday. I'll admit it, Father, I was showing off, trying to see how much I could reveal without revealing anything." He stood in front of Frank. "We both enjoy risk-taking, that's obvious from our mutual activities. But I got cocky, and you had a secret, and that threw us both off."

Frank wanted to attack the smug, tanned face, to shut him up so he could think. "Get out, Ray," he blurted, "or I'll call the police right now." Frank grabbed the phone and jabbed 911.

"Well, that's one thing cleared up. That means you haven't called them already. That's good, Frank, that's very good. Now think about it again. What could you tell them that would cause them to haul me away? That I made a tasteless joke at lunch that made you sick? All you have is a hunch. The only thing telling the cops would do is to create an exceptionally damaging situation. Let's be clear, Monsignor: Most of the money that you've helped disperse wasn't just dirty, it was filthy. It wouldn't look good if a drug-money-laundering charge ended up on the desk of the Cardinal or, dare I say it, the Pope. Neither of us wants to cause harm to the Church, now do we?"

Frank went over to the couch to get away from Ray Thomas, who continued unabashed, "Still, Frank, I was afraid you'd try to do something about this, even if you could never prove it. So I've decided to ask for your forgiveness."

"What?" Frank gasped and sat on the couch.

Ray Thomas approached and grabbed the arm of the couch. He lowered himself gingerly to one knee and crossed himself. "Forgive me, Father, for I have sinned. This is my first confession in a long time, and I'm afraid I have to tell you that I had your stepfather killed."

Frank looked at him in horror as the operator answered.

"Believe me, I'm willing to do a considerable penance, but you have to realize, as I'm sure you do, that you can't tell anyone now. What I've told you comes under the Holy Seal."

Frank dropped the cordless phone as the operator's voice poured out of the receiver, "Hello, hello?! Is someone there? This is the emergency operator." Ray Thomas reached over and pushed the "off" button as Frank rolled from the couch onto the floor.

Frank began to shake, and his eyes rotated up into his head. Ray Thomas' lips puckered in concern. "Epilepsy. That was another surprise that I found out about you. I didn't have time to discover how dangerous these fits can be." He watched Frank for a few moments dispassionately. "You're the expert in this, but it seems to me that God's will is being expressed here. It might be easier if He took you right now. It would be much better than both of us having to count on your ethical restraints. Let's face it, if you live, your life will be hell. However," he took out his handkerchief and wiped off the phone and the bamboo arm of the couch that he had touched, "you know me. Whatever happens to you won't be by my hand directly." He stood and stepped around Frank, whose eyes were closed and was still except for an occasional shudder. Methodically, Ray looked into the other rooms of the house. He returned to the shallowly breathing form on the carpet.

"Frank, if you're able to hear me, I want you to know that I was planning to give another big donation in the next year or two, you know, a few million that would put my name on a new gymnasium, something like that. But that would just add to the zillions of dollars' worth of unproductive properties you've already got, and I know you need cash. So I've come up with a better idea, a real act of contrition, because I really do feel badly about this mess we're in. I'll give the Archdiocese the condominium complex I'm planning for the Montero place. It works out for everyone. My company builds it, and then we set up a board of directors to run it for you. It'll provide a fabulous, ongoing source of new revenue for the Church that is invisible." He went to a window and looked out onto the empty street. "Of course, you know how this works. You and I have set up the Archdiocese as a silent partner in innumerable businesses since you've been in L.A." He moved to the door. "It's a great idea. Everybody wins, and we can put this unfortunate situation behind us." Using his handkerchief, he let himself out.

Inside the house, there was no movement for over twenty minutes, until Frank's eyes started to blink. Not far from his head was a low, open window. He looked out onto a patio with a small fountain and a statue of St. Francis. He lay quietly, hoping his body wouldn't short-circuit again.

Hummingbirds, robins and sparrows came to drink and frolic under the water dripping from St. Francis' hand. A lightheadedness, or aura, as he called it, hovered in his mind, letting him know that he was still vulnerable to another seizure. There was nothing transcendent about this kind. It was a "grand mal," the sort he'd been plagued with all his life.

Lying there motionless, he reconsidered keeping his inheritance and leaving the priesthood. But if he tried to step outside the institution, he became as big a threat as Ray was. He knew too much. Even if he vowed to keep it secret, the Church would never let him fade away. He would suffer the same fate as others who, over the centuries, had insider knowledge and had tried to disappear.

An upwelling of vindictive righteousness flooded him. The thought of revenge was satisfying until, in the quiet, he found himself agreeing with Ray. Even if he had convincing evidence that proved Ray's guilt, a murder trial would bring major embarrassment for the Church, and Ray would implicate him in their financial dealings. If that happened, Frank could end up in prison. The thought frightened him, but he told himself that it might be a relief, a way to leave this worldly path and live like a monk. After all, there was a long line of religious people who had gone to jail for the greater good. He thought himself a most unlikely martyr, but if that was what was called for, he was ready. Nonetheless, his problem was minor compared with what would happen if the Archdiocese had to reveal its financial workings: stock holdings, secret partnerships, interconnecting boards of directors. The Church would survive it—it always did—but the wealth of the Church would be exposed to the wolves that were always circling, hoping to bring it down and get rich. Those who had suffered sexual abuse were only the most recent chapter. Ray Thomas' greed and impatience could imperil God's domain. He had to be made to pay for his murderous arrogance without bringing in the police. But how?

The aura darkened once again, and Frank slipped back into unconsciousness.

21

Sunday, March 20, 2005

Peter watched as Judith approached their bed with two glasses of water. She offered him one, but instead of taking it, he rose up on his elbow, dipped three fingers in the water and sprinkled a few drops on her bare breasts. Her nipples hardened, and she sipped from a glass as he caught a rivulet crossing her stomach with his tongue.

"I can't remember why we haven't had sex every day of our lives together," he declared into her navel. She gingerly placed the glasses on the bed stand and knelt on the mattress, pressing into him.

"You were an idiot," she said with a quick inhale. He mumbled his agreement as he licked and nibbled his way slowly down to the inside of her thigh. Playfully, she pushed him onto his back, swung her leg over his head and lowered her clitoris near his face, bobbing in and out of range of his outstretched tongue. With a groan of satisfaction, she bent forward and took the tip of his erection into her mouth.

"You've been fucking someone," she giggled. "Good thing I

like her taste."

"Hey, look, there's a pussy in my face," he laughed. They fell silent, their breathing becoming rapid and irregular as the tension between giving and receiving increased. The sensations competed until Judith abruptly lifted herself up, spun around and flopped down next to him head to head. "I think 69 is a guy thing. It's too distracting for me."

"I'd be more than happy to settle for half of 69," Peter smiled. "Either half."

"Let's save it for a while." She saw the disappointment in his eyes, reached down, gave his rigid prick a gentle squeeze and added, "A little while." She untangled the sheet and pulled it over her shoulders.

Snuggling as their tumescence slowly deflated, they looked out through the orange bougainvillea that draped the door to the back garden.

"I want to hear more about what happened with Dr. Reed."

"You like my revelations?"

"I like what's happened: A priest tells you to pay attention to your wife; we finally went to see a therapist; the therapist wanted to see you alone, and he seems to have released you from your obsession."

"Now you are my obsession," he said, nuzzling her ear. "When did you say we had to pick up Sam at her little sleepover?"

"This afternoon," she said, shrugging him away from her neck, "and don't call me that, even in fun."

"You're right," he said, sitting up.

"So how did Doctor Reed help you deal with your issues surrounding Adrian Montero?"

"My issues?" Peter hesitated, then plunged ahead. "Okay, we've met four times, and yesterday afternoon we sort of struck gold. He must have sensed it was close to the surface, because he taped the session. He said I might not be able to recall all the points, and having a record would—how did he say it? Oh, yeah—'help me to reconstruct the narrative of my life.'" Peter got out of bed and walked naked to his home office, returning with a CD. "Doctor Reed is high-tech. He recorded us on his computer and gave me this CD." He put it into their sound system. "This is the second half of yesterday, when things really got heavy."

A gentle male voice filled the bedroom. "Peter, you told me earlier that you felt angry when your mom died. Can you remember how that felt now?"

"Sure."

"Where in your body do you feel it?"

"My shoulders. My jaw. My stomach just started churning."

"Who and what were you angry at?"

"The stupid fuck who was speeding down Federal Avenue and hit her." After a silence, Peter's disconnected voice continued, "She wasn't paying attention. She walked in front of a green pickup truck...an old Dodge. Bam!" He moaned as tears flooded his voice. "The side-view mirror hit her head...severed her brain stem."

"Who else were you angry at?"

"The ambulance driver who took all day, the hospital, the doctors."

"Who else?"

"My dad, a little. But it never made any sense to be mad at him. He wasn't there."

"Were you?"

"No. We'd been arguing. I wanted to go to an unchaperoned party. I didn't want to go on some stupid errand. She was dropping off a tuna casserole to a sick friend." The voice was quiet for a moment, then fired up, "I was mad at my mom—I still am—for being such a space cadet. Fuck! Is that what you wanted to hear?"

"When you think about your mom's death, you get mad at everyone, even me." There was a strained silence. "Anger is a normal reaction, but it can also be a defense."

"Against what?"

"That's what we're trying to find out. Who else were you mad at?"

"God, for a long, long time. I still am, at least the all-perfect, all-powerful God of my childhood."

"Who else?"

"I told myself it wasn't true," the voice continued reluctantly, "but I kept thinking I fucked up, that I could have done something."

Peter sat down on the bed, shaking slightly. He wrapped himself in a blanket as the sound of his own crying came from the speakers.

"Behind that anger is guilt," the therapist said after a while.

Peter's voice bubbled up through the sound of crying, "I'm Catholic, Doc." There was an attempt to laugh, but it was taken over by sobbing for nearly a minute.

"And behind the guilt there is tremendous grief."

There was the sound of nose-blowing. "I guess I've saved it since the funeral, because I didn't cry then. I remember my dad gave me one of his handkerchiefs, but I refused to use it. I thought I should be happy because she was going to heaven."

"Your guilt stopped you from the most natural feeling of all, mourning your mother," the therapist explained.

The sound of yesterday's tears continued, and Judith crawled behind Peter and held him as he cried again.

On the tape, Peter quieted and the therapist asked, "What part does guilt have in the Montero incident?"

Judith and Peter both looked up, waiting for the answer.

"Huge. I've been plagued with the feeling that I could have prevented it. I still feel that way, only I'm forcing myself to stop because it's destroying me."

"What does it feel like when you imagine not being responsible for either your mother or Montero?"

A shaky groan filled the room. "Terrifying. It's like the whole world will come apart, and evil will reign." Peter muttered, "Fuck, fuck, fuck," over and over.

"Stay with it, Peter," the therapist said.

"Evil is what my mother really believed in. She tried to make it sound like she was invoking God's love in her prayers, but to me it felt like she was stuck in a horror movie crying for help. Evil was everywhere, and I had to figure our way out."

Peter sat on the bed listening to himself, his head bobbing up and down in agreement, wrapping the blanket tighter and tighter and nestling into Judith.

"She'd get all airy-fairy mystical and positive and full of love to try to balance it out, but it all served to cover up how terrified she was."

"And you?"

"I was the perfect son, except a little manic...or really pissed."

"You thought you were the only thing standing in the way of your mother's chaos."

"Fuck, yes!" Peter blurted from the CD, but on the bed he slowly shook his head, saddened by his own angry response.

"There's the loop. Anger saves you from the fear, from guilt and from feeling helpless and scared."

There was a long silence until Peter said, "I was angry at my mom even before she got killed. I was planning how I was going to get away and make a lot of money so I'd never have to be trapped again...or scared."

"Can you see how avoiding feeling the fear has created this loop so that you never get out of feeling responsible?"

"Sort of."

"Unconsciously, people re-create situations from childhood looking for new answers to their old dilemmas. But without being able to admit the real feelings surrounding the original trauma, it's nearly impossible to arrive at a new place. So they— you—are stuck in an emotional loop. Why do you think you've been so obsessed by the Montero death?"

"'Cause it's not right for some asshole to get away with it."

"That's the anger part. What's the fear?"

"I'm afraid that if some asshole gets away with it that evil will reign and things will be chaotic…the same fear my mom had."

"And just because you're afraid of something doesn't make it true or inevitable, even if it feels that way."

"Wow!" Peter said after a few moments.

"Wow what?" Dr. Reed asked.

"Wow, it's not my fault she died, even though I was angry with her sometimes, even hated her. And, wow, even though she didn't tell me so directly, I really bought that I was responsible for our salvation."

"I'm curious. Your mother never taught you about forgiveness and redemption?"

"Sure she did. But all that was dessert to help us live with our guilt over our weak nature and our fear of hell. The real meat of the matter had to do with original sin and the devil. That's what she grew up on, and that's what she fed me. Dammit," Peter growled. "The God that she and the priests were teaching about exists because of their fear of Satan. One creates the other and teaching that to little kids is child abuse, emotional child abuse. I've got to get on top of this before I terrorize Samantha with the same twisted craziness."

After a period of silence, the therapist asked, "How are you feeling now?"

"Relieved," Peter answered quietly, "and exhausted."

"I'd say we're done for today."

"Wow is right," Judith said as she got up and turned it off. "Thank you for letting me hear that." She returned to their bed and kissed him.

He started to respond, then interrupted their kiss and rolled out of bed. "I need a couple minutes, okay? But don't go anywhere." Judith nodded sweetly.

Naked, Peter stepped out a door into a small garden off their bedroom and paused on the dew-covered grass. Beneath him, the cool earth felt firm yet yielding. Around him were blooming ranunculi: blood red, peach and velvety white that had recently erupted. He knelt down on his hands and knees and observed them. In time, a wave of euphoria swept gently over him, and he became aware that his mind wasn't interrupting his own pleasure. The harangue of voices, demands, obligations and guilt was silent. He hadn't trusted the silence yesterday, in therapy. He didn't trust that the ghosts in his psyche or ego or whatever it was would leave him alone, but reliving it just now had given him the same release. A welling-up of relief and gratitude brought him to his feet. He returned to the bed and snuggled up to Judith.

"Better?" she asked.

"Much," he said. "It's strange, but whenever I considered why I was so caught up with Montero, I never thought it had anything to do with my mom. If anything, I thought it was connected to my dad." He looked into Judith's loving gaze, reluctant to bring up something that was sure to break the mood. To his relief, she slowly dropped from view, licking her way down his body. "Oh, boy!" he exhaled. "Thirty-four and a half."

22

FRIDAY, MARCH 25, 2005

PETER LAY SWEATING ON the floor of an aerobics studio, euphoric, endorphins flooding his brain. Working out nearly every day since his experience in Ojai was starting to pay off. Between exercise and therapy, he was starting to find some joy in life, until he thought of Martin. It was tempting to ignore him since no one else thought he was in dire straits. Judith accepted Martin's situation and wanted to make his care part of their lives. She had urged Peter to visit his dad after the gym. Peter's glow dissolved. He might be able to live with this situation if he avoided it, but he couldn't face his dad, or what was left of him. The last place in the world he wanted to go was that nursing home.

The good news was that he was no longer obsessed with Montero, even though Frank had been calling for nearly two weeks. Peter had ignored him, but the priest's messages had only become more and more insistent and urgent without saying exactly what he wanted. When Peter had finally called him back two days ago, Frank seemed desperate for Peter's help in tracking down Mad Max. He said that even with the current scandal, the Archdiocese had enough pull with the DA that he would be able to keep Max out of jail if he would testify against whoever set up the murder. Frank couldn't really explain what had caused his change of heart, except what Peter had insisted all along; it was the right thing to do. Peter had put him off. He didn't tell Judith or his therapist about the call. He just sat with it. The offer was intriguing. If he was no longer alone in pursing this, it no longer felt like a compulsion. It was just the right thing to do.

Sitting in the steam room, he remembered it was Good Friday. All he could think about was that Christ had died for his principles over 2,000 years earlier. What was he going to do about his? Unable to ignore his question, especially on this day, he drove to the Senior Center. The same mixture of tourists, elderly and homeless roamed the long, narrow park. It was a gorgeous, sunny day, just like the day of the murder eight weeks before. At the desk a pleasant woman said that he didn't need the key as people were already in the Camera Obscura. He took the stairs and knocked on the door. It was opened by a man who was leaving. In the darkened room, he saw five young teenagers noisily pointing things out to one another as a thin Asian girl with spiked purple hair turned the wheel slowly. They were tripping on the passing panorama laid out before them. The boys' jokes and comments to the girls became more suggestive, and the girls teased back. Peter smiled, quite used to this verbal dance of hormones. In the glow from the table, Peter could see an older couple on the other side of the room. They were less than charmed by the sexy banter of the teenagers and started to leave. The view toward the bus stop came around slowly. And there, standing motionless at the edge of the scene, was Mad Max. "Stop!" Peter yelled and pushed through two boys to the Asian girl. He grabbed the wheel and turned it back until Max reappeared.

A mumbling chorus of "Hey, dude, watch out!," "Aw, shit!"

and "Fuckin' punk!" greeted his move. At the same time, the visiting couple opened the door to get out of the threatening environment.

Without looking away from the table, Peter yelled, "Shut that goddamn door!," which blew out the couple and set off laughter and more complaints from the teenagers. Back in darkness, Peter barked to the kids, "Chill the fuck out." This was received with sullen silence. Peter observed as Max stared toward the bus stop, nodding his head rhythmically. Mesmerized, Peter watched Max for nearly half a minute. The teenagers clumped together, whispering and giggling. When Max turned around and sauntered back into the park, Peter followed him with the wheel until Max walked out of the range of the mirror at the top of the Camera Obscura. Strangely calm, Peter looked around at the kids. "The patient man is rewarded," he pronounced.

Peter raced down the stairs, but came out of the center slowly, methodically. Max was leaning against a palm tree. Though Peter tried to approach nonchalantly, when he was twenty feet away Max noticed him and came out of his reverie. Max started to backpedal. Peter called to him as calmly as he could, "I need to talk to you." Without hesitation, Max turned and ran. Peter took off after him. Max dodged two homeless women lying on the grass, and within four strides, he was faced with a three-foot wire fence with a sign on it, "Shuffleboard Center—Seniors Only." He leapt the fence and ran through the shuffleboard game. Elderly gentlemen dressed in white developed florid faces as they shouted at the discourteous scoundrel who had broken the carefully observed boundaries in the park. Peter immediately followed, shouting, "Wait! Stop!" In a flash, they both vaulted the fence on the other side and raced up the path on the edge of the palisades.

Max turned to see Peter not far behind him and leapt a concrete barrier with a "Danger" sign on it. He pushed his way through some bushes and tried to pick his way down the extremely steep face of the cliff, struggling not to fall. Peter followed and found himself looking at Max's back only five feet below him, but sliding away quickly. He hesitated for a split second, then jumped. He landed on Max, slamming him hard into the cliff. As Peter tumbled past, he grabbed Max's shirt, and in a scrambled, head-over-heels ball, the two of them rolled and slid for sixty feet down the cliff.

Max landed on top and started to get up. He immediately screamed and crumpled to the ground, cradling a dislocated shoulder. Peter stood, badly scraped and covered with dirt, but not seriously hurt. He looked around him. They had landed among the debris at the base of two giant date palms growing at the bottom of the cliff. They were only about thirty feet from Pacific Coast Highway, but a thick tangle of vines and shrubs blocked them from the motorists whizzing by. He looked up and saw a canopy of green palm fronds obstructing the view of anyone on the cliff trying to see what was going on below. Shakily standing over Max, Peter caught his breath and exclaimed, "Okay, now you're going to tell me a few things."

"Who the fuck are you?" Max stammered.

"Why were you at that bus stop just now?"

"What the fuck are you talking about? Hey, dude, you fucked up my shoulder." He scowled at Peter, his face contorted with pain and fear.

Peter pushed his shoulder a little and demanded, "Answer me!" as Max cried out.

Gritting his teeth, Max moaned, "I wasn't doing shit until you started chasing me."

"I was chasing you 'cause you were running away. Why were you running away?"

Max winced and said nothing.

Looking into Max's eyes, Peter hissed, "What happened at that bus stop?"

Max's eyes widened. "Nothin'."

"It was eight weeks ago tomorrow," Peter insisted and tapped his shoulder lightly.

Max grimaced silently.

"Tell me, you son of a bitch. I already know, but I want you to tell me." After no response, Peter pushed him on the shoulder again, harder.

Max cried out, "If you know, why do you need me to tell you?" He looked away and, with his good arm, grabbed a broken bottle lying in the dirt next to him. He flung it and hit Peter on the forehead. As Peter grabbed his head, he fell forward on top of Max. Max screamed in pain and then passed out. Peter lay on top of him holding his head, his hand getting wet with his own blood. He couldn't tell how much of a cut he had. He lifted himself off Max and knelt next to him. Max began to stir. His eyes opened as blood dripped on his shirt from Peter's forehead.

Peter glared into Max's eyes pinched with pain. "I saw you push that old man into the bus. I want to know why, and you're going to tell me."

Fear intruded into Max's pain.

Peter pressed his cut with one hand, and his voice softened. "You're not so tough. You feel guilty. That's why you came back to the bus stop. I knew you would."

"You a cop?"

"No, I'm a crazy fucker who's been waiting for you for almost two months, and now I've finally got you."

Swearing under his breath, Max finally gave in. "Some guy paid me to do it."

Peter felt lightheaded with victory. "Who?"

Max hesitated until Peter pointed at his shoulder again. "We didn't exchange names, man. Some construction guy who was letting me do some clean-up work around there." Max whimpered and looked away.

"Why did they want him killed?" Peter continued.

"How the fuck should I know?" He paused, then added in a low, scratchy voice, "He was just an old man. I watched him for a couple days. He could hardly get around. He was gonna die pretty soon. I figured I was doing him a favor."

"How much was this old man's life worth?" Peter demanded.

"Five thousand dollars." He lifted his head and looked at Peter earnestly. "That was the only reason I did it. I needed some money so I could get myself together." He moaned with pain.

Peter stood and stepped back a foot. "Come on."

Max looked at him, fear amplifying the pain. "Where?"

"To the police."

"You're fuckin' insane, dude!" Max spat out.

"Come on," Peter shouted, moving closer.

"You can jump all over me, but there's no way I'm gonna tell this shit to a cop." He looked at Peter defiantly.

Peter blinked, trying to stop the blood dripping into his eye. He pressed his forehead with his fingers, suddenly unsure.

"You can't prove shit!" Max's eyes brightened as he watched Peter wilt. "And I ain't gonna do time for this."

Peter stared sullenly at him from one eye. "How could you cold-bloodedly push someone you didn't even know in front of a bus?"

He sneered at Peter with a nonchalant arrogance. "It wasn't hard, once I decided to do it. Like I said, he was old. Besides, it's hardly anything worse than what's been done to me."

Peter looked away from Max.

"A guy like you couldn't understand that."

"What do you mean, a guy like me?"

"You look like you always had it pretty easy."

Peter picked up the broken bottle that Max had thrown and jabbed it toward him. "You piece of shit!"

Max stared at him without blinking. "See how easy it is."

Trembling, Peter threw the glass away. "It's easy to want to.

Doing it is something else." Their eyes locked again in mutual loathing. "Who in the hell are you?"

The man remained silent, but his eyes now had a thin veneer of arrogance, made cocky by winning the last verbal joust.

"I've been calling you Mad Max, but that's wrong 'cause he was actually trying to do good. You're just scum."

"And it's assholes like you who think they know everything and stick their noses into other people's shit."

Peter shifted his weight, ready to kick Max.

"Fuck you," he swore as he propped himself up on his good elbow and answered. "My name is Louis Diggs, with two 'g's.'"

"From?"

"Brattleboro, Vermont. 129 Crescent Street."

They looked up as horns blared and tires squealed on the highway, but the accident was averted. "I know you, Louis. You're some kind of mean, but you're not really a killer. I've known it since I saw you do it. I knew you'd return to where you killed Adrian Montero because you felt guilty."

The man scowled and hung his head.

"What?" Peter demanded.

"He never had a name before."

"And kids." Louis swore quietly and looked up as Peter continued. "His stepson wants to help you if you're willing to finger the guy who paid you."

"And then what? Let the guy who killed his dad go free? You're fuckin' nuts."

"He's a priest."

A glimmer of hope crossed Louis' frowning face, but he dismissed it. "He'd have to be a fuckin' saint, man!"

"He's not, not by a long shot. But, fortunately for you, he's a man with a lot of powerful contacts. He'll get an attorney to plea bargain with the cops for you. He thinks you'll probably get immunity for giving evidence. You get to do the right thing." He paused. "We all do."

"Fuck you!" Louis struggled to his feet, wincing, his left arm hanging uselessly. "I like my chances better out here on my own."

"Listen, asshole, you don't seem to understand. I described you to the police the day you killed Adrian. Right down to your big Adam's apple and your loopy way of walking. I told them where you ran after you did it. There are people on that bus and in that building who will remember your ugly face once they see you in a lineup." He reached to his hip and pulled out his new cell phone from its case. "I've got both Sergeant Jones and Monsignor Greening on my speed dial. Who do I call?"

23

Continuing: Friday, March 25, 2005

A N ARIA SERENADED MARTA through the headset of her portable CD player:
"Marta, Capuchina d'Oro
Marta, en jardin bella rosa"
Halfheartedly, she mouthed the words as she splashed through the diaphanous skin of water spread across the wide, glittering beach. The fluid sand was a tapestry of pink as it reflected the flaming clouds in the sky above her, but she didn't see. She came to a halt. What had once been her favorite piece of music was a concentration of falsehoods. She wasn't a cup of gold in a beautiful garden. She was a lost soul unreachable by the beauty or grace of God. She stopped and yanked the earphones from her head. She grabbed her CD player from her waist and strode into the numbing water, not caring about her wet shoes, and flung all of it into the waves. She trudged back to the flat, wet sand and continued along the ocean, glancing up at the sunset throbbing on the horizon with a look of grim satisfaction.

God always tested her. He'd give her things and she'd fall

in love with them, but eventually she had to give them up. Big things like her mother and the garden, but little things, too, like music. She believed that she was being led to God by giving up more and more worldly pleasures. Besides, this was the day of Jesus' greatest sacrifice. The Catholic part of her accepted that salvation was all about renunciation, and that fit nicely with her native instinct to live lightly on the earth.

She relaxed her stride and looked up again at God's rosy complexion. For many years, she had allowed herself the ritual of watching the sun go to its watery grave at low tide. It was a vital part of staying in contact with Pachamama and the wilderness of the ocean. She was paying attention to God Himself and to His reminder to live in beauty. She didn't think she was supposed to give this up.

The whole ocean was retracting as far as it could, draining the beach into a stage for this recurring natural drama. All the fluids in her body seemed to react. Her whole being was drawn back, concentrated, in communion with God's work. It was like her period, only it wasn't painful; there were no cramps in paradise. For years, this walk along the beach to see the sunset at the time of the full moon and low tide had been a special indulgence. In winter she'd left work early to get to the beach and still get home in time to have her father's dinner on the table at 6:15. She felt a yearning for the predictability of those days, and told herself she mustn't live in the past.

The top of the full moon mushroomed up from the eastern skyline. Marta thrust her arms out and spun. She was home, in the center of the universe. Arms outstretched, her left hand now lifted the glowing yellow moon as her right hand pushed the flaming sun under the sea.

A crowd of sandpipers scurried after the receding water like wind-up toys, poking the wet sand for their food. Marta spun again and followed after them. There was no one to cook for, and there was no boss to make excuses to. After several lapses on her part, her boss had talked her into taking a leave of absence "to deal with her family tragedy." They tried to make it sound like a temporary change, but Marta was sure they wished she would leave for good. She was different. She had no ambition. She defied categories. She'd never married, but she wasn't a lesbian. She'd lived at home, yet she'd worked all her life. She could be pleasant enough, but she never had many friends and never married. She never had a "liberation" like other women of her generation. The feminist revolution had passed her by as she was caring for her dying mother, looking after her father, making a living and leading a moral life. She was born, and remained, old-fashioned.

With the sun gone, the pinks in the clouds were mixing with streaks of chartreuse and turning to purple. The light was slowly being extinguished as the tide hovered and the opaque waters prepared to creep back onto the land. She was afraid of walking on the beach after dark. Most everyone was, or should have been. Marta reversed direction and began to walk back to the end of Pico Boulevard, where she had parked. Over the years she'd read about terrible things happening on the beach at night, and she thought about them too often. She was afraid even though no one could hurt her anymore. That wasn't the reason she'd taken Adrian's pistol. It had begun as a way to keep him from killing himself, something she'd obviously failed at. But she had kept it, and now it kept her safe.

She could feel its weight in her backpack. She carried it there with her Bible, her purse and a few leaves of coca. She had told Frank about it once when he'd pretended to be worried about her safety. Not that he understood what a woman had to be worried about. He claimed he was afraid she would hurt herself. He tried to make it sound like he was concerned that she didn't know about guns. She'd told him that the man at the store who'd sold her the .38-caliber ammunition had been very helpful. He'd shown her how to load it. She had even learned how to clean it.

He'd given her some tips on shooting, though she refused his offer to teach her more at a firing range. She didn't want to get involved with any oddballs.

A vibration against her ribs startled her before she realized it was her cell phone. So few people called, except the silent one, the one who never said anything.

"What do you want, Frank?" she said after she read his number.

"What? Oh," Frank said, still not used to doing away with the rudimentary courtesies that email and caller ID had made obsolete. "I, uh, well, I have some amazing news for you. Wonderful news!"

"What is it?"

Frank hesitated. "Where are you?"

"Taking my walk at the beach, like I told you this morning, not that you remember anything I say."

"Where exactly?"

"Just south of the pier, Frank. What is this news?"

"Do you remember Peter Winston, the fellow who said Adrian had been pushed?"

"Of course I do."

"He's found the man who did it."

Marta cried out, "Someone really pushed him?" She stomped about, splattering mud and water, yanked between doubt and euphoria. "I don't believe it, Frank," she shouted into the phone.

"Marta, it's true. I told you that what happened to Adrian wasn't your fault. You don't need to blame yourself. If anything, it's this man you should hate."

Marta shrieked, then cried out, "This is the man who bought our house?"

"Not exactly. He worked for that man. But he's the one who killed Adrian. He confessed it."

"Where is he?"

"He and Peter are up the coast from you about a mile. Peter is sort of holding him captive."

Marta wheeled around and began walking north. The lights of the Santa Monica Pier glowed above the beach in the dusk. A chill wind came off the water, and the clouds dulled to slate. "Why haven't the police arrested him?"

"It's complicated, Marta. Peter has it in his mind that the one who's really responsible is this man's boss, but he doesn't know how to bring him to justice, so he called me to help."

"Did you call the police?"

Frank evaded the question. "It could be a while before they show up."

"These people are evil, Frank. They are trying to destroy our family, our ways." Marta walked resolutely into the murky shadows beneath the pier. She stopped, slipped her backpack half off and got her gun. "I'm going there."

"They are evil, Marta, but I don't want you to get hurt. The situation could be dangerous. I need to know: Do you still have Adrian's gun?"

"Of course." She continued deeper into the darkness under the pier. "Where are you? Aren't you coming down here?"

"Yes, but the traffic is horrendous."

Disgusted with her brother, but resigned to having to do the hard things herself, she demanded, "Where are they exactly?"

"Peter told me he'd wait by the water roughly parallel to that little restaurant next to the bike path. It's the place you told me you went with some people from work last year." The sounds of the arcade overhead drowned out whatever else Frank said as the connection broke up.

24

EARLIER: FRIDAY, MARCH 25, 2005

AFTER HE GOT OFF the phone with Frank, Peter took his belt and made it into a leash by fastening it to the wrist of Lewis' bad arm. He was sure he'd try to run away again if he could. They waited until the light at the California Street incline stopped the traffic on Pacific Coast Highway and made their way across four lanes toward the beach. The few people who even noticed them from the comfort of their cars saw a couple of dirty bums whom they hoped wouldn't try to clean their windows and ask for change.

The pain in Louis' shoulder seemed to have put him into shock. Either that or he was struck dumb by the predicament he faced. They walked in silence across a big, empty parking lot and trudged across a quarter mile of sand to the ocean. When they got to where Frank said to meet, they sat watching one of the most beautiful sunsets that Peter had ever witnessed.

When the sun disappeared, they both looked around self-consciously to find a full moon, the cause of the extreme low tide, ascending slowly in the east. The physical beauty only served to make Peter feel even more apprehensive, but Frank had insisted that they meet him there. He had said they needed to remain in firm control in order for this situation to come out right and that he was going to bring out someone to take things to the next level. All Peter knew for sure was that he was glad he wasn't trying to resolve this alone anymore. On his own, he'd be at a dead end. His threat to Louis had sounded convincing, but it was bullshit. It was true that two other people had remembered seeing someone who looked like Louis, but, of course, they hadn't seen him do anything wrong. As long as Louis didn't know that and was in physical pain, Peter had all the leverage he needed.

The beach was empty except for them. Louis lay back on the sand to get away from the cold breeze. The clouds hovered above them like purple bruises as the sky morphed to gray. It was nearly dark when Peter noticed a hooded figure far down the beach churning their way with determination. Louis sat up, and both of them followed the figure's progress, its long skirt sweeping across the vast, darkened expanse of the beach at low tide. Peter couldn't be sure, but he guessed that Frank had decided to dress up for the confrontation in all his ministerial glory.

Suddenly, a voice boomed out from behind them, "Gentlemen, which one of you is the guilty party, may I ask?" Half-frozen, Peter and Louis twisted around to the sound.

Struggling to his feet, Peter asked, "Who are you?"

The dapper older man, wrapped in a scarf and a three-quarter-length cashmere overcoat, replied with a note of authority, "You first, young man."

"Peter Winston."

"And you, my tattered friend?"

Louis muttered his name.

"Well, if I had to guess, I would say it is you, Louis, that I am here to see."

"Who the hell are you?" Peter said.

"Let's just say that I'm an interested party."

"Did Frank call you?"

"Exactly." The man's eyes narrowed suspiciously as he looked past Peter and Louis. They turned to follow his gaze. The hooded figure was closing fast on them, and over the rumble of the waves a raspy woman's voice erupted. "Which one of you killed my father?"

"Marta?" Peter exclaimed. "Jesus, what the fuck?"

"Who was it?" she insisted and stopped, ten feet away.

"Marta, you know me. I'm Peter Winston, but how…?"

"Just tell me who is who, Mr. Winston."

Peter pointed to a terrified Louis, who was laboring to get to his feet, and said, "He pushed him, but," and he swung his arm toward the other man, "if this is Ray Thomas—and I bet it is—he's the one who hired him."

"That's ridiculous. I've never met this man."

"But you are Ray Thomas, right?" Peter insisted.

"Assuming that's true, what…?"

"And you've been waiting over ten years to get the Montero house."

Louis saw Marta's gun first. He promptly kicked Peter in the balls and ran zigzagging toward the surf, holding his bad arm while the belt dangled from his wrist. The two shots Marta fired wildly only propelled him faster. When he was ankle-deep, he dove into the water. Barely visible when his head rose again, he was shielded from all but the most practiced sharpshooter.

Peter was on the sand clutching his groin. As he struggled to catch his breath, he looked back and forth from the fierce-eyed Marta to Louis disappearing under the surf.

Rooted to his own spot on the sand, Ray Thomas called unctuously. "Marta, you can't believe this crackpot. I had nothing to do with that murdering bum. I'm here to help." Marta glared at him. "At your brother's request," he added with smooth sincerity.

Without taking her eyes off Ray Thomas, she called out, "Peter, why did that coward say he killed my father?"

"He was paid to do it," Peter shouted.

Marta screamed at Ray Thomas, "Why are you here?"

"I want as badly as you to catch that murderer."

"Liar!" she shrieked. "Why didn't you go after him?"

Ray Thomas' brief hesitation spoke volumes before he found his voice. "Don't you worry. We'll get the police down here in a few minutes and catch that son of a bitch." Emboldened by his own words, he approached her, holding out his hand for the gun. "Let's not do anything foolish."

The first shot missed, but the next bullet found flesh, knocking him down to one knee. He clutched his thigh, his face contorted. "No, stop! You've got it all wrong. Frank and I…"

Marta stepped closer and steadied the gun with both hands. Bellowing, he pleaded, "We've made millions for the Church. God dammit!" Marta put him out of their misery with a shot to the head.

Peter watched in horror and a little awe. The wind and roar of the ocean swallowed the pop of the pistol, and in slow motion Ray Thomas fell back on the sand. Marta drew close and stood over him for a long minute until his heaves and twitches ceased, then she flung the gun away. She knelt down, and with a dismissive pass of her hand, she closed Ray Thomas' shocked eyes.

"Marta," Peter called out over the chorus of wind and surf.

She crossed herself, slowly stood and looked at Peter. "You were right, Mr. Winston." An otherworldly calm inhabited her voice. "Thank you."

"Thank me? Marta, I'm sorry, but I thought you might have been behind your father's murder." He hesitated, and she gazed at him unperturbed. "I made a lot of phone calls trying to scare you into doing something foolish that would expose you."

"This wasn't foolish." She looked out to sea, then back to Peter. "At least you cared."

He stepped closer. "How did you know we were here?"

Marta seemed to ignore his question as she looked around her, taking in where she was. To the east, the full moon was lifting into the sky, while the cliffs of the palisades lay in shadow. "It's all part of a vision, Mr. Winston. I didn't understand it at the time. That's often the case with me." A sad smile crossed her face, and she murmured, "Now I do: like mother, like daughter." In the growing light of the moon, her features relaxed.

"But why are you here?" he pressed.

She eyed him and responded to the version of reality that he insisted upon. "Frank called me."

"He told you to kill Ray Thomas?" Peter gasped.

"No, it's never that direct in this family." She sighed and seemed to deflate back down onto the sand, her heavy skirts encircling her.

"Marta, the police are going to find out about this." He kneeled next to her.

"Yes, of course. They, too, must do what they must do."

"But…"

"We aren't as free-willed as we like to think. Nor are we alone." She drew a large X in the sand. "The gods are with me."

The ocean and wind masked the inhaled "thup, thup, thup" sounds of the police helicopter until its blinding searchlight lit them up and the down draft from its blades placed them in the middle of a sand storm. Shocked and disoriented, Peter reached out to Marta to comfort her, but through squinting eyes he saw her peering up at the machine above as if it were some redemptive angel. Peter sensed movement out of the corner of his eye. Sergeant Jones and three other cops came quickly out of the shadows into the cold white light illuminating the crime scene. As Jones came closer, he motioned urgently to the helicopter to leave, and they heard him swearing that "the fucking idiot pilot" was blowing away evidence.

Saturday, March 26, 2005

I T WAS JUST AFTER midnight. Peter sat alone in the interview room, a cold cup of coffee before him. Detective Hererra, his interrogator or interviewer, Peter didn't know which, came through the door for the umpteenth time. Hererra ran his slim fingers over his thin, sculpted moustache before he spoke. "You chased this guy for two months, and you didn't even make him show an ID when you finally got him?" Peter ignored him. "There's no Louis Diggs anywhere in Vermont, nobody around his age in the system at all."

"Fuck!" Peter pounded the table. Brown sprinkles of coffee erupted in a circle around the cup, which didn't tip over. "Fuck me and fuck this whole mess." He shot a glance at the detective. "I guess I was a little euphoric over being proven right. It's not easy being the only person who knows the truth."

Hererra returned a surprisingly sympathetic look. "Like I told you when they brought you in, I remember you from the report sent to us from Traffic. Anyone who hands his kid to a stranger to chase after a perp is either crazy or a genuine hero."

"Or both," Peter added.

"Or both." He smiled a grim smile. "Anyway, I tended to believe you'd seen a murder two months ago. But that doesn't explain tonight, especially since we still don't have any evidence of your guy."

"So you think that a millionaire developer just randomly decided to take a nighttime stroll on the beach and got whacked by a deranged woman whose home he'd recently taken over, and that I just happened to come by?"

"No, I think you convinced the grieving family members that there really was a murder plot and got them to set up a meeting down there. The complication has to do with Louis Diggs. If we find him, you better hope that he admits to being there tonight. Otherwise, you're involved in a second murder mystery you've observed but can't explain."

"There's no murder mystery, Detective. Marta killed Ray Thomas. She admits it, and I saw it, just like I saw a guy I used to call Mad Max kill Adrian Montero. The mystery was why, and that's been solved. Ray Thomas set up the murder of her father out of greed and Marta got revenge."

"But you can't prove what Ray Thomas did."

"Mad Max told me that someone paid him to kill Montero, and that had to be Ray Thomas. It turns out that I was bringing the bait to pull Ray Thomas into the open."

"So you admit you're an accomplice to Ms. Montero?"

"Shit, is that what you think? I told you three fucking hours ago that I was waiting for Frank Greening, not his sister. He's the one you should be grilling."

"You like to tell people how to do their jobs, don't you? What you need to understand is that as far as I'm concerned, this Mad Max character either doesn't exist or is irrelevant. You see, the only other person besides you who attests to his existence on the beach is the shooter, who also told me several stories involving a jaguar, a burning circle and dozens, if not hundreds, of macaws and parrots. You got a problem, Mr. Winston."

"Then fuck you. Either arrest me or let me out of this hellhole. I'm not talking to you anymore, Motherfucker."

"Watch your language, Sir."

"I just saw someone get shot in the head, Detective. What the fuck do you fucking expect?"

Hererra glared at him for a few seconds, then left. Peter was released and dropped off at his car, parked near the Camera Obscura. The patrol car drove off and he wearily clicked open his door. Across the street, the headlights of a black BMW flashed.

Peter ignored it. The driver's window of the BMW lowered, and Frank beckoned to Peter as he began to open his door. Peter didn't know whether to be terrified or enraged. He was both.

Frank stepped out of the car, his priest collar a subtle adornment beneath a handsome blue blazer in the cool, clear night. Peter held up his belt-less pants with one hand and crossed the street. Frank gestured toward the passenger door. "I'm not going anywhere with you," Peter declared.

"We need to talk," Frank replied, his face unexpressive, "that's all."

"More lies?" Peter spat out.

"You'll decide," Frank answered calmly.

"I can't believe they let you go," Peter said as he sank into the soft leather seat.

"I was thinking the same thing," Frank responded, slipping behind the wheel.

"They were questioning you, too, right?"

"When they weren't with you."

"Fuck!" Peter rubbed his face. "I figured Hererra was getting information from you because he got more suspicious every time he'd come back into the room. You lied to them about Lewis," he spat out.

"Or you did."

"Motherfucker!"

"Detective Hererra and I agreed that you were obsessed with Adrian's death. They suspect that you're delusional, maybe schizophrenic. I suggested that was taking it too far. I said that you'd been very worked up, obsessed if you will, during our eighteen hours together in Ojai, but I didn't think you were, you know, completely crazy."

"Fuck you! I told them you made those calls to Marta and Ray Thomas. They'll be able to prove it once they get the phone records."

"Oh, they know. I already told them that I had to warn my business associate and dearly departed friend that you were trying to prove your crazy theory with some poor homeless fellow you'd probably beaten up and kidnapped, if he existed at all. By the way, that's when Detective Hererra began to wonder if you were delusional." Frank dispassionately observed Peter's squirming and growing astonishment and horror as he realized he was the mouse and no longer the cat.

Peter gasped, "But why?" Frank said nothing, just looked at him, cool and detached. Gradually, Peter collected himself enough to ask, "What about Marta? Don't you care about sending her off to prison?"

"Prison?" Frank scoffed. "She'll end up in a mental hospital run by an order of nuns. I'm sure she'll settle in and function like she was part of the religious order. It will be the answer to a childhood dream." Frank paused and cocked his head. "By the way, did they ever ask you about your harassing phone calls?"

Peter sat stony-faced, but even in the dim light Frank could see panic flit across his eyes. "When Marta first complained of someone trying to freak her out, my first thought was you. Marta agreed, when she wasn't attributing them to various Andean deities. I told Hererra, but I guess they couldn't prove it was you since you cleverly used public phones each time."

"You must really hate her," Peter finally responded.

"You have no idea how I feel. You never did, and your ruse to destabilize Marta was pathetic. It shows you don't understand Marta or me, even though you chose to meddle in both our lives. I will tell you this, which I believe you've already observed. Marta is a lost soul. She was born into the wrong century and culture. Once Adrian sold the house, she became completely ungrounded, literally and otherwise. I told the police I called to let her know about our phone call, the phone call you instigated, by the way, that began this whole unfortunate incident. Did I know she was going to be on the beach at that time? Possibly; she walked there often. Did I know she was carrying a gun? Less likely, though I did mention that she must have taken it from Adrian. Most important, did I know she'd kill someone at that impromptu gathering? Hardly. And why should she, except that some hysterical history teacher insisted that her father had been assassinated, and then had tried to spook her for two months. Plus, who the hell knows what you told her on the beach."

"You bastard!"

"Marta always wanted to give her life to the Church, and, as luck would have it, I am able to help her achieve her dream."

"You're heartless!"

"In Ojai, you were quite willing to acknowledge our similarities, so you know that's not so. What just happened to Marta may seem more radical than what you tried to do for your father, but not much more." Peter bristled, but Frank continued, "It's become obvious that Marta's capacity for managing her life has been lost. You were there, so you know she fulfilled herself by avenging her father's death."

"And you sent a friend to his death."

"How could I know what was going to happen?"

As the truth of this soaked in, Peter's adrenals pumped more alarm into his system. "My God! You didn't care who she killed, did you?" He opened his door, readying his escape. "Getting rid of any one of us, Ray Thomas, Louis or me, would have broken all possible connection back to the Church."

"Close the door," Frank demanded, losing patience momentarily. He collected himself. "You weren't in danger. You were only the messenger."

Peter's eyes opened wide. "Ray's last words were to brag about the millions you two had made for the Church! But your partner in God knows what sort of corruption was responsible for killing Adrian, so you had to resolve Adrian's murder without revealing the secret relationship you and Ray have. This looks like revenge, but that's not what it's really about, is it? You didn't care about Adrian. He was someone who tortured you when you were little. But you had a business problem. You were in danger of losing your power, and you're addicted to it. So, when I called with Louis, or whoever he is, you were ready to take action. You had to make a sacrifice, but, hell, the Bible's full of them."

"You have only a partial understanding of what's behind this moment of justice. Be glad for it. Enjoy the resolution."

"Your job is to be aware of any situation that can financially damage the Archdiocese and the Catholic Church. You understood what you had to do. You did what the Church has always done in these situations. You made the problem go away."

"What are you going to do about it, Peter, get in touch with your inner Visigoth and try to bring down the Church?"

"You can rationalize anything, like a Nazi."

"A crude comparison, especially for a historian, Peter. Evil exists. But it isn't intrinsic to any one act. A man must choose whether to succumb or to fight it. We're both fighters, I'll say that for you."

"At one point you called me a fundamentalist, but you're a fanatic. I may like things to be black and white, but you're willing to destroy all shades of gray."

Frank sighed, tired of the conversation. "Justice has been served, Peter. That's what I wanted to tell you, why I waited for you tonight. We got our man. You figured out who was guilty, and I figured out what had to be done." He motioned for Peter to let himself out as he started the engine. "Be glad it's over and thankful that you survived."

26

SUNDAY, MARCH 27, 2005

ALL AFLUTTER IN A gauzy pastel dress, Samantha ran across the lawn to Peter, who sat alone. "Look how many Easter eggs I found, Daddy!" she exclaimed. Together they counted five dyed eggs before she squealed off with other kids to search in another part of the garden. Peter looked around. He found no joy in the blooming Icelandic poppies that surrounded him. There had been no joy in anything in the day and a half since being dismissed by Frank.

Judith broke away from the other drinking and eating guests. "Feeling any better?" she asked as she approached. She had pushed hard to get him out to their friends' place in Mandeville Canyon for Easter brunch.

Peter took a sip of his Bloody Mary and shrugged. "I'm feeling every way possible: enraged, relieved, hopeless, relieved, confused, relieved…everything except religious."

"Do you think you'll ever go back to church?"

"Besides to arrest someone? I don't know. But I do think my days as a private investigator are over."

Judith sat next to him and gave him a kiss on the cheek. "Finally, some good news."

He put his arm around her, and they sat for a while, soaking in the sun. Into the warm, scented air humming with bumblebees and the exaltations and laughter of the children, she said, "I want to visit your dad on the way home today." When he didn't respond, she added, "You've got to start sometime."

Peter withdrew his arm from her shoulders and, finally, broke his silence. "I tried to suffocate him, right after he broke his hip."

"Oh, my God!" She burst out and turned away. After a while, she asked, "And?"

"And I came very close, but I couldn't go through with it." Peter looked at her trembling back. "I tried to talk to you about my agreement with him, many times."

She whipped around and opened her mouth to yell at him, but caught herself. "And now?" she finally asked.

"I don't know what to do, but I can't keep avoiding him, and secrets between us really fuck things up."

She took his hand, and they sat looking at the blanket of yellow mustard blooming on the hills above them. "I knew there was something else," she sighed. "Come on, we've really got to go."

Over Sam's protests and after collecting her dyed eggs, jellybeans, chocolate Easter eggs and other candies, they left the party. Driving slowly down the narrow, canyon road, Peter regretfully announced over his shoulder, "Sam, we have to visit Grandpa for a little while."

"I don't want to go, Daddy. It smells funny." Her nose wrinkled up.

Caught off guard, he asked, "How do you know?"

"Mommy took me there."

Peter glanced at Judith as his surprise mingled with guilt. "Well, I don't want to go, either, but I have to."

"I don't like it there." Sam pinched her lips, her eyes looking up, remembering something intently.

"Why not?" he asked.

"'Cause Grandpa is mean," she said defiantly.

"How is he mean to you?"

"He pretends he doesn't know me."

Judith sighed, but her look at Peter said it was his turn to try to explain.

"Honey, Grandpa isn't pretending. It's for real." He stopped at a stop sign, turned to the back and saw her confusion. "Grandpa isn't trying to be mean," he struggled to explain. "His memory is gone, and he doesn't know what he used to know. He's sick: sick in his brain."

"But Grandpa doesn't think he's sick, because I asked him."

"He doesn't know he's sick, but he is, and there's nothing that can be done to make him better." He started driving again.

"Is Grandpa going to die?" Sam asked, sounding more curious than sad.

Peter's voice cracked, "His memory has died, but he might live for many more years."

"Does Grandpa remember that he's alive?"

Peter frowned. He admired yet hated her question. She had no idea of its tormenting implications. "Well, he knows he's alive, but…" he stopped. "I guess he doesn't remember it." There was a silence, then Peter began again, louder, "Memory is a difficult concept to…" and he stopped again, aware that he was about to launch into a lecture, and that his audience couldn't care less.

Judith tried a new tack. "What would be interesting, Sam, is to visit Grandpa and try to see things like he does. Try to imagine what it would be like if you had no memory." Peter watched Sam in the rearview mirror as Judith added, "Make it into kind of a game, okay?"

"I don't want to play that game," she said.

"And afterward," he continued on into bribery, "you can have some of that chocolate egg. Is it a deal?"

"It's a deal," she agreed

Judith turned on the radio. Peter understood the signal. Sam might take a little nap if they stopped talking. He was happy to oblige.

As the car was filled with a Mozart Mass, Peter recalled sealing his own fate when he had said, "It's a deal," to his father many years before. Now he was breaking the deal. He defended himself in his head: *I'm not willing to risk spending my life in prison. I'm lucky I wasn't successful the first time.* He nervously glanced back at Samantha, as though his thoughts could be heard. She was nodding off in her car seat.

Peter was afraid that it was only a matter of time before he would come up with a dying trick that wouldn't draw suspicion. Right after Ojai, he had talked with Evan, a gay friend in New York, who had seen many pals and his own partner die of AIDS. Peter hadn't asked directly, but he was sure Evan would be up to date on ways to end a person's life without going to jail. Safe dying was probably more trendy than safe sex.

He looked over at Judith, who gave him a smile. He wasn't alone in this anymore though there wasn't anything Judith could do to help. Unless and until an assisted suicide law passed in California, Martin was stuck in misery. Even then, it probably wouldn't help someone in his condition. The divine fervor of "Gloria in excelsis" filled the car, and Mozart temporarily soothed Peter's throbbing mind.

A honking SUV woke Samantha up after ten minutes. Peter turned off the radio, and in the silence Samantha sang through "Rock A Bye, Baby," over and over, until her parents joined in. Soon, they were at the Fontaine Nursing Home

In spite of telling Judith that he didn't want to know anything about it, she had already assured him weeks before that this place was one of the best. They were buzzed through locked doors that didn't open from the inside. As they clicked behind him, it felt to Peter like a minimum-security prison for people who could no longer take care of themselves. Most families weren't able to look after a five- or six-foot baby who couldn't control his bowel or bladder, especially if he were inclined to wander off or be violent. As they walked down a hallway, Judith mentioned that the staff was generally efficient and concerned, though the patients were usually kept sedated in varying degrees. With rare exception, this was the last stop before the grave. It looked to Peter like it could be a long one.

Someone in a white uniform directed them to an enclosed patio, where a staff member was playing a game with eight patients as players. She started to sing "The Good Ship Lollipop." A moment passed, then someone from the group shouted, "Shirley Temple!" The others smiled and nodded, and the game continued.

Peter spotted his father strapped into a wheelchair off to the side, gazing at a bush covered with red camellias. Judith stood with Samantha watching the game, while Peter sat in a chair next to the frail, old man and said, "Hello, Dad."

His father looked at him with a friendly face and said, "Hello." Peter looked into his father's eyes and saw the blankness behind the smile. He didn't know if it was better or worse to not be recognized.

"I'm Peter, your son."

"Of course!" The old man's eyes winced with an apparent attempt to hang onto what had just been said. "These flowers are…" and he fell silent and looked away.

"They're beautiful," Peter managed to reply. "Do you like to garden?"

"M'hm." He leaned out of his wheelchair and touched a flower gently. "I'm going home."

"You're going home?" Peter asked in spite of himself.

"I am?" his father asked, but a clouded look crossed his eyes, and he fell silent. He had already lost track. A moment later, he looked up with a smile and said, "Aren't these beautiful?"

Peter reached out and squeezed an ant off a stem. "You've got quite a job keeping the bugs off."

"Yes," he said, "…a job." He picked idly at a small scab on his arm until he noticed Samantha coming toward him. "Hello… Adorable. What's your name?"

"Samantha Winston. You know me, Grandpa."

"Samantha," he repeated, "Sure," and the conversation dwindled to an uncomfortable silence.

The activity behind them continued. "I'm thinking of an old-time band leader whose first name was Artie," announced the staff member. Suddenly, one of the patients stood and began to sing "Begin the Beguine," Artie Shaw's biggest hit. Peter, Judith, Samantha and the patients stared at the old guy, who was now really into it. After a moment, Peter looked back to see if his dad could understand any of what was going on. To Peter's amazement, he was mouthing the words along with his fellow resident in a low but distinct voice.

Peter choked up and nudged Judith and Sam. It was the Martin of a long time ago. Peter remembered being very little when his father sang to his mother in the kitchen as she cooked dinner. She pretended to be embarrassed at the attention, but Peter could tell they were happy.

Words tumbled from his dad's mouth, but there was no expression on his face, like a wooden puppet. He stopped when the other singer finished, though no one except Peter, Judith and Sam was aware he'd been singing along. As the other patients offered scattered applause for the impromptu concert, the staff member went over to the beaming, old singer and gave him a big hug. The gesture was caring, but it struck Peter as patronizing. She was hugging him for not having lost every single one of his marbles, somehow normalizing what was a tragedy. Martin had wanted to die with all his marbles. That was all he had asked, but what if he couldn't get what he'd wanted?

Samantha beamed, "That was nice, Grandpa."

"What?" he said.

"Your song."

"No…song…sing." He mumbled, "When I was…mmmm."

Sam's lower lip trembled, and she hid behind Peter's shoulder. The old man leaned out from his wheelchair trying to follow her. When Sam reappeared, he raised his eyebrows in delight. Sam giggled and ducked back behind Peter. Her next reappearance excited her grandfather even more, and he laughed aloud. Sam laughed, disappeared again and reappeared to mutual elation. Back and forth she went in rising hilarity with her grandfather until she reappeared one more time and he was looking far away.

Sam disappeared once more and tugged on Peter's shirt. Peter thought it was a signal that she'd had enough. Certainly, he felt that way, but Judith whisked her away and left Peter with his dad.

Martin looked at Peter with zero interest, then stared off into space. A tidal surge of grief flooded through him and he was inundated by helplessness. His father was still present, barely, if only in the back and forth of peek-a-boo, that universal game that laughs at separation by promising return. But Martin was detaching, disappearing through that same door he had entered as an infant.

All the debates they'd had over life and death made sense now. They'd shared a bond, forged in blood. It had often been expressed in their desire to control death. He'd long been critical of his father's need to maintain the illusion of control. But he now saw his own fantasy: he wanted to amend death's decree by demanding, "Yes, we all die, but we really live forever: God says so." It was peek-a-boo on an eternal scale with daddy, and us, always coming back.

He cried for them both until the weight of grief lifted as naturally and quickly as it had descended. Peter pulled himself together and began to talk as though they had been checking in every day. "I saw a murder, Dad. I tried to solve it, but it ended up that a second person died." He hesitated, "A priest caused one of the deaths, maybe both. You'd tell me that I was naïve to think that the Catholic Church wasn't capable of murder and fraud, but I didn't think they'd let a priest run the show. In the last big scandal, they had an outsider do the dirty work so they'd have a layer of denial. You loved that story. If you could remember anything, you'd remember Roberto Calvi. You know what's really ironic, Dad?" Peter's volume had risen, and he dropped back into a stage whisper. "After the Calvi fiasco, Frank Greening was part of the effort to reform the financial management by moving it back under Church control. And look what happened to the reformers: 'Power tends to corrupt, and absolute power corrupts absolutely.'" You taught me that Lord Acton quote when I was only ten."

Martin became agitated, twisting around against the straps that held him in the wheelchair and uttering a few random words. When he settled back, he looked at Peter with suspicion.

Peter took it personally. "I could take you out of here, but there's nowhere that would be better." His father stretched uncomfortably and looked past him. Peter got up, stood behind him and began to give his dad's shoulders a gentle massage. After his dad settled down, he continued his tale. "I could have been killed the other night, and I was damn near arrested. One of the detectives had the nerve to warn me not to harass Frank like I had his sister. I denied knowing anything about it, but if I keep playing private eye, they might get a fucking restraining order on me. I think that, at least, the cops took me seriously when I told them that Ray Thomas and Frank were involved in some kind of crooked deals that were making millions illegally for the Church." His dad sighed with contentment.

"Frank should pay for his sins, but it seems quite possible that his undoing would destroy the Archdiocese and create an unimaginable crisis across the U.S." Peter stopped moving his hands, caught up in his explanation. "Even before I ran into Father Frank, I was worried that the biggest religion in the country was in danger of collapse. In the 1950s, there were over 50,000 guys training to be priests in America. Now there are fewer than 2,500. As long as they keep their all-male, secret hierarchy running the show, they will crumble from within. You'd think they deserve that, but I'm not sure. If the American Catholic Church crumbled, it would seriously disrupt this society. I think we would see a complete fundamentalist takeover." Martin began looking around, and Peter got back into the massage. "Anyway, Frank is just another powerful person who does bad things for good reasons. He's no worse than Thomas Jefferson, the hypocrite who created American democracy."

Peter sat down and Martin regarded his son with serenity. "I know what you'd say. Why am I surprised by human nature?" Peter continued, "I do take some solace knowing that Frank has a conscience. He isn't a psychopath. That means he will suffer. He knows that he's a liar and an accessory to at least one murder. When his guilt catches up with him, he's going to go through hell or, at least, the dark night of his soul's journey. That's my prayer, but maybe it's bullshit. After all, he set up his own sister. And then he had the balls to compare that with what I'd tried to do with…with you." Peter swallowed the last words. Through tears, he looked up to see Martin watching him. "I'm sorry you ended up here, Dad, I'm so sorry."

Martin looked at this unhappy being, and a spark flickered in his eyes. He opened his lips and said "Sorry" quietly, but clearly. Peter watched as his father then twisted his mouth trying to hold onto the impression or urge or whatever it was that had somehow fired a few million select neurons to allow that to be expressed. But the old fellow drifted away again, like a leaf falling from a tree. He landed inside a sweet, vacant smile.

Peter wiped his eyes. "You used to insist that memory was an ethical and political act. You loved that Milan Kundera statement: 'The struggle of man against power is the struggle of memory against forgetting.'" He smiled tenderly. "You liked it when I went into history: 'Honorable work,' you called it, because so many people selectively forget in order to survive or live with themselves. Neither our brains nor our emotions can handle the stimulus, from petty meanness to major traumas. It's too much. I guess that means that if I can handle it, I'll bear witness to the truth about Frank. And, obviously, I have to remember for both of us. I remember you, and as long as someone remembers you, you exist."

Peter saw Judith and Sam returning. He leaned forward, his face directly in front of his father's. "Dad, is there anything you need or want?"

The wrinkled face turned to him, his countenance mirroring Peter's seriousness. His lips puckered like he was thinking. Then, he smacked his lips, but no words came out. "Of course," Peter began laughing, "you're hungry! When's lunch in this joint?" he chortled. His father laughed back, a jolly, oblivious laugh.

An attendant approached and offered to wheel Martin into the dining room.

Peter leaned forward and kissed Martin on the cheek. "It's a tragedy if I remember what's missing, but otherwise, you've become some goofy Zen monk, totally in the moment." He stood as Sam ran to him, arms raised high. He scooped her up. "Goodbye, Dad. I'll see you soon."

27

Sunday, April 17, 2005

FRANK HAD CELEBRATED A Mass every morning since Good Friday. He would have presided at more if he could have. He reassured himself that the situation was finally under control; the police weren't suspicious, and Peter Winston had been thoroughly intimidated. Still, Frank barely slept more than an hour or two at a time. He tried to forget his diet, but he had no appetite. He was moody and snappish with Sal. He thought that the death of Pope John Paul II should have been a worthy distraction from his own problems. Indeed, as the brutal politics of succession that had been under wraps for years erupted, the Cardinal considered sending him to Rome to be his eyes and ears. He was needed. But his boss had achieved his high station because he was an excellent judge of men, and it was obvious that Frank wasn't himself. The Cardinal knew not to demand too many details about the cause of Frank's malaise, but he finally insisted, rather than recommended, that he take some time off. That didn't mean he couldn't say Mass. That was the last thing a priest was stopped from doing. The religious knew that was his lifeline to God, and sanity.

He told himself that God understood and accepted that he had done what he had to do, but it didn't mean he didn't need help in overcoming his guilt. Negative thoughts and fears could kill; nowadays, everyone accepted the connection between mind and body. It was gratifying how science had finally caught up with the Catholic belief in transubstantiation. If prayer could help cure disease, then faith could turn bread and wine into the embodiment of Jesus Christ. Neither could be proved physically, but both could be shown to make people feel better. Each Mass he said was a prayer that he would find some peace so he could get back to his regular life. That was why he had done what he'd done to Ray and with Marta, so he could continue his work.

"Peace be with you," Frank said as he handed out the communion wafers to a class of third-graders who had come to Mass that morning. Their sweet, solemn faces helped him ignore the corrosive thoughts in his head. "Peace be with you," he repeated, beaming love and grace to each little child receiving the Blessed Sacrament from him. Awash in a sea of innocence and love, he found himself asking God to forgive Ray Thomas for his sins. With that, he felt the first flush of grace, of resolution. Forgiveness was the clearest sign he knew that healing was at work. Soon he would begin to look for new and better ways to continue his fundraising for the Archdiocese. His prayers that his recent extraordinary efforts to protect the Church would be rewarded by a more humane leader had not been answered. In fact, he was sure that the new pontiff would prove to be the worst of Pope John Paul II, rigid without charisma or charm. There would be no thaw in the dogma wars, no reconsideration of the issues of celibacy and birth control.

His disappointment that he probably wouldn't live to see the advent of more progressive church doctrines lifted as he worked his way to the end of the line of children. Each one's gaze mesmerized him with the purity of his or her trust and faith.

He came to a woman whose patient smile instantly told him that she was their teacher. As he turned to the last pair of eyes in the long line, he found Peter glaring back at him. Frank lost his grip on the platter of wafers, and it tumbled to the ground. A communion wafer landed on Peter's brown loafer. With a flick of his ankle, he sent it skittering onto the floor, where it was ground beneath Frank's heel as he hurried about, urgently gathering and protecting all that he believed in.

Peter walked to the back of the little church and stood in the shadows. The oldest institution on earth was rotting. Along with his faith. He still felt compelled to bring down Frank and his scam even if that meant…what? Embarrassing the Catholic Church back into a movement no bigger than the Unitarians? Peter laughed at himself, at the inflation of his role. He still had the yearnings of an absolutist—a Catholic, Marxist fundamentalist. He couldn't bring down the Church any more than he could bring about a communistic paradise, any more than he could insure his father's happiness. He couldn't do these things and he was tired of feeling he had to try. He was a good enough son. Good enough. He would bear witness to history in the making. That might help. It had to be enough. In the meantime, the planet was melting. He unlocked his bicycle and headed for home.